FOUR LETTER WORD

Four Letter Word

New Love Letters

Edited by
Joshua Knelman & Rosalind Porter

Chatto & Windus
LONDON

Published by Chatto & Windus 2007

2 4 6 8 10 9 7 5 3

Some material in this collection has been previously published as follows: 'Lubyanka, 2 September 1918' by David Bezmozgis; 'Diamonds and Soot' by Douglas Coupland; 'Give Up' by Jonathan Lethem; 'You Would Look Away' by M.G. Vassanji and 'Love In Eight Chapters' by Juli Zeh in *The Walrus* in July, 2005. And 'In Reference to your Recent Communications' by Tessa Brown in *Harper's* in May, 2005.

First published in Great Britain in 2007 by
Chatto & Windus
Random House, 20 Vauxhall Bridge Road,
London SW1V 2SA

www.rbooks.co.uk

Addresses for companies within The Random House Group Limited can be found at:
www.randomhouse.co.uk/offices.htm

The Random House Group Limited Reg. No. 954009

A CIP catalogue record for this book is available from the British Library

ISBN 9780701180935

The Random House Group Limited supports The Forest Stewardship Council (FSC), the leading international forest certification organisation. All our titles that are printed on Greenpeace approved FSC certified paper carry the FSC logo. Our paper procurement policy can be found at www.rbooks.co.uk/environment

Typeset by SX Composing DTP, Rayleigh, Essex
Printed and bound in Great Britain by William Clowes Ltd, Beccles, Suffolk

For Jess

LOVE LETTERS

INTRODUCTION

On 4 May 2000, I was one of millions of people to open an email with the subject 'I Love You' containing an attachment 'Love Letter For You'. Launched by a Filipino hacker, the love letter virus 'Love Bug' first appeared in Hong Kong before quickly spreading to Europe and then to the United States, infecting servers and costing companies an estimated one billion dollars in lost time and recovery.

In the UK, both the House of Commons and House of Lords were hit, leading to a shutdown of email that lasted a few hours. 'The message was noticed before lunch. It was a message sending love to you, which is the sort of message a lot of us here don't expect to be receiving,' claimed the deputy sergeant at arms for the House of Commons at the time. Which begs the question: who are the people who would expect to receive such a message?

Most of us don't check the post in anticipation of scented envelopes stuffed with locks of hair, though many of us have received a fervent card; a flirtatious email; a suggestive text. Often we save them and reread them to remember a moment in time or a phase of life, even those from relationships long dead.

Over time, a hierarchy to this kind of semantic courting has developed with the ambiguous text at the bottom and the email only a bit higher up. A card may prove a touching example of someone willing to take the time to find a stamp, seek out an address and locate a post-box, but the letter – with all the noble attributes of the card and no space restrictions – is perhaps the supreme medium to befit a message of love. Also, it harks back to a chivalrous age full of men attaching scrolls to pigeons or throwing bottles into the sea and aligns the writer of the love letter with a whole tradition of literary seduction.

Written on something highly flammable and sent precariously by post or slipped underneath a door, there has always been something slightly risky about the love letter. Someone delivering it to the wrong person who then got the wrong idea; letters getting lost and therefore never replied to.

'How is it that I have just received your seventh letter,' writes Denis Diderot to his young mistress Sophie Voland in 1762, 'when you have only four of the nine I have written you, including this one?' It's possible to see how the margin for miscommunication here might become so wide that it, not the declaration of love itself, is in danger of becoming the main subject of their letters.

Email may have removed the fire hazard, but has its own set of potentially catastrophic contingencies. Any form of writing, it seems, demands that one worry about practicalities. The speed of the post or the Broadband connection has the power to send a lover into a fit of nervous rage when no reply comes and, even worse, the written word can hang around for ever. Long after the flame has been extinguished, those pleas of passion you jotted down might still be in her underwear drawer. And if you suddenly become famous? What's to stop him from selling your letters to the library which bought the rest of your papers?

The reclusive writer J. D. Salinger took the poet and critic Ian Hamilton to court when Hamilton tried to quote from various letters of Salinger's deposited in libraries and archives. Hamilton argued that since the letters were in the public domain it was only reasonable that he be permitted to reproduce them. And although he lost his case and had to resort to paraphrase, anyone can look at Salinger's letters in their entirety in the libraries and archives. Nothing, it would seem, is sacred.

Unlike a phone call or a conversation, a written declaration of love is a thing: a thing which exists in the world (often for a very long time) with the power to conjure up an emotional disposition, which is why, on occasion, we ask for them back, destroy them, prevent people from publishing them or keep them.

Something that has survived thirteen house moves is a Valentine I was given when I was five. 'Dear R,' it reads (his mother, or possibly our teacher, having written out this bit, though the statement itself is in my enthusiast's own hand). 'I want to love you. Happy Valentine's Day, From P.'

I adore this card. I remember P well, perhaps because I've had his Valentine for all these years. Sometimes, when I come across it, I feel the urge to write back – I want to clear up the ambiguity, an ambiguity that's intrinsic to most love letters. 'Dear P, Does this mean you don't love me? That you want to, but can't for some particular reason? Or are you asking my permission to do so and if that's the case, well then yes. Yes. Yes. Yes.'

In addition to this souvenir I have folders containing hundreds of pieces of correspondence from friends and family; colleagues and tutors. One folder marked 'random' holds papers from people I've never been particularly close to. Most of them are birthday cards but there are also a few love letters (some of which are intentionally anonymous).

Significant members of my family, good friends and exes all

have personalised folders, as do people who fall under the general heading of 'flirtations' since I somehow feel it's worth keeping the artefacts of relationships that never quite happened. Why I've been hauling around every expression of even the most vestigial of feelings says something about how sentimental I am but also about how, in this speed-dating age, traditional modes of courtship still have value.

The reasons for keeping bits and pieces from relationships that did happen are more straightforward. Without the pile of junk in A's folder, I'm sure I would have forgotten, in lieu of more impressionistic memories, that he sent me a postcard every day (the same postcard, in fact), for a month after we first met.

'This is the third,' he wrote, 'in what is fast becoming a series of postcards.' A few days later, after I'd gone away on holiday, 'It was GREAT to speak to you last night. I have to admit to missing you, especially when I'm walking down the street' (?). Later still, 'I have taken to crossing my fingers in order to simulate your presence' (??) and, finally, 'I guess it's pretty obvious that I miss you . . . Right now I feel emotionally dead.'

Since I don't have copies of what I wrote back, appreciating these postcards involves an imaginative reconstruction of the early days of our relationship. What was it about walking down the street with me that had been so bloody great? What I do remember is falling for this person not when I first met him, but soon after the postcards began to arrive.

'Dear R,' reads a card encased in a large envelope. 'Wishing you a very happy birthday, Love G.' In the envelope is a disc containing every email G and I exchanged – something deemed fit for a birthday present long after we'd split up. We wanted, it would seem, evidence certifying that those halcyon, dating days really had existed, but they also – quite unintentionally – serve as a reminder of the quotidian reality that followed as the infatuation stage wore off, expressed through angry emails and unquestionably dull ones too. 'Here is F's address,' reads one. An email containing nothing except a link to a website that does currency exchanges (even though we never went anywhere together) is another.

The folder to which I've returned most often is a wad of printed-out emails, postcards and bone fida love letters from L, with whom I had an on-again, off-again relationship.

'Dear R. It was lovely to meet you last night.' Then a very long, very charming preamble, ending with, 'It's coming up to the anniversary of our having known each other for forty-eight hours. How to celebrate?'

Even during our 'off' phases, every letter from L was filed away neatly – every email printed out – because somehow I'd known that a material record of our written communication would be of value to me. I've often returned to L's folder because I sometimes think it holds clues as to why so many things worked out yet, overall, the whole thing didn't. More than what we said in passing, our letters and emails contain a degree of authenticity about the way we felt because we put some thought into what we meant before setting it down on paper (before beaming it off into cyberspace), offering our words to one another with the awareness that giving them to someone meant forfeiting ownership.

Like any published writer, the author of the love letter can never take anything back. Words – unlike the actual feelings they connote – cannot simply be loaned. L was a journalist, well aware of how permanent the written word is and paid to use language to dress up a story in an alluring way. And he was good. They never failed, these letters, to lift me out of some dark mood or stretch of ennui, even if I did suspect a degree of contrivance to them. Because all writing is an affective art form – the manifestation of a voice meant to move the reader in a premeditated way – which is why love letters can be so exhilarating and so convincing; which is why so many people opened the 'Love Bug' email.

Even though he got caught, the Filipino hacker was no dummy. He observed our collective hunger for a demonstration of something so ethereal it's not always possible to demonstrate it, and with prescience, he lured us to him with a false promise of words. Because with words, anything is possible. Through words, even our most ardent desires can be fulfilled.

Over the past year, Joshua Knelman and I asked some of our most esteemed writers to apply their skills to the form of the love letter – to resurrect this dying custom and remind us of how seductive words are. The brief was purposely simple. Each piece had to be addressed to someone (or something) and concerned with a heightened state of emotion. The result is a montage of sorts – a picture of what love looks like in the twenty-first century; a collage of methods and moods.

You won't find a lot of high romance here, although we certainly didn't discourage this. There is quite a bit of humour, a fair dose of sarcasm and a mountain of grief. We were hardly surprised by the degree of darkness in some of the letters, but were slightly amazed by how many typify love as a feeling that evolves through absence, rejection or death. A few of them don't even involve another person; a number take on the form of an apology.

What they do have in common is that all are works of fiction, although some may have been inspired by actual events. Each is unique, evidence not just of the incredible creative diversity of our leading writers today, but also of the intricate sophistication of love, and each – I suspect – will have the power to move you.

Rosalind Porter
April 2007

LOVE LETTERS

JONATHAN LETHEM

Dear E(arth),

I am writing to tell you to give up. You may already be a winner, the kind of winner who wins by losing, rolling on your back and showing me your soft parts, letting me tickle and lap and snort at your supplicant vitals. Perhaps I should put this more forcefully: GIVE UP. You stand no chance. Resistance is futile, futility is resistant, reluctance is flirtatious, relinquishment is freedom. I love you and I am better than you in every way – grander, greater, glossier, more glorious, more ridiculous, energetic, faster in foot races and Internet dial-up speed, hungrier, more full of sex and fire, better-equipped with wit and weaponry. I'm taller than you and can encircle you with my lascivious tongue. Admit this and admit me. By opening this envelope you have been selected; from among the billions upon trillions of amoebic entities, you've been plucked up from the galaxy's beach like a seashell by a god. Something in you sparkled for a moment (terribly unlikely it means anything much in the scheme of things); absurd that noticing you squeezed somehow on to the agenda of one such as me. But I was amused – don't ask me why, it's practically random, like a lottery. Yet you'll never be able to spend the wealth of my love, to run through it and waste it like the hapless lottery winner you are. Though you may try, you'd never spend it in a dozen profligate lifetimes. My eyes settled on you in a weak moment, and you'll never see another. No, I'm an edifice, an enigma; to one such as you my science is like magic. Don't delay, act now, give up. You have been selected by a higher being from another realm to be siphoned from among your impoverished species to join me, to be seated in the empty throne beside me (only because I'd never troubled to glance to one side before to notice a seat existed there – not, somehow, until my gaze lit on you) where none of your lowly cringing fellows has ever resided. You're unworthy but you'll be made worthy by the acclaim of my notice. I say again, I'm superior to you. You're tinsel, static, a daisy, a bubble of champagne that went to my head and popped, and I don't even know why I want you and you'd better not give me the chance to think twice. You'll find I've anticipated your responses and attached them below (see attachments, below). They're feeble and funny, helpless and endearing, and you've already blurted yes take me yes how can I resist yes I give up yes. So do I as I say now. You've already done it, you're in my arms like an infant, a ward, a swan. Give up, you gave up already, you're mine.

Love,

M(ars)

CHIMAMANDA NGOZI ADICHIE

Emeka,

That round-mouthed surprise a woman shows (is supposed to show?) when a man proposes has always annoyed and puzzled me. Surely a couple whose relationship is strong must have talked about marriage instead of following the script of the silly 'ambush question' from the man and then the woman's response of grateful surprise as if she were receiving a glorious gift she had never imagined would be hers. Are you smiling reading this? It's not funny-oh! So, really, why was I surprised when you sent me that ridiculous text? We had talked about marriage, hadn't we? Well, *you* had mostly. Still, reading your – *do you think we can begin to discuss the possibility of getting married soon?* – I felt first surprised, then amused, then frightened and then this stupid crazy joy that I still feel.

You know, you're wrong when you say that it's remarkable how similar we are. Of course we are similar – except for the little fact that I am significantly more attractive – but it isn't remarkable at all. Many other children of Nigerian academics read Enid Blyton and wondered what the heck ginger beer was; read every single book in the Pacesetters series; and read every James Hadley Chase. These are not at all proof of how right we are for each other – if they were, then you would be right for one out of every two campus-raised women I know.

Your father graduated from Ibadan only two years before my father did. If your family hadn't left Nigeria just before the war we might even have grown up together in Nsukka and maybe all of this marriage talk wouldn't be going on because we would have known each other too well, you would have been my brother Okey's friend from secondary school and you would always see me as Okey's scrawny little sister. So no, there's nothing remarkable about our shared interests. But the day you told me that your favourite part of Mass, the only reason you still go to Mass sometimes, is when the priest says 'as we wait in joyful hope', I was startled. I didn't tell you then because the coincidence seemed a little too pat but it's my favourite part of mass too. *O di egwu!*

So since your text came yesterday, I have been recalling the ways we are different, how you like beans and macho novels and the rainy season and I don't. It's suddenly important to me that we not be too similar. You know I have always been suspicious of anything close to perfection, anything too neatly put together. Always wanting to find bumps in smooth surfaces, as you tell me. It frightens me, how easily I now speak in the first-person plural. Yesterday, just before you sent the text, Aunty Adaeze called me and asked whether I would get leave for Christmas to go to the village. I said that we were hoping to get time off until after New Year's so we could go to Uche's wine-carrying and return to Lagos in January. She started laughing and said, 'Ah, I asked about you and you are telling me "we".' After I hung up, I began to think about how used to you I am and began to wonder how many other times I had said 'we' without even realising it.

Yesterday, too, I realised that I have never told you how much I like you – this before your text, by the way. Love is different. Love is ridiculous. Love can just happen, as it did to you when you saw me and asked Ifeanyi to introduce us (exactly seventeen months and three days ago) and to me as you tried to charm me with your watery knowledge of Achebe's work, but like requires reason. And yesterday I marvelled at how much I have come to like you. I like that you know when to leave and quietly shut my door and that when you do I never worry that you are not coming back. I like your cooking (I have never complimented you because I keep imagining those silly women who over-praise men for cooking, and those silly mothers who like to say, 'My son can cook-oh, so no woman will use food to tempt him'). I like the way your butt looks in your jeans, that flat elegance that you don't like me to point out, and I like that you make futile attempts at the gym to grow muscles we both know you never will and I like that you underline sentences in books to show me. I like that you like me and that your liking me makes me like myself.

I will, by the way, never write anything like this to you again. So smile all you want now, *atulu*. I remember when I was a kid, reading books in small dusty Nsukka, and often encountering characters eating bagels. It was an elegant word, bagel. I wanted desperately to have a bagel. Years later, in New York City (on our first visit to America as a family), I was flattened to discover that a bagel is a dense doughnut. I imagine you saying 'From where to where with this story?' as you read this. Well, my point is that I never wanted marriage and so perhaps it will turn out to be something good, unlike the bagel which I wanted and which turned out to be remarkably boring.

I have been reading your text over and over since yesterday and I have never felt so alive. So, yes, I suppose we should begin to talk of the possibility of getting married soon.

Chioma

ADAM THORPE

My Lord, I now propose to read a letter from the late Colin Stock-Tremlett, dated 29 May of the same year. Your Lordship will find it at tab 3 of the bundle of written materials relied upon by the defence. I would like to point out that the accused has in fact no gas supplied to his home, and subsequently – his curiosity aroused – intercepted this letter before it reached the person for whom it was intended.

Marilynne,

You said your husband never opens bills. Thus the disguise. This is not from British Gas, from some mad or mistaken clerk (do they still have clerks?). This is from the man you met on Saturday, at the Arts Festival's private buffet do. The solicitor. The solicitor called Colin, although you said you'd no memory for names. The solicitor who hated being a solicitor, who was forced into it by his father and his grandfather, custodians of the family firm since 1928, as a perusal of the crooked little house in Northcombe Lane and its buffed brass plaque will tell you. Remember?

I hope you are reading this on your own, or at least not within squinting distance of your husband. I imagine you have tremendous self-control beneath your vivacious exterior, so that even if this lovingly faked gas bill has magically transformed itself into a billet-doux at, say, the breakfast table – with your husband opposite, grinning over the toast – I know you will not look alarmed and give everything away. I know you will carry on reading me quietly as if examining the estimated consumption, the VAT, the glossy rubbish that always accompanies the pecuniary hurt (a mere pinprick to you, I know). Or perhaps fold me carefully, to peruse later in the privacy of your bedroom.

Because you know already what I am about to say.

How many hours were we together? Intermittently together, at that? Four, I calculate. Derek Bintwell's cottage is small, though very charming (I dealt with the original transaction, and he paid through the nose for it), and the kitchen table too large. Thus we were all pressed around the food when I first glimpsed you. I had brought the unpopular rice salad, needless to say. Do you remember me telling you this, right at the beginning? It made you laugh. My heart leapt. My own wife never laughs at anything I say. But you laughed, showing your perfect teeth.

You were trying to find a place for your superb avocado mousse, which reminded me of a delicate tabernacle under threat from elbows and knives; I cleared a place for it and helped you lower it on to the scrubbed deal. Our fingers touched. The very first proper thing I said to you, as we were lowering the dish together through all those greedy hands, was: 'That's going to go down a lot better than my effort.' You asked me which my effort was. I pointed to it and said: 'What someone tomorrow's going to call "the unpopular rice salad".' That's when you laughed. We were practically shouting, of course, because the din in the kitchen was dreadful. People talk too much. They talk all the time. Those involved in the festival are particularly loquacious. In a word, they are bores. Actually, they are ghastly, most of them. Culture snobs. Refugees from Ascot, they look like, except that the horses have more brains. I could tell you a thing or two.

A solicitor tends to see the worst side of people. I never wanted to be one.

What I realised, once we'd broken out into the relative peace of the garden, was that you were different.

You were beautiful and exotic, of course, that goes without saying. But your beauty was at one with your voice, your laughter, your 'attitude', as the young(er) say. It sparkled in your eyes as you looked at me, patiently listening to my nervous twaddle, which you seemed to appreciate. I was nervous because you were having a serious effect on my middle-aged composure. It was dusk, the gnats were busy, the moon was rising huge and swollen above the rustling corn (the location of Derek's cottage, although enviable, is not for hay-fever sufferers like myself), and I was experiencing the most intense flush of happiness I can ever remember. I wanted to fling off my tie and shoes and run about the garden with you, hand in hand. I wanted to take you in my arms – not violently, of course, but tenderly – and dance for hours in the balmy air. Instead, I talked: mostly about myself, about my oh-so-thrilling life, filling you in on the local area, the Rotary Club, my solitary weekend hikes, the way in which our respectable family firm had been inveigled to sponsor the festival's modern art installation – those ridiculous rubber fire buckets in the High Street, which have been the inevitable subject of angry letters to the *Chronicle*.

I made jokes which you found amusing. You even found my sneezes amusing – or the way I turned them into something comically self-deprecating. You called my sense of humour 'English, real dry'. I had the sense that you had at last met someone who wasn't a polite Home Counties bore. I filled your glass with the festival's indifferent Chilean red, and talked wine. Every comment you made, however brief, was worth its weight in gold: intelligence shone from your every sun-gilded pore.

Thank God most of the invitees were stuffing their faces in the house.

Then, when I asked you what you did, you said: 'Nothing.' 'Nothing?' 'Zilch. My husband's loaded. He's older than me. He's fat and old. He gets drunk. There he is.'

You Americans, you have such a frank way with words. I looked and there he blew. I was so very pleased to see that he was, in fact, disgustingly fat. He was dressed in a crumpled white suit and was talking to Sarah, Derek's estranged wife – the festival broke their marriage and gave me yet another case, but that's by the by. And I could see he was pretty old, although the folds of stubbled blubber on his face made any precise calculation impossible. He bellowed something and then let forth a very deep and wheezy laugh. (Sarah was chatting him up well, on behalf of next year's festival.)

I turned to you and said, 'It's either him, or the polar bear.' You frowned, remember? Not understanding, not at first. I elaborated: 'The right of our species to be rich and fat, versus the survival of the polar bear. No argument, is there?'

'Don't say that too near him,' you murmured, leaning towards me and raising your lovely eyebrows; 'he gets dangerous when crossed. I mean that. That's why he's a millionaire. *He keeps at least three guns.*'

Wrapped in your scent, I could scarcely summon a coherent reply.

Now, my dearest Marilynne, I don't want you to think that I am prone to insulting people, millionaires or no. I am not even particularly bothered about the polar bear: in the long run, it'll be just one more rather spectacular extinction in a planetary history of extinctions that have mostly gone unnoticed, unhindered.

Let me explain. The previous night, I had been watching *Planet Earth* on television, and feeling particularly low. Deep in a 'funk'. Pointless and pessimistic. I had not been to any of these extraordinary places passing before me on the screen. Neither would I ever be going to any of them in the future, were I (or they) to stay intact long enough for me to do so. My wife Jane hates travelling, and we always end up in Wales where we bicker in front of the fire. Now I was slumped on the sofa, while she was checking her spreadsheets in the dining-room (she is in the social services, and has little time for anything else). I felt plump and horrible, watching these doomed creatures and habitats. As you know, I am on the thin side: the feeling was purely psychological. Thus, when I saw your husband guffawing on the lawn the very next evening, my revulsion was for something that I had only just felt in myself. But – and this is the important point – it was now outside me. It had fled me like a diabolic spirit from a possessed body. This is because *you* were there in front of me, filling me with a sense of freshness and exhilaration. I no longer hated myself – or the human species!

I think I might be avoiding the L-word. I am cautious, generally. I see situations through a legal lens. Cut and dried, pros and cons. Objectively. We have to remain above reproach, we local solicitors. Not that all of us do. But this one does. That's what our reputation is built on, in this area. Honesty, honesty – and extreme confidentiality.

When I was eighteen, however, I had long, greasy hair and played the drums. I wanted to be a rock drummer, a star like Phil Collins. I took drugs, I went for long walks and even wrote poetry. Then I grew up. Actually, my mother died, then I had a severe attack of shingles and, on my recovery, I was a changed person. I studied law and slipped into my grandfather's and father's shoes. I met Jane on a camping trip in Derbyshire: she had precisely the same type and colour of rucksack. Like yourself, we are childless, much to my father's consternation – the firm's line will be broken, the blood in the ink will run dry.

We are childless due to chemical incompatibility.

While I was talking with you in Derek's garden, I felt the drummer within me stirring. I have never felt this with any woman, including Jane. It goes far beyond the physical. Ah yes, I found you extremely attractive, with your very dark and flamboyant head of hair, your large green eyes, your delicate chin, your general shapeliness of body (just ever-so-deliciously tending to fullness and roundness in that long, low-cut yellow dress, with its Spanish frills, that was quite unlike anything those faded festival-committee baggages were sporting), but I am speaking of elements of attraction far deeper than flesh.

And then came the clinching moment.

Do you remember what you said? Probably not: the wine was flowing freely by the end. You had briskly recounted your difficult small-town childhood in Nebraska, your abusive uncles and drunken half-Comanche single mother, your first husband's attempt to start a vineyard in California, your violent separation and his subsequent suspicious death in a car crash, your brief spell as a go-go dancer in Las Vegas, your two (or was it three?) abortions, the reconciliation with your mother, your five-year wanderings in South America, your time out on the pampas as a female 'gringo' gaucho where you think you met a famous German ex-Nazi whose name I forget – while all this was naturally fascinating to me, putting my own brief, rebellious phase into cruel perspective, it was something you said just before Helen Dipley (Festival Treasurer) came over to us that hurled me into the state that I have remained in ever since – of complete and utter adoration.

I asked if, while on the pampas (trying to comprehend the endless, lonely grasslands you'd described), you were not near any reasonably sized town?

And your reply came without hesitation: 'Honey, we were *so* not near any town of whatever darn size, it wasn't true!'

I mentally recorded that sentence, as I'm wont to do in my

profession. For a start, no one had ever called me 'honey' before, except in an amateur production at my school, when I played a waitress in *Annie Get Your Gun*. Second, the sentence was very wittily formed, and completely naturally so. If you remember, I gaped as if wonderstruck, then laughed. Our eyes met – properly, I mean – in the thickening twilight.

And then you said: 'I like you.'

I was opening my mouth to respond in similar albeit stronger fashion, when Helen Dipley came trotting up with some major, all-hands-on-deck crisis concerning the sponsors of the printed programme for the harp concert in the Methodist Hall. And then, as you know, we were never left alone together for the entire remainder of the evening.

So this is my reply to your 'I like you'.

It could be boiled down to just three words. You can guess which those three words are.

No, I have not been able to stop thinking about you over the last few days, even through the most atrociously, grindingly dull piece of legal tittle-tattle. Most of my work concerns divorce and property and petty crime, often simultaneously. I am not popular with the local police, who lie in wait for me in hedgerows, trying to nab me speeding. This is because I am honest and stand up for victims of local injustice, however uncouth those victims might appear to be. So, you see, I have my moments.

The quiet knight.

Shall I come galloping to you, my dearest Marilynne? Shall I wrest us from our mutual unhappiness?

In short, do you have any excuse to see a solicitor?

Piningly yours in hope and expectation – and, of course,
in the very strictest confidence,
Colin

LIONEL SHRIVER

From: Alisha Garrison [mailto: Alisha.Garrison@gmail.com]
Sent: 12 August 2006
To: Kaminsky, Seymour <skaminski2@aol.com>
Subject: No Games

Seymour,

I realise that all the how-to books on love – which would also admonish me never to drop the L-word even in passing at this early a juncture – would command me to wait to contact you until days, perhaps even weeks have elapsed since our reluctant parting. I shouldn't seem too eager, too desperate, too 'needy'. And after getting no sleep whatsoever last night, I ought really to be taking a good long nap! But when I got home to Shepherd's Bush, I was so agitated, so excited, so intoxicated with the sudden gloriousness of life in general that sleep was out of the question. We dispensed with so much in fast-forward; surely we're already beyond childish romantic games. I cannot, I will not be coy. Acting politic, hard to get, unhurried would not only be a lie, but would besmirch with scheming and calculation the clarity, honesty and instant mutual recognition that we discovered so serendipitously. So though it's only been a few hours, they already seem squandered. All this time I might have been writing to you!

First things first: You said this address was the best way to reach you since your mobile had just been stolen. (Being set upon along the South Bank by a gang of ruffians no more than ten years old must have been so, well, unmanning! But I admired that you told the story honestly. Most men would have put fifteen years on their assailants just to save face.) I promised to lodge my phone number in your email queue, since all we could lay hands on at Mandy's party was that grubby napkin on which you scrawled 'skaminsky@aol.com'. I'm touched you were already so concerned that these fragile, paltry digits that could nonetheless prove the password to so much happiness be stowed in a safe place. So enter this in your mobile's phone book when you replace it. For that matter, have it tattooed somewhere private, on a patch of skin I never want another woman to glimpse again! (020) 7274-6738. (I know, I must be the only woman left in London without a mobile. You see – before last night! – I fancied my solitude, and wending my way through the city had no desire to be reached – perhaps in any sense.) Please ring, my sweet. I know you don't have a landline, but such a marvellous man must have many friends with phones! I cannot wait to hear your voice again. This is such a frustratingly cold medium in comparison to the heat of your touch, the warmth of your smile, the glow of your expression when you catch my eye.

Of course, the disadvantage of writing so quickly is that I have little to report – yet everything to report! After a single night, you have utterly transformed my whole landscape. Even on the tube home, all the passengers looked so fascinating, pulsing with poignant stories that broke my heart. Do you know they stared at me? I know I looked a tad dishevelled (your fault!), but I don't think that's why I drew so much attention. I think I had a look. I was exploding with satiety, with a positively obnoxious self-satisfaction! They all appeared so miserable in comparison. And even the colours have changed. You know that A.A. Milne poem, from *When We Were Six*, I think – The cold is very cold; and the hot seems so hot? (Isn't it funny that we grew up with the same enthusiasm for Pooh – although I do hope you don't spot a scatological fascination in the word. As you discovered, my sexual inclinations are deliciously normal!) It's been like that. The yellow's so yellow, and the black's so black!

Oh, and I can't bring myself to shower. I can't bear to wash away the smell of you, which makes me giddy, like sniffing glue. (Not that I sniff glue! Isn't it funny, that you can write 'like sniffing glue' and have no idea what that feels like, yet at once be certain that you have lit upon absolutely the perfect image?)

I'm torn between telling you everything you need to know about me for pages and pages, and getting this off so that we can talk and arrange our next rendezvous. Because I'm not embarrassed to admit that I'm free this very night, I'll tear myself from this email and send it hurtling to your computer. I'll stay in this afternoon and await your call.

Already pining,
Alisha

From: Alisha Garrison [mailto: Alisha.Garrison@gmail.com]
Sent: 14 August 2006
To: Kaminsky, Seymour <skaminski2@aol.com>
Subject: Double-checking

Seymour (and I've been thinking about your name – 'See more' – it's metaphorical, isn't it? You make me *see more*, for the vividness of colour has not abated. And 'mour' recalls 'amore,' as in 'That's amore!' You make me see amore!)

I hope you don't mind my re-sending that first email a few more times over the weekend. I've had trouble with Google in the last several weeks; I've had hardly any mail at all, which is quite impossible. In fact, in the previous year several other gentlemen – who shall go nameless, since I'm not a manipulative sort of girl who would try and make you jealous! – have informed me that they never received an email that I most certainly sent. At your end, AOL doesn't have an exactly sterling reputation for reliability, either. Isn't it rumoured that the company is going bankrupt? Partly because customers like you are so exasperated with uneven service provision? The Internet is not nearly as sure a form of communication as we've been led to believe! And I should loathe for us to founder on so capricious and arbitrary a matter as a technical glitch.

Even if you did get one of the notes in bottles that I dropped into the ocean of cyberspace, maybe there's something about that particular message that won't send properly. I can't say that I'm any kind of computer wunderkind, but wouldn't it be just my luck that that email of all emails was doomed, marked like Cain for destruction! So I thought I'd send a fresh one. In case you never received the earlier one, my phone number is **(020) 7274-6738**. Commit that to memory, recite it as you fall asleep! (Look at me, already bossing you around like a wife of twenty years. Don't I have cheek!)

Of course, you can't have had time to get a new mobile yet, and I know how hard it is to find a working phone box on the street these days. They say that it's only a matter of time before BT eliminates them altogether. And you may very well have tried to ring, borrowing a friend's mobile or something. (I *do* think it's best to keep a landline for just such emergencies as this, even if you claim that with a good price plan it's unnecessary. Whoops! There I go, bossing you around again!) You see, while I did try to stay in for the weekend to await your call, I'm afraid I ran short of provender, and had to nip off to the supermarket for a few things on Sunday afternoon. Although my telephone provider should have recorded any message, I've had simply dreadful experience with One.Tel's voice-mail service. You would not believe how many times I've been told later that someone *definitely* left a message, and I never got that interrupted dial tone indicating that it was awaiting me, much less listened to a recording of any description. The system simply eats messages for breakfast! Honestly, Seymour – See-amore, my new pet name for you! – nothing seems to work as faithfully as need be when so much depends on the successful meeting of electrical wires, the twist of mere cables!

Then again, you may just be terribly busy. I could tell how responsible you were, and however powerfully you might want to distract yourself work has to come first. Perhaps you're saving ringing me up as a little treat for yourself. If so, think of me as a sweetie in your pocket that's going to get all sticky and gooey if you let it sit there too long. Unwrap your little candy, darling! I can't receive private calls at work, so I've taken a personal day today. And I've laid in so many provisions that you'd think I was a Mormon awaiting Judgment Day! (I confess: I was hoping to lure you to dinner, and wanted to make sure that I had all the fixings just in case you rang and said you wanted to call by at the last minute. Isn't it funny, how you have to plan, even to be spontaneous?) So I shouldn't have to leave the flat at all. That way I don't have to depend on One.Tel!

I *do* hope you like smoked salmon. With wheaten soda bread, a squeeze of lemon, capers and thinly sliced red onion. As for the red onion, I'm of two minds. It provides a wonderfully sharp counterpoint to the salmon, but I wouldn't want to spoil our breaths. On the other hand, if we both eat raw onion, doesn't that rather cancel out the unpleasant effect? Goodness, these days to be lucky at love a girl has to be a biochemist!

Trying to be patient with the slings and arrows of outrageous fortune that technology is err to,

Alisha

From: Alisha Garrison [mailto: Alisha.Garrison@gmail.com]
Sent: 26 August 2006
To: Kaminsky, Seymour <skaminski2@aol.com>
Subject: Drop dead

Seymour – or how about See-mort?

Who do you think you are? Or, more to the point, who do you think I am? Some harlot who isn't even smart enough to charge? Some vapid vessel for your seminal fluids, like a toilet bowl? Didn't you appreciate that you were dealing with a woman of some cultural sophistication, so that if she stoops to a cliché like, 'I don't usually do this' she's only making that trite an assertion because it happens to be true?

I suppose you'll also be happy to know that I kept the smoked salmon for so long that it spoilt, which I thought was metaphorical. Something that started out fresh and delicious and nourishing gradually grew slimy, rank and poisonous! So I fed the salmon to my neighbour's Pomeranian – our lovely dinner literally going to the dogs!

It's been two weeks! And don't tell me you didn't get my last email either, because I sent it at least a dozen times, and from my neighbour's computer as well for good measure. (In case you imagine that I brutally use people, like a certain someone who shall remain nameless, I was comforting her about her dog.) I ran out of personal days, and had to ring in sick – anathema to me, since I am renowned for my integrity. That's why the floor manager never questioned whether I was truly ill. In fact, unlike *some* people, he seemed very sympathetic! Which, as it happens, he should have been. Because I am sick. Of you!

Did you assume that because I was willing to slip off to Mandy's guest room I was cheap? Could you conceivably imagine that I pour out my heart like that on a nightly basis, to just anybody? I am a very private person! And now I feel I have entrusted my innermost thoughts, my deepest yearnings and longest-lasting passions, like my love of Pooh – and that's with an H, you dirty-minded cretin! – to a rake and a charlatan, like throwing my finery into a sewer!

So this morning I finally took a shower, and I'll tell you I did so joyfully, I did so singing! 'I'm going to wash that man right out of my hair!' I belted, at the top of my lungs! I rinsed away every dandruffy flake of you, every rancid trace of sweat, every sour drop of your foul testicular emanations.

You would be foolhardy in the extreme to make use of the phone number I entrusted to your keeping. Please destroy it. I assure you that were you to ring now I would not only fling the receiver to its cradle, but direct One.Tel to change my number forthwith!

Icily,
Alisha

From: Alisha Garrison [mailto: Alisha.Garrison@gmail.com]
Sent: 31 August 2006
To: Kaminsky, Seymour <skaminski2@aol.com>
Subject: Please forgive me

See-more, my dearest,

I'm terribly sorry for that last email. I fear that when I wrote last I'd had a drop too much to drink, and you know how in an information vacuum one's mind can run rampant.

Can we just agree to draw a line, and start from scratch? I'm not saying that you like playing games any more than I do. Still, even if we touched our very souls against each other that night, in an everyday sense we know each other only so well, and you may have got the wrong impression of me. I'm usually very guarded, if anything too civil and polite, so that people take a long time to get to know me, and sometimes mistake me for frosty. You should know first-hand that I'm anything but frosty! I suppose it was such a relief to let that guard down and show my true colours – those yellows so yellow, and those blacks so black! – that I may have got ahead of myself.

Tell you what: let's pretend I never wrote anything at all. This time around, we can take it slowly. Maybe we shouldn't have let our passions run away with us that night. What would you say to rolling back the clock, and meeting for lunch, or a drink, or even an innocent cup of coffee? Perhaps we need to get to know each other on an ordinary level, before we see to the touching-souls part. Isn't it funny, that I know your truest, deepest nature, but I don't even know your middle name, what languages you speak, or whether you play the piano?

Hoping to see you soon – and on my best behaviour!

Alisha

From: Alisha Garrison [mailto: Alisha.Garrison@gmail.com]
Sent: 31 August 2006
To: Kaminsky, Seymour <skaminski2@aol.com>
Subject: I'm frightening myself

Seymore – as I see less . . .

I know I shouldn't be writing to you, but I don't know to whom else to turn. I can barely drag myself out of bed, and after my taking those two weeks off work the floor manager from Asda rang to inform me that 'my services would no longer be required'. I don't have any appetite, and when I looked in the mirror just now I almost didn't recognise myself. For the last two days I've barely eaten anything other than the last two pints of Banana Split Häagen-Dazs, and my cheeks are cadaverously sunken.

Outside the sun is beating, bright and mocking, but my head is swirling with darkness and dread. When I lean out the window I feel the summer air sucking me out; I look down and I'm drawn giddily to the vertiginous plummet to the pavement from my first-floor window. The knives in my kitchen glitter with allure like jewellery. I can't gaze upon my top sheet without envisioning it twisted and looped from the overhead light fixture, swinging, tempting me with its release. The oven door gapes open and offers up its hot-breathed maw, except that I read somewhere that natural gas these days has had the lethal component removed, and the Sylvia Plath route has been confounded. I don't think that's very considerate, do you? Just because you work at Asda – or used to work at Asda – doesn't mean that you don't deserve a poetic departure.

I was happy before, or whatever it is you call not knowing what you're missing. I was living on bread and water, and for one night I tasted cake. Oh, See-more, I cannot return to a prison diet once more. So if you read about me in the papers, just know that you blessed this poor inmate with one glorious night of freedom and escape. If I only truly lived for one night, so many of us sad little moths seeking out the light never live at all. I suppose that I'm lucky. But if I'm so lucky, why do I feel so doleful, so despondent, so beyond caring?

Sorry to trouble you,
Alisha

From: Sam Kaminski [mailto: skaminski2@aol.com]
Sent: 31 August 2006
To: Garrison, Alisha <alisha.garrison@gmail.com>
Subject: Re: I'm frightening myself

look lady i dont know if this guy yr writing scammed u with a fake email address or weather yr completely whacked and he's a fig newton of yr imagination (haha) but im a new jersey boy born and bread and u and me never spent no night together eating cake or nothing. id never have loaded yr emails to begin with what with the virus alerts and stuff cept that the subject line of the first one made me mistook it for having to do with the video game i was bidding for on ebay (dark messiah of might and magic and some dipshit beat me out). so dont stick yr head in the oven on my account especially if it dont even work. and if you don't mind me tossing in my two cents from the peanut gallery if yr buddy 'seemore' did palm off a bullshit address and flee the scene of the crime so to speak the guy's a fucking smart cookie (or fig newton haha) sam

DAVID BEZMOZGIS

Lubyanka, 2 September 1918

My dear Mika,

Though you have made it clear that you do not care for me, my heart nevertheless insists that I address you as 'my dear'. I know this will only irritate you. It irritates me too. My love has brought neither of us any happiness. But don't think that I resent you for this. On the contrary, I am grateful. At a time of revolution, love is a bourgeois indulgence. In rejecting my affections, you reminded of this. I am ashamed of the woman I was in Kharkov. I wanted romance so desperately that I forgot myself. For those two days, I allowed myself to imagine that I was once again a girl of sixteen. When I saw you, I saw the last man who had treated me with tenderness, spoke loving words to me, and made me feel like more than a rag dragged through the dirt. Seeing you, it was as if the twelve years of prison and loneliness had evaporated.

You will never understand, but I have lived for twelve years in permanent blackness. Even in the rare moments when my vision cleared, I saw before me only my black life in the prison camp. Many times I wished for the strength to bring about my own death. Many times I cursed myself for having survived the explosion in the hotel room. What had my survival brought me? Only misery. A girl of sixteen, half blind, imprisoned with no hope of clemency. But then came the February Revolution, the amnesty, and the doctors who restored my vision. And then, as if by fate, there you were in the street buying a newspaper. How else to explain your presence in Kharkov, standing in the street where I took my afternoon walks?

This is mere sentimentality I know, but amnesty from prison and reprieve from blindness made us foolish and optimistic. I shudder to think of the image I must have cut running towards you. I felt myself a young beauty, but what I must have looked like! Hysterical, a madwoman, coat flapping, hair wild, pale and gaunt. Like a witch from a fairy tale used to frighten children. I saw the truth in your eyes but I refused to admit it. Though now, sitting in my cell, I see quite plainly the disgust on your face. I have seen much more of it these last days. I no longer care. I accept that I am a woman who does not inspire warmth in men, and I will never again beg like a dog for a scrap of kindness.

I have no illusions, Mika. I know what awaits me. I know what to expect from the Bolsheviks. Sverdlov, Lenin's pet jackal, has come to witness my interrogation. Naturally, I refuse to speak in his presence. They send one after another of their lackeys to pry information from me. They do not believe that I was capable of acting alone. Perhaps you also cannot believe this? But it is true. Before this letter reaches you, you will have read in the newspapers that I shot at Lenin. I do not think I succeeded in killing him. If I regret anything, it is only that. He is a traitor to the Revolution. I lay the responsibility for the treacherous peace with Germany and the dissolution of the Constituent Assembly at his feet. I have told my inquisitors as much and so expect that they will not censor it from this letter. That this letter reaches you at all I have entrusted to Yakov Peters. He is the only one among them who has treated me with even a semblance of decency. In his youth, like you and me, he was an anarchist. History has turned him in one direction, me in another, and you in yet another. What will come of it all I can only speculate. But when the doctors fixed my eyes, I had hoped that I would look upon a better world. For the first days, I saw beauty all around me. I saw potential in all things, including myself. Of course this sensation did not last. It did not take long for the world to assert its true nature. The Revolution was betrayed and you confirmed my inadequacy as a woman.

For years I had consoled myself that, in prison, blindness was a sort of blessing. What, after all, is worth seeing in prison? But even liberated from the tzar's prison I recognised that I was not free. For the workers of the world, liberty remains an unkept promise. We remain prisoners of the bourgeoisie and of the false prophets of the Revolution. And so I am not sad to say goodbye to this world. I have done what I could to further the Revolution. I will die as I have lived, a Marxist and a Socialist revolutionist.

I will end here but for one request. Mika, I know I have no claims on you and no reason to make demands, but as this is the only letter I am permitted to send, I ask that you write to my brother Berl in New York. Tell him he was right, I was not made for a long life. Tell him also that I do not want our father to recite prayers for me.

Yours,
Fanny

This letter was discovered among the papers of Yakov Peters at the time of his arrest and execution by the NKVD in 1938.

CHRIS BACHELDER

To whom it may concern:

I am writing to recommend Charles Valentine for any love-related position – professional, academic, or personal – for which he might apply or be considered. I have been a love educator at the high school level for more years than I would care to disclose, and I can say without hesitation that Charlie is the most gifted student of love I have ever seen. In comparison, all of the other students I have taught and all of the students I will yet teach in my long slow slide to retirement – my previous and subsequent recommendation letters notwithstanding – are what we in Love Ed. call Raisin Hearts. By all other reliable measures an average and uninspired student (see transcript), Charlie is, in the discipline of love, a prodigy and a genius.

Bear with me as I create an analogy based on bicycling champion Lance Armstrong. Much has been made of Armstrong's natural or genetic gifts; he has, as I understand it, *three lungs*, no doubt a considerable asset in the Alps. But we all know that an extra lung in and of itself does not account for Armstrong's preeminence. He also has spent a good deal of time on his bicycle, making himself better than everyone else. Without work ethic, a freakish genetic mutation is nothing more than a freakish genetic mutation. To achieve elite status in any pursuit, one requires a combination of innate ability and determination, and what I am trying to tell you now is that young Charlie Valentine, Perlis High School class of 07, possesses precisely this combination in the field of love. Even as a sophomore in Beginning Love, Charlie instinctively understood what many – my former husband Dennis, for instance – will never, *never* understand about intimacy and affection. But he has also developed his gifts with real initiative and self-discipline, devoting himself to his studies, devouring the love canon.

I will never forget walking into Beginning Love nearly three years ago and seeing skinny Charlie sitting in the back row with his notebook open to a clean white page. I and everyone else in town knew that his father had pushed his mother down a flight of stairs when Charlie was just an infant, and that Charlie had spent his youth in a series of foster homes, some of which were case studies in pernicious love. I certainly expected him to be a typical Perlis youth; that is, I expected him to regard his own heart, and the hearts of everyone around him, as an old piñata, bludgeoned, shredded, plundered of all sweetness. And yet Charlie quickly proved me wrong and he almost immediately distinguished himself as an affectional savant. While he lacked the conceptual framework, critical vocabulary, and familiarity with the canon that he later would develop, he somehow had a native empathy and a real sense for the art of love. In the second week of class, months before the Communication Unit, Charlie respectfully engaged J.T., one of a dozen or so students vying for the position of class clown, explaining that J.T.'s unruly in-class comments were, like all sarcasm, 'corrosive to genuine trust and intimacy'. The ensuing period of silence – broken finally by the sobbing of a jilted cheerleader in the hallway – was the most powerful six or eight seconds of my teaching career. And while I may be a fatalist, I don't consider it mere fatalism to say that I will never feel another moment like it, in or out of the classroom.

While most of his peers enthusiastically desist their formal love education after the required Beginning Love, Charlie enrolled in my Intermediate Love, an elective, during his junior year. Intermediate Love, as you may know, is basically a course in boundaries, responsibilities and needs. To begin the Needs Unit, I administered, as I do almost every year, the Mortenson Passion Vector Diagnostic Exam (popularly, the Passion Grapher), which measures the relative warp of the subject's amorous desires, interests and goals. Students answer 234 questions and, with the aid of Passion Grapher software (what a racket), their responses are converted into a graph of passion vectors. The straighter the lines, the healthier the lover. I probably don't need to tell you that the Passion Graphs we derive at Perlis High usually look like bonsai trees – a typical junior's vector will loop back to cross itself or veer wildly off the edge of the page. The software version we use at Perlis is no doubt dated, but still, we had students whose passions' coordinates were literally unrepresentable in two-dimensional space. There are crooked needs and then there are *crooked needs.* But Charlie's passions? Strong, lovely, majestic blasts, right down the middle of the diagnostic fairways. These vectors looked like they had been drawn with rulers. (It is a testament to his romantic discretion – often mistaken here as shyness – that Charlie has not taken a girlfriend at PHS.) I sent the results to Dr. Mortenson himself, and he replied, six months later, by denouncing me and my 'hoax'. Nobody's desires are that straight, he wrote, and particularly not those of a sixteen-year-old foster kid from the sticks.

The final project in Intermediate Love is a Personal Love History. The PLH requires students to investigate the types of familial and romantic love they have experienced – the forces that have shaped their predilections and capacities – since childhood. The purpose is to understand one's heart as the product of specific circumstances. (The implied logic that once students understand their own hearts they will subsequently act in their hearts' best interest has always struck me as a form of optimism that borders on mental illness, but the curriculum comes down from on high.) Charlie's PLH was of breath-taking scope and tone; he covered four generations of his family, and his 53-page treatment of his ancestors' staggeringly warped passions – accounting for more than two dozen love-induced felonies over a century – was both firm and empathetic. Judicious throughout, the PLH was by turns clear-eyed castigation and tender memoir. One of the writing samples you will find in Charlie's file is a short excerpt from this masterpiece.

You will notice from Charlie's transcript that he has not taken Advanced Love, but please note that our county does not offer Advanced Love. The official explanation is that there is not enough student interest, but the real reason is that Advanced Love would likely include a Sex Unit, and the school board has prohibited sex education in county schools. However, for his senior year, Charlie, on his own initiative, planned an independent study with me that has extended and expanded his intense exploration of love. He developed his own massive and diversified reading list, which includes work from many genres and disciplines – poetry, fiction, religion, philosophy, psychology, and even biology and chemistry (though he remains passionate in his position that the sciences will never be able to account fully for love). Late last fall, Charlie created a love tutoring center at the high school, staffed by volunteers that he trains. Within weeks, Charlie opened up a second center in the basement of the Perlis Baptist Church, open nights and weekends. It is far too early to determine what kind of effect the centers are having at school and in the community, but social services did report a slight drop in abuse, neglect and abandonment during the Christmas holidays, typically the high season for love-related mayhem.

I hesitate to mention one last point about Charlie's recent studies because I fear it may negatively affect your estimation of his candidacy. But if this is the case, then your brain is as weak as your heart. Lately, the scope of Charlie's focus has broadened considerably to include politics, economics, government and history. In our weekly meetings the last few months he has begun speaking much more expansively about love and justice. I'm not sure I know what he's up to, but if I had to guess, I'd say he's developing a theory of love and revolution. Many years ago I surrendered all hope of any meaningful change in the world, but Charlie's interest in the intersection of love and political economy has stirred some long dormant part of my heart.

It is true that almost every student I teach snickers and punches a classmate whenever I mention the *love canon*. And it is also true that many of them think *eros* is the plural form of the kind of sharp projectile their camouflaged daddies shoot at large game. Many are pregnant; many have black eyes; many are so damaged that they will never give themselves fully; many are so damaged that they will never stop giving themselves fully; most are reckless, blind, angry, and deranged by lunatic desires. Most are so irrevocably lonely and love-starved as to be unreachable by love. Inevitably, Charlie's talents seem miraculous in a town like Perlis. Nevertheless, I am certain that Charles Valentine would be, even in the most love-enlightened community (and please do tell me where that might be), an exceptionally gifted and promising student. Charlie has my respect, my envy, my blessing, and my very highest recommendation.

He also has my heart. I imagine by now it is obvious that I am deeply, deeply in love with Charles Valentine. One evening last winter I saw him in the parking lot of the mall theater. I had had, it is true, a couple of tall vodka tonics, and I asked Charlie, out of earshot of his drug-addicted foster aunt, if he would like to come to my apartment some time ('or now') to drink lemon liqueur and chat in front of my gas log fireplace. Of course it was wrong – let me count the ways: he's eighteen (actually seventeen at the time), I am decades his senior, he's my student, and all of the boats in this town have glass bottoms. But he is an extraordinary boy and the wind was so cold and my phone sometimes goes weeks without ringing. I like to believe that Charlie hesitated just a moment before he declined my proposal, doing so in a way that allowed me to retain my meager stores of hope and dignity and professionalism. In fact, his rejoinder was so tenderly delivered as to make me feel, for just a moment, worthy of expert love. I remember his cheeks were blasted red by the wind and his hair stood up funny in front. As usual he was not wearing proper winter clothes, and he shivered slightly as he pointed out to me that he might compromise his grade in the independent study if he were to come to my apartment. He added – and here his tone was elegant, rich and complex – that I would likely find him much less interesting and desirable the moment he ceased to be so scrupulous in his passions. This, I concede, is probably true. Such is his empathy, such is his understanding of the paradoxes of love!

This recommendation completes Charles Valentine's Love Credentials File. You, holding this letter, you with your scars and rusty scalpels, you do not deserve Charles Valentine because nobody deserves him. If by some fluke you find yourself in his midst, I implore you to receive him with gratitude and with reverence.

Here he comes, Raisin Hearts. Here comes my Charlie and he is not mine, not mine, not mine.

Sincerely,

Paula Gates
Director of Love Education
Perlis High School

A. L. KENNEDY

Another room. We still have these in common at least: the so very many rooms. Not exactly empty, hardly full, and the small unbalanced weight of us soft inside them while we look at the distance between the window and the wardrobe, the bathroom and the table, the nightstand and the necessary bed – if they give us nothing else, there always is a bed. The cities outside, they don't matter. I am in my rooms and you are in yours and the distance between us too deep to see.

And the travelling. We both know about that – one loneliness pursuing while we hide in the rush of another – our type of flight.

The way to Norwich, I remember, was very cold. Trains stammered and wandered and stopped in the damp, flat country and the sleet kept coming, nothing to stop it, and my coat still smelt of holding you, which is to say of that goodbye which seemed hardly final at all and also like tumbling over into nothing, no one.

Although I am an adult, we are both of us adults, and quite aware that we can live without anybody, anything. There are very few losses we won't survive after our fashion: keeping ourselves from the thoughts we would rather not have and breathing and blinking and swallowing as we should. We look very much like other adults, are credible.

Such a bad journey, though, to Norwich and I wanted to call you and say how many hours longer it lasted than it ought to have done, how many baths I took to try and warm my hands, my body, rinse away what won't be shifted.

Little Formica unit in that room, bible and a hairless carpet, television bolted to the wall, fawn kettle, three custard creams I didn't eat and this space I could almost touch, could have occupied a month before, a week before: the shape of myself on the bed and calling you, feeling better, understood.

Like being in London and back in that place I can't go to any more – where the rooms have good, thick walls and little kitchens, proper sheets – and meeting the way we did then: on the run and gently, perfectly unhinged. Dinner when I couldn't find the restaurant, doped up and stitches in my mouth, and you came out looking for me when I phoned and then I circled round, holding your voice in the receiver, and watched until I saw you walking up towards me, talking me in.

Talking the way I hadn't, didn't, don't – about penguins' eggs, dentistry, lamp oil, cruelty, theft, forgiveness, coming quietly, the possibility of losing everything, the possibility of writing on the dark. And we said we were glad that we were alive: more precisely, that we were glad of each other's lives, if not our own. Which is the way that joy comes in – quietly and written on the dark.

The rooms always come with their different shapes of darkness: lintels and blades of shadow where we stumble in the small hours and cannot find the glass, the switch, the door-knob, whatever it is we are reaching for and think we need. Sitting perhaps in that room in Cologne and beyond the generous window and the sense of expensive confinement is a streetlamp and the cemetery wall, a view on to old graves, and I think I need to try and make you laugh – nicely hard and always worth it – and I think I need to do that and I think I need to see the black flame of your hair – suggesting the black flame in your head – and I think I need to see the way your beard grows when you leave it – as if it would like you to seem ridiculous – and I think I need to feel the way your stomach flinches under touch – that nice shyness – and I think I need to see you smile and I need the way you smell when you haven't washed and I need to see you smile. I need to see you smile.

But I'm wrong, of course: I don't need it. What I have must be enough. No one survives without having enough. I have the light from the smoke alarm in the ceiling, the pinprick of red ticking on and off, and I have this tiredness and this fear that all there is left will be waiting by myself while dying comes closer, travels. You said you were afraid all of the time. Now that's how I am, too, but I can't tell you.

And I did nothing to help you when, from the first time, you helped me. Dying in a plane crash, never finishing another sentence, being ugly, being selfish, being useless, being hurt – the stupid fears a stupid person has – you lifted them very precisely away, as if you knew what you were doing and knew me. The good I found in you I never showed you properly. I was not convincing.

Now I'm in this room, in New York – thick rain clattering down the skylight and it's my late evening in the middle of your night: even our days separated, staggered apart. My luggage has gone missing and this would be funny if I could make it a story for you – another disastrous journey that wouldn't much matter, because we're all right and care that we're all right. Only I have no story, because you don't want one.

I have this which you won't read. Whatever form of words I find, it will make no difference – there's nothing more you'll let me say to you. I work in invisible ink, unsay myself in rooms I don't want and don't know and I keep on the road to stay ahead of so much silence, to be beside you in this one way, travelling as I know you're travelling, running.

I never was sure what we believed in, except each other, but since I am helpless and you may be too, I make us a prayer every night which asks if you could be happy, if you could be safe. Then I would have almost enough.

My love never was any better than that.

JEFF PARKER

From: WheelerDealer@yahoo.com
Date: Wednesday, November 22, 2006 11:42 AM
To: jnotice@moose-mail.com
Subject: a little catch-up

Dear Jana,

Hi, I found your address online. It might be weird to get an email from me after so long.

I don't rightly know where to begin. I often remember those days in '94 and '95: You and I, two spry young HTML coders who couldn't get enough of each other. What really did it for me was how you brought our work back to the bedroom. Serious. I loved that. If you had been one of those, 'Fuck me with your big dick' kind of girls, I don't think we would have made it as long as we did. But there was this one thing you would scream – I can hear your voice right now: 'Open carrot, div, align equals right, close carrot, indent, open carrot, image, space, source equals harder dot harder dot harder dot jpeg, close carrot, outdent, open carrot, backslash, div, close carrot.' I couldn't control myself. And you didn't have to worry about referring to external javascripts or style sheets or database query strings which is what it's all about now, so technified and unerotic. Those days, the early days of the Internet, were much simpler times. Give me a basic scripting language over object orientation any day.

It's not the reason I'm writing. I haven't really told you anything about me yet though, have I? If you're interested, I kept on with the coding, moving up here and there as the technology changed. Eventually I bought a book on SQL and learned databases. It was a good move at a good time from a career perspective. The past five years I've been in database design. It's interesting, when you're building databases all day you focus in on one thing, you know, the primary key. Everything else is relation, relation, relation. Does this other thing relate to my primary key? If so, how? If not, how to organise the relation?

Coming around to it, finally, my wife – yep, I'm married – wants to have a baby. We've been trying for a while and with no results. I suggested she get a fertility check-up and she kind of half got offended. Ah, that's not true. Lisa doesn't get offended. Everything is ironic with her. But she got ironic offended and said I needed to get a fertility check-up too. I said, 'Look, it's not me okay. I've been responsible for two abortions in my life.' Lisa thinks this is a trip. She accuses me of bragging about my abortions. But I'm a good sport and I went and did the jerk off into a cup thing. The results came back showing her pond fully stocked. Me? Low sperm motility, which means the percentage of moving sperm and their quality of motion. I'm telling them that their results must be off, to retest, and they say things like, it's not the first time they've had a guy who can't make babies suggest a history with a woman who claimed they made a baby. I about punched him for, in effect, calling into question your good name – you know how fond I've always been of you, Jana, even after we split. I checked around on the Internet and certain people's sperm motility does decrease over time, especially if they're mountain bikers or some new studies show that cellphones actually have an impact. But I don't ride and I don't talk so much on the cell, surely not enough for that. Quite the opposite. I sit ten-hour days in a one-thousand dollar ergonomically correct office chair, comfortably resting my balls on an indentation which keeps them, as I code, warm and balanced.

Sometimes things seem so far away though it's like you don't really even remember them. You can start to feel crazy because part of you is so sure your life went like this and another part of you feels this panic because maybe you misread something all these years. I don't know what I'm really trying to get at. I just think about you sometimes, especially when something like this comes up. I hope it doesn't create bad memories or something. Where are you in the world?

Solid Gold,
-Dealer

From: jnotice@moose-mail.com
Date: Wednesday, November 22, 2006 12:14 PM
To: WheelerDealer@yahoo.com
Subject: Re: a little catch-up

Dealer,

Conceivably it'd be nice to hear from you. But do you have to be so pornographic? I'm not like that any more. Let's agree to keep our electronic reunion strictly business. You wrote me for a reason and I'll discuss that point with you because it's having some bearing on your life, which I don't feel completely comfortable about. (But I'm not accepting your friend request on MySpace, and you really should write people before just adding them.)

I never told you this, but I came down with a condition while we were together. It's somewhat rare, often misdiagnosed, leads to break-ups, divorces and single-parent children and lifelong sex phobias. So the fallout in our situation pales in comparison. We hardly even knew each other.

I was never pregnant. That was an excuse to keep from having sex because I started getting headaches. At first I thought what was causing the headaches was the screaming. I always hated HTML. I did that for you, because I very well knew you loved it. If I have a gift it's knowing what people love. But soon there was like a lightning bolt in my head. It's called Sexual Headache. It means a sudden excruciating headache when approaching orgasm or afterwards, also known as Orgasmic Headache. It is believed to be vascular and sudden rupture of a cerebral blood vessel can occur. So it's dangerous.

I was stupid and insecure. I didn't want to tell you I was getting headaches. I thought you'd hate me. On top of that the old sex-headache cliché. So I told you I was pregnant. I invented the abortion saga, carried it out for months. Those times I wept, it was because I was imbalanced. I began to hate me and to hate you. The doctor told me it was impossible to tell what caused Sexual Headache, but that he was sure if I didn't have sex, it would solve the problem. The abortion story bought me time. When you dropped me off that day, and I ordered you not to come in, it was because I had scheduled an exam, a consultation on birth control. Nothing more. The consult took about twenty minutes, and I sat in the waiting room while you sat in the parking lot, to give you the impression it took longer than it did.

The rants that came out of me, things like, 'I can't live with what we've done', fueled the guilt. In truth I couldn't live with the headache I got while we were doing it. And the thing is, I'm grateful for all of it. I didn't have the strength to break up with you otherwise. I didn't have sex with anyone for more than a year, but when I did, it was fine, great even – and no headache. It never occurred again. The cause of my Sexual Headache was you.

I don't want to seem heartless, Dealer. I do have nice memories of you. But honestly, the capillaries in my brain feel constricted just emailing you, like the effects of a hangover. I'm sorry to hear about your motility and I wish you and what's her name the best of luck, but don't write again.

Jana

From: WheelerDealer@yahoo.com
Date: Wednesday, November 22, 2006 12:16 PM
To: jnotice@moose-mail.com
Subject: Re: Re: a little catch-up

You always were a neurotic bitch. Thanks for fucking out my world.

From: WheelerDealer@yahoo.com
Date: Wednesday, November 22, 2006 12:20 PM
To: KkrazychickK@gmail.com
Subject: quick question

Dear KkrazychickK,

Hey. Nice email handle. It's got great symmetry. So yeah, this is Dealer. It's been a while huh? I tracked you down online. Looks like you're working for some yoga place – sounds hot!

To be honest I'm in a bit of a panic here. I'll give you the condensed version: my new wife – yep, married – wants to have kids. We haven't used protection in years because I guess you could say we were never really not trying. I assumed the reason nothing ever happened in the kid way was that she couldn't have children. This made sense to me in terms of karma, that I would fall in love with a woman who couldn't conceive. I figured I'd aborted my chances at children and now by the natural laws of the universe, I would not have them. I remember the abortion you had when we were together. That really broke me up. The funny thing is, I've been diagnosed with low sperm motility. In other words, my boys can't swim. They lack umph. But I'm trying to figure out if this is something that's happened over time, or if it's always been this way. Obviously, it can't be the latter, because you got pregnant when we were together. Right? Well, of course you did. We had that little scare afterwards, with the blood in the toilet. And you called the doctor and it was just a normal clot. I know this must seem weird and probably unpleasant. I'm just trying to clarify. I've had some disturbing revelations of late.

Hope everything's okay in your life.

Solid Gold,
-Dealer

From: KkrazychickK@gmail.com
Date: Wednesday, November 22, 2006 01:07 PM
To: WheelerDealer@yahoo.com
Subject: Re: quick question

Hey you, that's so strange. I was just thinking about you the other day. The owner of a studio I work at was interested in building a database of her clients and asked me if I knew anyone who did that stuff. I said that I did but I hadn't talked to him in a few years.

I'm teaching Pilates and Bikram Yoga at a few places in Oakland. Do you know what Bikram is? It's like hot yoga. So, yeah, it is hot, about 106 degrees to be exact. The poses are designed to tourniquet your body with long, low-impact stretches, which you hold, cutting off the blood flow, then release, and your blood surges through you again, rushing oxygen to every tissue. It's the life. Nothing but good feeling from me. You're probably right about the karma. I don't want kids.

Listen, about that abortion back then, I've got to be honest with you. I wish I'd known how to get in touch with you because I've needed to for a while about this very thing. I ended up in a twelve-step program not long after we split. I had it coming even then. One of the steps was to apologise to everyone you had hurt and/or lied to in one way or another.

You were at the top of my Had Lied To list. I was cheating on you with four or five guys. You tended to use condoms whereas they didn't. So I doubt it was yours. In fact I can say for sure that I doubt it was yours. I know whose it was. I remember exactly when it happened. You would have been at work, which is when I would meet with this particular one. It happened just like I always imagined it would, mystically, under a tree, in the rain. But it wasn't you. You were the only one who stepped up to the plate though. I figured because you had experience from that other girl, the one you got pregnant before me. You knew how to deal with things. Good because I didn't want to have anything to do with that guy. You were really sweet during all of that. I'd like to send you the money you paid for it. What was it, like four hundred dollars? What's your address?

Kisses,
Kim

From: WheelerDealer@yahoo.com
Date: Wednesday, November 22, 2006 01:09 PM
To: KkrazychickK@gmail.com
Subject: Re: Re: quick question

You've got to be kidding me. Four or five guys? Under a tree? In the rain? Are you sure that wasn't a movie? Or maybe you're misremembering. Time is like that sometimes. Especially with all the pills you were doing.

The database stuff isn't hard to learn. Well, I take that back, the query languages take some time, but the actual design of the database is pretty simple. You have a number of entities with different sets of data, but each entity shares one thing in common. That's your primary key, which forces entity integrity by uniquely identifying entity instances. Then there's your foreign key, which enforces referential integrity by completing an association between two entities. These keys can be as meaningless as an ID number or as meaningful as a last name.

I am still trying to picture this: you under a tree in the rain, being mystically impregnated by one of four or five men you are sleeping with during the time I am at the office learning the principle of the primary key. You could say that I feel right now like the keys connecting the associations of my life have just been blipped. It's primary key rule numero uno, that each instance of its entity must have a non-null value. When it's pulled out from under you, it's a crusher.

Pilates and Yoga? You must be in great shape. Could you send me a pic? Are you born again and everything now?

Solid Gold,
Wheeler

From: KkrazychickK@gmail.com
Date: Wednesday, November 22, 2006 01:35 PM
To: WheelerDealer@yahoo.com
Subject: Re: Re: Re: quick question

Yes, it's what happened. Time I'm very clear on. The mistakes add up quick.

I know in my heart that there's something out there, Wheeler, something governing the universe. But I don't believe in God. I didn't fall for that part of it. I only fell for the part that could help me. It's not selfishness though. I know in my heart by helping me it helps the rest of the world too. I was corrosive before. Now I am galvanic.

I don't get any of what you said about keys.

Seriously, send me your address. I'm waiting. Atonement, at last . . .

Kim

ps: Here's a shot they took for my instructor profile. It's the Dandayamana Dhanurasana pose. I can do that shit all day long.

From: WheelerDealer@yahoo.com
Date: Wednesday, November 22, 2006 01:38 PM
To: KkrazychickK@gmail.com
Subject: getting over it already

You look totally collapsed in on yourself there. I mean you look really good one-footed, twisted around yourself. I think I can safely say you are the hottest woman I ever went out with. You were probably my best chance at natural selection. Of course back then you were so fucked up it probably would have had some defects or something. But present wife included, you are definitely the hottest. That's no dis to Lisa. Lisa is amazing. She's totally ironic, and she just deflects things. And she'll try anything but in moderation. I think she knew all along that it was me, that I was the problem. And she let me blather on about my abortions and how it had to be her. I'm still fucked over all of this. Did you ever have dreams about the kid, Kim? I have dreams about the kid all the time, and not only that one. I dream about the other one I supposedly (long story) aborted with that neurotic bitch. I've had such vivid dreams I woke up in the morning and thought I heard the both of them, two boys, chattering away downstairs in front of the TV. They'd be five and eight now if they ever really existed. It never bothered me. Never. Not until now. I carried them with me and that was enough, and now I find out I was carrying nothing all along. It's like the opposite of that Jesus and footprints in the sand story. You don't think something like that will affect you, but it does. It affects you.

Solid Gold,
Wheeler

From: WheelerDealer@yahoo.com
Date: Wednesday, November 22, 2006 02:10 PM
To: KkrazychickK@gmail.com
Subject: indecent proposal

What does a guy have to do to get an invite to the Bay Area and a complimentary body tourniquet?

From: WheelerDealer@yahoo.com
Date: Wednesday, November 22, 2006 02:20 PM
To: gogogadgetsoul@gmail.com
Subject: where we stand

Well, babe, I've been searching for answers. Things are

confirmed: I was a dope, duped. My boys never swam, Lisa. I hereby drop my claims on the good people at Fertilocertainty. I hereby restore their good name. My abortions were fictions all these years. Those cunts. I could understand one, but two. Where do you find girls like that? It's been a grand deception. I just thought of something funny, babe: False sense of sterility. But that's not quite it, is it?

Solid Gold,
Wheeler

From:gogogadgetsoul@gmail.com
Date: Wednesday, November 22, 2006 2:35 PM
To: WheelerDealer@yahoo.com
Subject: Re: where we stand

Dealer,

I'll see you tonight. We'll make it. There are drugs to teach your boys to swim or machines to do the swimming for them. And in the end, it's just another project of mine. If it doesn't work out, I'll find another project. This is how well I understand me. The ROOMBA robotic vacuum is already tempting. It's like a puppy except instead of shitting and pissing all over the place, it cleans. It's cute, adorable even, a little toaster-sized cross between Knight Rider and R2-D2. Don't worry about your ex-cunts. I'm more than you could ever ask for.

xo,
Lisa

FRANCINE PROSE

Dear Franz,

Having outlived you by so many years, I often feel a bit uncertain about what you will and won't understand. For example, what would you make of the phrase, zero to sixty in sixty seconds? That was how it was for us, my dear. One minute we were at Max's apartment, perusing your vacation snapshots, which you handed me, sacramentally, one by one, over the table. A minute later, you were writing me letters, and then not writing, and I would write, or not write, a letter wouldn't arrive, you'd write me an entire letter about the first letter not arriving, and so it was on, our great love affair, zero to sixty in sixty seconds.

It was all about the letters. The letters were our subject. Other couples had children, gardening, kisses, the theater. We had four hands, two typewriters, paper, two desks in distant cities.

But first, we had those snapshots: a mountain, trees, a stream, rocks, you and Max posed in some village square. I was glad to have them to look at. No one wanted me at that dinner. I was Max's brother-in-law's cousin, a family obligation passing through Prague *en route* to her Budapest sister. Not powerful, not beautiful, a secretary from Berlin. The pictures gave me some privacy, and besides, it was interesting to secretly watch you secretly watching me. Who were you? I'd forgotten your name. It wasn't a name I'd heard. You were young, unmarried, nice looking, though other girls might not have thought so.

So many of your letters, dear, were childlike demands for truth – where did I go, what color hat did I wear, how well did I chew my food – that it seems a little strange that so much lying should have gone on. Right off, I only pretended to be interested in those (to be honest) rather boring vacation snapshots. I didn't want to be at that dinner, but I knew no one else in Prague, and the meal was free. I knew how they felt about me, too, so that when Max pointed out that my food was getting cold while I lingered over the photos, it gave me pleasure to say I found it disgusting when people were no better than pigs, obsessed with stuffing their faces.

It wasn't exactly a sacrifice. The food at Max's was awful, those quivering lumps of animal fat my Prague relations ate. But when I said that about eating, you nodded wildly, and then seemed surprised to feel your own head bobbing up and down.

The conversation kept drifting to some dreary literary business you and Max had to settle. There wasn't much I could add until someone mentioned needing a manuscript typed. It was as if I had left my body, and was watching myself hold forth on the fascinating subject of *my life as a typist*! I said I no longer typed any more, the firm hired girls to do that, but I saw nothing demeaning about the job, in fact *I liked to type*. How innocent you and Max were, dear, assuming that a woman stupid enough to like typing would be too stupid to know what effect it might have on a writer to hear that a woman *liked* to type.

You smacked the table and stared at me. I'll admit, I liked the attention. So when the conversation drifted back to this or that magazine or publisher, I took advantage of a pause to remark how hard I was working, studying Hebrew in my spare time. You had mentioned Palestine, earlier in the evening.

Hebrew! How impressed you were! A braver, bolder spirit possessed you and made you declare that you not only wanted to go to Palestine, but you were planning to go this year! And then that bold angel or devil leapt from your head into mine, and made me say I would go with you. You asked if I meant it. I nodded. We shook hands on it, then and there, comradely and businesslike, with Max's family watching. An agreement had been reached, a deal had been transacted.

You were never going to Palestine. I understood that, soon enough. And though at the moment I meant it, I wasn't going, either. So let me return, for a moment, to the subject of lying.

I wasn't studying Hebrew. I'd been thinking I might want to.

Dear, every couple tells little white lies that don't seem false at the time. They say they love something they don't really love, only because the beloved loves it, and for a moment they do love it, because the beloved does. That's what is known as falling in love, though how could you have known that?

And now, my dear, a question that I can only ask you: What, do you think, would be the point of a man lying to his diary?

When your diaries were finally published, you had been gone for decades, but even so I felt a chill – a chill of conscience, you might say – at reading the intimate journals of a man to whom I'd once been engaged. Not once, as you well know, but twice. I am only human, as you were always so eager to point out, so perhaps I can be forgiven for admitting that I opened the volume directly to the date of our first meeting. As intimate as our courtship had been, I still feared that I was prying. And my punishment for this tiny sin? It was instant, dear, and cruel.

How shocking to learn that what you saw in me – that what

attracted you – was what you called my emptiness. *A bony empty face, displaying its emptiness openly* was the exact expression that, I believe, you used. *Bristly, unappealing hair, a big chin, a broken nose.* I know I was never a beauty, I had trouble with my teeth. But I wouldn't have called myself *empty.* Far from it. I was full of many things, energy, for one. I had supported my family since Father left us for his younger, more cheerful family on the other side of town. I traveled, I had an excellent job, friends, money, professional respect. I was a woman who had done well for herself even if I didn't write books, like you and Max and your friends.

And if I'd written *that* to you, my dear? No one could ever correct you, because you always agreed with them and went further. You were a worm, a dog, a feral creature fit only to haunt the woods and crawl on the floor and beg for table scraps. Besides, those few times when we saw one another, I *did* feel myself empty out, like a spilt cup waiting to be filled by one precious drop from you.

No one else has ever made me feel that way in my entire life – the life that you despised me for wanting, and warned I would never find with you. No one else had the power to turn me into a melancholy ghost of myself, sighing and wringing her hands, too weak and indecisive to move from the sofa to the chair. There would be no point in saying that it wasn't fair. You would only go on for pages of self-laceration, like the pages in the letter that included your marriage proposal. A girl wants to show such a letter to her family, her friends, her co-workers. But I couldn't. You had made sure of that.

How much have you kept up, my dear? That is so hard to know. These days, women do what they please, they are just like men. But in our time, our circle, it was considered awfully *modern* to agree to go to Palestine with a stranger one had just met. It wasn't something a girl would forget, but I tried. I told myself it was a joke. And then I received your first letter. The trip to Palestine was on. We needed to discuss it. Meanwhile, you felt you should warn me that you were careless, casual, lazy about correspondence. All lies, I need hardly say.

And then the second letter, the one I pretended to lose. I didn't know how to answer it. I don't know what I expected. Polite chat about your family, a remark about the office, the weather in Prague, but not those pages of complaint about the torture it had been for you to write every word you sent me. Was I supposed to be flattered, dear? I put it out of my mind, until a friend mentioned she'd heard that I was engaged in a very lively correspondence with a certain Doctor Kafka, and I said yes, a lively correspondence indeed, and so it was decided.

It wasn't just the speed of it, the zero to sixty in sixty seconds, but the fact that you and yourself and our love affair took off and left me behind. I was good with numbers. If I'd had the time or the interest, I would have computed the ratio: the small number of our meetings compared to the large number of letters before and after, the notes arranging every detail and then reporting that you had changed your mind and then changed it again about whether the meeting would even take place.

Certain things did interest me: that note you enclosed with the flowers you sent me. 'The outside world is too small, too clear-cut, too truthful to contain everything that a person has inside.' I recognised your handwriting, but you didn't sign it. And what on earth did it mean? A more conventional woman might have been scared away for ever. And you, with your famous imagination, why could you not imagine the scene in which my family and friends gathered round and said, Flowers! Show us, dear Felice! What does your young man write?

There was so much you never forgave me for even as you claimed to take all the blame on yourself. For example, my so-called failure to understand your work. Oh, I understood it, all right. But how could I not have been jealous of the rival that, as you seized every chance to say, you loved so much more than me. How could I not have resented the hungry beast that had to be fed, and whose need for care and feeding meant you could never have a life. A normal life was all I wanted, dear, and what you claimed to want – at the beginning. A house, the voices of children, country vacations, Sunday lunch. You had your fantasies, and that was mine. Both were equally unlikely. Those Sunday lunches were as improbable as a machine that painfully tattooed the names of one's crimes into one's flesh, though maybe those things were the same for you. How would I ever know? By the way, dear, I've spent much of my life – my normal life – in America, which, I feel I must tell you, might be hard to recognise as the country you described in your book.

Since we are, as we frequently were, speaking of forgiveness, perhaps this is the moment to tell you about something for which I feel I might need to be forgiven. And that is the sale of the letters, dear, by which I mean your love letters to me. I don't know if you know about this yet, it has only just happened. I have no idea how you get your information, or if you get any at all. Though matters of finance were always far below the lofty plane on which our love transpired, I must confess that I received, for them, the not inconsiderable sum of eight thousand dollars.

I agonised for a long time, as I'm sure you can believe. My deliberations are worth noting, if only because you were always the one who got to play and replay every theme and variation, to trace and retrace every baby step forward and backward in your thinking about this or that.

I thought about your reading Grillparzer's letters, and Kleist's, and I wondered if you could imagine some as yet unborn disciple of yours poring over your letters that way. I thought of how lightly you took it when my mother and sister found them, and how your only concern was that they should realise that, despite the passion and intimacy of our correspondence, we had spent only a few heavily chaperoned hours in each other's presence. If they'd known you, they might have realised that, but that is not my point. I am merely consoling – or justifying – myself by recalling your lack of outrage at having something so tender exposed to unsympathetic eyes.

I am not the sort of person who adds things up, who divides life into debit and credit columns marking who did what, and who owes what. I have always thought that my not being that sort of person was among the many reasons that my marriage was so happy and lasted so long – until my late husband's recent death. And yet I think that, in our case, some accounting is required. While I was pretending to have lost that second letter, you wrote 'The Judgment' in one night. While you were worrying about the flowers and the card you sent, you found relief by writing that terrifying description of that poor young man waking up as a bug. And then there was that meeting in the Berlin hotel room, a conversation that now, my dear, would be called an intervention. My friend and my sister helped me demand that you be honest and stop lying. Forever, you would refer to that afternoon as 'the tribunal'. Who was being judged, dear? Who was being punished? You went off with Ernst and his sexy girl, you had a good time, you had fun. And I stayed in Berlin, feeling as hopeless, as cursed as you claimed to feel every day of your life. Later, you would write *The Trial*. Don't I get any credit for that?

Which isn't to say I don't owe you some things: a tendency towards paranoia, a compulsion to analyse every word in an attempt to fathom its hidden meanings. That is how I first heard, in my grown children's voices, the unspoken mathematics of how much my care might eventually cost, and which of them would assume it. It is they who urged me to sell the letters, so maybe you were right about the danger that children posed to your life as a writer. Or maybe you would have wanted them sold. Those letters were never written to me. They were messages from you to yourself, from you to yourself and the world. But even so, as my family has so often, and so unsubtly pointed out, I am old, my love, and your letters were all that I had.

With love,
Your Felice

GRAHAM ROUMIEU

Dear Santa,

I guess it probably be long time between time you get letter and actually get chance to read. Bigfoot also get a lot of mail so understand it take long to get through all of those word. Words hard read, especially when come from sad heart.

Bigfoot heart sad like kitten who choke to death on pretty ribbon.

Suppose you already know how Bigfoot feel.

Then again, maybe you not. You only know what everyone do, naughty and nice. Bigfoot not know if you know how they feel afterward. Maybe you have no time any more to look at bigger picture. Maybe just not care. Maybe want stay cold and impartial in judgement. Bigfoot can only guess. Sit here in dark room and cry and guess until maybe just die from too much guess. Santa think of Bigfoot as nothing more than bad kid? Is that how?

Ten year now, no phone call, no letter, no hello-visit-down-the-chimney leave Bigfoot only to wonder what going on in Santa head. Bigfoot admit I do something awful. Thought Bigfoot mean more to Santa than that though. All time we spend together, like father and son, two cool mythical bachelor dudes out on town, two kindred spirits; how can throw all away?

Like I said, Bigfoot know I do something wrong. Betray you for dirty lady in dirty bar wrong thing to do in hindsight. That woman not worth it at all, she simply just another filthy Starfucker tramp that want to screw Bigfoot for trophy value. Just like ladies you warn me about.

But, I no listen.

I NO LISTEN

I NO LISTEN

I NO LISTEN

;ALDJSFALN;SKIHLS;LHK;BANO NO NO NONO!!!!!!!

I let her seduce Bigfoot with long painted fingernail and big curly hair. Her teeth so sharp and hand so fast. Bigfoot spray scat all over barstool but she only come on stronger. We make out real hard and mate right there right on floor of TGI Friday's. Love.

In pool of liquor and glass and other fluid I ask her marry me.

I just did it. It just come out like excited barf.

She say 'YES, YES I MARRY BIGFOOT!' and I so happy!

Thought greatest moment of life.

I so happy. Say to her have to go tell best friend Santa that I find woman of dreams and want him be best man at wedding! I tell her all about Santa, how fun, how we go like party sometimes. How Santa can come over and hang out with us and barbecue at new Bigfoot family compound.

Then things get weird. She glare at Bigfoot and she say 'I no believe in Santa, so he no can come to wedding. Only loser believe in Santa. No marry if Bigfoot believe in Santa'.

Bigfoot was confuse. Also now terrified because she hiss all scary as stroke Bigfoot real hard as Bigfoot mill over deep moral and philosophical dilemma. Kept looking for you to come back from bathroom but you must been taking big milk and cookie dump because you gone way way too long.

Sometimes think Santa never intend to come back from bathroom.

Bigfoot feel pressured and crack, say worst thing Bigfoot ever say in life. Was hoping sound of hand dryer or flush toilet would drown out so Santa no hear. Bigfoot say that I no believe in Santa either. Just want make her happy. Ladies like hear what ladies want hear. Bigfoot just want be happy.

Me know now it worst thing Bigfoot ever say. Make Bigfoot sick just to think about. Guess you did hear what I say. Maybe you magic power of know everything help you know. Either way, obviously you catch wind of it because Bigfoot no have seen you since.

You know how lonely mythical life be. Felt like Bigfoot only have one chance at true happiness. Felt like Santa would totally understand. Thought Santa understand too when no invite Santa to bachelor party or send any kind of wedding invite. Figure you just shrug off, figure you probably pretty busy anyways and might not be able to make.

Marriage a sham and fall apart after a month. She just after Bigfoot money and when that all gone she gone too. Worst part is she leave Bigfoot on Christmas day. No woman, no hope, no self-respect, no Santa beard to cry on, and worst of all find lump of coal in stocking.

I mean fuck, maybe I have it coming but you not think you could use a little restraint you heavy-handed fucker? Really push Bigfoot over proverbial cliff. Is any wonder Bigfoot try kill self by eating all of Christmas tree ornaments?

No, it not.

Anyhow, have been ten year since go by. Have try and try get hold of you. Notice you change you number, you still live at North Pole? Have sent many letters like this but no response. Expect not to get anything from this letter either. If you are reading, Bigfoot really want you to know you still mean a lot to me. You beacon of light for Bigfoot and I only truly realize when you gone. You mean a lot to Bigfoot, man. Kids write and say nice stuff to you all the time but they only want toys. See through that and know what Bigfoot write come from heart. We kindred spirit.

Santa, I know I fuck up. Know I deserve be treated like piece of shit Bigfoot am. Even so, try, try, try to find way to forgive. Not because of Christmas stuff you obligated to do but because Bigfoot need you and is that not true meaning of Christmas?

Love your pal,
Bigfoot

GAUTAM MALKANI

Dear Mum,

Did Dad write letters to you? I know he sent you the odd bunch of flowers when you were both young (I suppose the correct word is courting) because I found the little message cards you kept. I was clearing out some old crates and boxes in the attic earlier today and I found them in a shoebox full of your old postcards, photographs and even your old, expired passports. I'm writing this letter up in the attic, away from Kate, because she always complains that I never write letters to her. I tell Kate I live with her, so why would I write to her? If I lived with you, then I probably wouldn't write to you either.

Anyhow, I was going through the old crates and I found a letter I wrote to you when I was at school which I've kept hold of all these years. So I thought I'd give it to you now – albeit about twenty-five years late. And somehow I've ended up writing this letter as well, which I suppose makes this a covering letter for the original one.

You're probably wondering what on earth I was doing writing to you while at school. If I remember right, it was part of an English lesson. It was when I was in Mrs Arnold's class, which means I must have been about eight or nine years old. You remember Mrs Arnold, don't you? I think she'd asked us to write a letter to a hero or a person we admired. She was always setting us bizarre tasks like that. Perhaps she secretly hoped someone would address a letter to her. A love letter, perhaps. After all, we may have been allergic to girls back then, but I remember lots of boys in my class were infatuated with Mrs Arnold. I wasn't, of course. I didn't have any childish crushes on anyone. Actually, I think we weren't supposed to address our letters to real people. They were meant to be to a character from a story. That was the rule. But I addressed mine to you, and all the other kids started teasing me. Especially Keith Mackenzie. Remember how I used to complain about him?

Anyway, I'm sorry I didn't give the attached letter to you when I wrote it. I was being a bit pathetic, I suppose, embarrassed because Keith Mackenzie and the others had laughed at me. It wasn't as if any of them knew about Oedipus or even Norman Bates back then – presumably most of them still don't. But nonetheless, they considered it weird of me to have written a love letter to my own mum. Maybe it was, but I was nine years old. Who else was I supposed to love? Or even like? I didn't even care much for Madonna or that girl from *Grease* – Sandy, I think – I only hung those posters on my bedroom wall to show people that I was all right, you know? I'm sorry if some of my posters offended you – you'll be glad to know they weren't in the boxes of junk I was sorting through today because I threw them all out when Kate first moved in. During my first cull. She doesn't like clutter, you see. She's into minimalism and feng shui (which she pronounces 'fung shway'). She forced me into the attic today because apparently I've contorted my Chi. She always mocks my tendency to hoard things – somehow she always mocks me, full stop. You're going to say you told me so, right? That I should have known better. I know I've discussed this with you many times before but finally I can appreciate why you never liked Kate. I suppose it's as well you don't have to live with the consequences of me ignoring your opinion and I hope this letter doesn't disturb your resting soul or anything. It's just that when I found the old letter and decided I had to come by and leave it on your gravestone, I thought I'd add a few more words while I was at it. Keep you up to date.

I suppose I just want you to know that I've come to realise you didn't like Kate because you didn't think she was good enough for me. Perhaps I always knew this and I always knew you were right. Perhaps that's why I've never written Kate a love letter. I've never even written the little message card when I've given her flowers. In fact, I don't think I've ever written too much inside her valentine, birthday or Christmas cards either. Just 'Dear Kate', then whatever the card has to say, then 'from Michael'. Not even 'love from Michael'. That's minimalist, right? Kate keeps things even less cluttered by throwing all those cards away the day after I give them to her. You'll be glad to know my junk in the attic didn't include any of Kate's cards to me. That's just as well, seeing as I need to clear more space up there to make room for her body . . . only joking – it's just as well I've inherited your dark sense of humour.

I was thinking this same thing just the other day. I was smelling your perfume and found myself trying to decide what aspect of your personality it most clearly resembled. And I decided it was either your sense of humour or that elegant way you carried yourself. I often carry your last bottle around with me – the little glass pyramid leans perfectly against my ribs. And no matter how much de-cluttering I'm forced into doing, that's one thing I'll never throw out. Scent is pretty strange, isn't it, Mum? I can't tell whether that bottle contains the scent of the perfume or the scent of you. The obvious answer – that you smelt of the perfume – doesn't really suffice. After all, I imagine even your shampoo smelt the same as your perfume and your hair still smelt of shampoo even if you hadn't washed it for weeks.

I have a Muslim friend who says a son can never thank his mother enough. I can see what he means by that. That's why I actually found myself in tears when I came across the enclosed letter. If only I'd just given it to you back then. I wish so much that I'd just given it to you then. I hate myself for worrying about what people like Keith Mackenzie said. For being embarrassed about getting called a mummy's boy. How can I have been so stupid? There's nothing wrong with being a mummy's boy, is there Mum? I remember I even felt ashamed of myself at the time. But I didn't know you wouldn't be there one day. I mean, how would I have coped if I thought one day you might not be there? I wouldn't have bothered going to school in the first place, would I? I wouldn't have bothered watching TV or riding my bike or doing anything, Mum. But seeing as how it'd be impossible for me to thank you enough even if we both lived together for ever, it probably makes no difference whether I carry on writing this letter or whether I just end here and let you read the original one.

Lots of love
from Michael x

To My Mummy,

Hi Mummy!

Mrs Arnold wants us to write letters to someone from a story. Keith Mackenzie told everyone he's writing his letter to John Travolta. What an idiot, right? John Travolta is not a character, he is a real person. Keith says he is famous and he will never meet him, but that doesn't make him not real, does it, Mummy?

I told Mrs Arnold that Dad always says I have the most lovely Mummy in the whole wide world and so she is letting me write my letter to you. Sometimes Dad says I look like you. He calls me his Heaven sent son because he says that's where I came from. But I don't remember living there.

I hope he remembers to buy you some flowers for Mother's Day instead of forgetting like he did last year. I want to buy you some red roses but I don't have any money.

I hope you like my writing. I am using a pen now, not a pencil. And I am checking the spellings in the dictionary. I even checked the word dictionary but I didn't have to look it up because it's on the front cover. I hope you like the letter I wrote to you yesterday, and the one the day before that and the one before that one. But I didn't write those other letters as part of lessons. I did them during break time. I wrote them to say Thank you Mummy. Thank you for being my mummy and thank you for being so lovely. I wish we had some new pictures of you. Dad still cries when we look at pictures of you. I don't even want to ask him to send you this letter because he might start crying again like last time. But I can't send it by myself because I don't know your address. Whenever I ask Dad where you live, he says you swapped addresses with me the day I was born. But I still don't know what that means. Why can't we live in the same place? All my other friends live in the same place as their mums. Then I wouldn't need to write you letters.

Lots and lots and lots of love from Michael xxxxxxx

MIRIAM TOEWS

Dear Cadence Loewen,

Thank you so much for your letter, and I appreciate your concern. And yes, of course, do feel free to pray for me. I don't mind at all. When I first received your letter I didn't recognise your name, but something happened recently and I realised that I know you! Your mom and dad were good friends of mine way back in the late 70s, early 80s. I apologise if my calling them your mom and dad upsets you. Maybe you don't see it that way, and that's perfectly understandable.

The last time I saw you was when you were just a few weeks old, just days before Jackie and Tim, your birth parents, had their accident. A bunch of us were hanging out, smoking pot in this field behind the golf course, near Kokomo Road, and Jackie and Tim drove up in Tim's brother's old Vauxhall. Smoking pot, by the way, is something I don't do any more, don't worry, but we were all young back then, seventeen years old, and there wasn't much else to do. So Jackie and Tim drove up and were all excited and happy and wanted to show everyone their new baby, you. Cadence, they said, these are our friends, and yours, too. You were so beautiful, and still are, by the way. When I saw your photo in the newspaper I almost had a heart attack, you look so much like Jackie did at that age.

Tim let us all hold you, even though we were a little stoned, and we all started crying, even the guys. We were so blown away by you. Everything about you was perfect, you had Tim's little ears and Jackie's long, skinny fingers, and they were so crazy in love with you and each other and life and the whole big, amazing idea of being your parents. They didn't do any drugs that day, or ever again, I'm sure of it. And they didn't smoke around you, or play music too loud, and Jackie was always pulling your little toque over your ears so you wouldn't get cold, and telling everyone to be very, very careful with your fontanelle, that soft spot on a baby's head, before the plates of the skull fuse together.

Look, she said, you can see her heart beating in her head. She'd pull your toque up a tiny bit so we could have a look. Tim told us you loved Warren Zevon and Jackie had embroidered the words 'I like to rock' on this little sleeper you had. Tim said 'Jackie was like this machine, man, in labor. She was total business, told everyone to fuck off, she was doing this thing. She was taking charge. She was amazing, man. I love her so much.' Jackie said she just couldn't stop staring at you. She couldn't believe that you were hers. She said she wished she could always stare at you, all day and all night, all the time, for the rest of your life. That would be her full-time job, she said.

And then we all built this little monument to you out in the field. We made it out of rocks and sunflowers and we all wrote little notes to you with lipstick because nobody had a pen, welcoming you to the world, and we put them under the rocks and some of the guys poured a little bit of Wild Turkey over it, like a toast to you, to a long, happy life, and we spelled out the name C-A-D-E-N-C-E with little rocks in a circle around the bigger monument, and then we all sang that Cyndi Lauper song, 'Time after Time', because it was the only one we all knew the words to, and it seemed appropriate, even though it was also cheesy.

So that was quite a while ago, almost twenty years ago. Most of us left town after high school. Then, a week ago, I got the news that my mom was very sick and so I came back home to help my older sister take care of her. I was sitting at my mom's bedside, looking through the local newspaper and that's when I saw your picture in the announcements section and thought holy shit! It's Jackie! Except of course it wasn't, it was you. I showed it to my mom and she told me that after Jackie and Tim's accident, Tim's parents had raised you. She said they did a very good job, too. She mentioned that Tim and Jackie's deaths had been so hard for them to accept because they hadn't been saved or baptised before they died, and how they agonised over how they would tell you that, how it would make you feel, knowing you wouldn't ever be able to see them again, not even in heaven. She said you have perfect attendance at church and sing in the choir and even teach Sunday school to the little kids. That's amazing. And now you're off to do missionary work in Belize. Wow! I wish I'd been that focused when I was nineteen.

Cadence, I do wish you all the very best with your work, and in life, now and in the future. It was an honor to have met you that day out behind the golf course, and to have had Jackie and Tim as my friends. They were such great kids, and parents. I know I have a reputation in town as a God-hating atheist, but it's not true. I'm an agnostic, really, and I think about the existence or non-existence of God all the time. One thing that does bring me closer to 'embracing the idea of God' as you very aptly put it, is my memory of all us kids in that field. I can see us all perfectly, the sky, the sunflowers, Tim's brother's old Vauxhall parked in the clearing, Jackie showing us the soft spot on your head, your little I Like to Rock sleeper, and your tiny fists, and how we all gathered around our home-made monument to you, holding hands, singing, a circle of love and happiness and reverence for your precious life, and such joy in the moment. All because of you.

Again, Cadence, I do wish you all the very best in Belize, and wherever else you may be. I'll be thinking of you.

In friendship,

Miriam

p.s. By the way, Warren Zevon died recently, but his music still rocks, if you're interested in checking it out.

JAMES ROBERTSON

I start to compose this in my head on a cold February morning, as I set out for you in the car. The village is in a mist of sleep when I leave, and Coupar Angus, Perth and Crieff are just stirring, each a little livelier than the last, as I drive through them, heading west and north. A huge, slightly squashed white moon keeps pace with me even as it fades and sinks. I think of my wife, still in bed, and then I think of you. My heart beats a little faster at the prospect of a whole day spent with you, and the many projects, commitments and words that have been jostling in my mind begin to separate and detach, clearing like the lines of mist from the air.

It feels strange, and slightly silly, to address such sentences, such sentiments, to you, utterly indifferent as you are to me. In fact, I will shortly stop writing *to* you and write instead *about* you, thus I hope avoiding any embarrassment – not yours, of course, since you neither take nor give offence, and are beyond and above any such squirmings of the human heart. It is myself I don't want to embarrass by referring, coyly or otherwise, to your 'many other lovers' or by decrying the 'cold heartlessness' you show to us all. I remember being warned by a teacher, decades ago, of the dangers to good writing of anthropomorphism. He was referring to animals, but he might just as well have been speaking of mountains.

I stop in Comrie and buy some food for the day, then drive on. I am heading for Beinn a' Chreachain and Beinn Achaladair, near Bridge of Orchy. I attempted these two Munros almost a year ago but had to retreat, fifteen minutes from the top of Beinn a' Chreachain, because the wind had risen greatly during the long walk in and was so strong on the final ridge that I couldn't stand up. I made several efforts to do so but each time the wind bashed and buffeted me and dumped me on the packed snow and ice as if I were in the ring with a heavyweight boxer. It was frustrating, but eventually I had to concede defeat and go back the way I'd come. So now I am trying again, intending to retrace my steps and, with luck, complete the big circular walk I was denied last time.

By the time I reach Loch Earn the day's bright, cloudless beauty is revealed in full. Expanses of dead bracken on the braes above the northern shore stretch like sheets of gold cloth, and even the brown larch plantations seem to shine in the low sunlight. I have driven this twisting road countless times, but it is always new. On the other side of the water rises Ben Vorlich, one of the first mountains I ever climbed. (I was eleven or twelve, and probably did it in wellies or some other unsuitable footwear.) Its profile, along with that of its neighbour Stuc a' Chroin, is familiar to tens of thousands of people, since, seen from the south, they dramatically announce the start of the Highlands north of the Forth valley. Between the two mountains is a bealach or pass, with a steep ascent from it up the east side of Stuc a' Chroin. Too late a start defeated me once, and bad weather a second time, before I finally managed to get up this mountain: and on that occasion it was snowing, and the climb demanded considerable effort. I had never before used an ice-axe in earnest, and I remember the sense of triumph as I hauled myself up to the summit ridge. It is, I know, a scramble of no difficulty for any real climber, but for me it was exhilarating, and I will never forget it.

Glen Ogle, Glen Dochart, Strath Fillan – every mile of road takes me further from cities and towns, deeper into the Highlands. There to the north-east is the great sprawling mass of the Lawers range, and the lesser but more rugged Tarmachan hills beside it. A few miles further on, to the left, the twin peaks of Stob Binnein and Ben More loom, the road passing right under the bulk of the latter. (Once, on a Saturday three days before Christmas, I had the whole of Ben More, usually a popular mountain, to myself: I remember being quite sure, as I stood at the icy summit watching long, flat, sun-flushed clouds crowd over the ranks of peaks to the north-west, that there could not possibly be a better gift in all the shopping centres of the world than the view which was being presented to me alone.) And then, beyond Crianlarich and Tyndrum, where the road climbs up on to the great wastes that stretch from Loch Lyon and Loch Rannoch in the east to Loch Etive in the west, I feel an immense liberation: there is no turning back now, the day is going to be fine, I am committed. For the next few hours I will be beholden to nobody but myself.

I used to believe that I went to the mountains in order to think. But when I considered this more carefully I realised that, whatever the intention, the effect was the opposite: I went and I did *not* think. The physical effort of climbing two, three, four hills, the concentration on underfoot terrain, the crossing of burns and rivers, the watchful eye kept for changing weather, the sighting of birds and other creatures, the sometimes tedious journey back out and the tired triumph of completing it – absorbed with all these immediate concerns, I had no inclination or indeed ability to think in any coherent, structured way about other things. Neither the plots of novels nor the meaning of life are worked out by hill-walking.

But something does happen to the mind on these days: it empties, refills, reorders itself. Superfluous or temporary files are sent to the recycle bin; the brain is defragmented. It is a cleansing experience. I return, not with fresh stories written or problems solved, but with the *possibilities* of new narratives and solutions. This is the effect of the day's journey: but where has the journey taken me?

Where is it people go when they go into mountains? When they go alone, as I nearly always do, are they going anywhere other than into themselves? A number of apparently contradictory things, it seems to me, happen simultaneously to the lone hillwalker as he – or she, although the single walkers I meet are almost always male, especially in winter – leaves road, car, bicycle or both behind and pushes deeper and higher into places where there are no mobile phone signals and no human habitations: he is both magnified in himself and reduced in the landscape; he becomes stronger and more vulnerable; more self-reliant and more at the mercy of nature. And this double effect, that works on him externally and internally, is at once exhilarating and sobering, disturbing and calming. There are times, walking alone, when he senses another striding effortlessly beside him.

Certainly there are moments when I slip outside myself: there are two of us then, and both are renewed and re-energised by this dislocation, which is not quite ever a complete dislocation. The great Gaelic poet Sorley MacLean captures this sensation in his poem 'An Roghainn' ('The Choice'), although the circumstances in which he was writing were very different: he describes walking with his reason beside the sea, how they were together and yet how his reason kept itself at a little distance from him. On mountain days, my reason and I walk, sometimes together and sometimes a little apart, but I am not sure which of us stays in the body, and which has stepped outside.

I am by no means a really dedicated hillwalker, out every weekend whatever the weather, let alone a skilled climber. Work and other commitments mean that my days in the hills tend to be single and spaced well apart. I wish this were not so. I'd much prefer to spend more time outside, engaged in this one-sided affair with the mountains, and less in front of a computer screen. Obviously I am not alone in this desire, but one of the advantages of my writing life is that I can sometimes choose, on the strength of a late-night weather forecast or an early morning sky, to abandon work on a weekday and take off. As a result, on many of my outings I meet hardly any other walkers or climbers at all. It is just me and the mountains, and whatever physicality or philosophy it is that joins or separates us.

I have written this much when I begin to pick up echoes of voices other than Sorley MacLean's in what I am saying. I realise that all I am probably doing is restating things that have been better said by other writers. I go at once to Nan Shepherd's book *The Living Mountain*, her testament of love for the Cairngorms, written at the end of the Second World War but unpublished till 1977, and I find the following passage. She is trying to explain the *feyness* she feels, 'that joyous release of body that is engendered by climbing'. Surely, she writes, she's not such a slave that she cannot be free unless her flesh feels buoyant. There is more to the 'lust for a mountain top' than that. An exchange of some kind takes place between her and the mountain; place and mind interpenetrate till the nature of both is altered. And at the end of the book – a brief book, which yet contains vast traverses of thought – Shepherd articulates what I was groping for a few paragraphs ago:

> . . . as I grew older, and less self-sufficient, I began to discover the mountain in itself. Everything became good

to me, its contours, its colours, its waters and rock, flowers and birds. Knowing another is endless. And I have discovered that man's experience of them enlarges rock, flower and bird. The thing to be known grows with the knowing.

. . . It is a journey into Being; for as I penetrate more deeply into the mountain's life, I penetrate also into my own. For an hour I am beyond desire . . . I am not out of myself, but in myself. I am.

For an hour I am beyond desire. Perhaps this is where walking alone in the hills really leads: to a place where nothing is yearned for, nothing is required, nothing is lacked. It is strange that Nan Shepherd says that this sufficiency grows, in part, from becoming less *self*-sufficient, but I think she is right. And there is something else. *Man's experience of them enlarges rock, flower and bird.* I wrote in a poem once,

'I didn't see a soul
All day on the hills' would be a chilling tale if there was
Nobody to tell it to.

If the landscape is not known, not touched by human thought, then it is truly inhuman, and in that sense desolate and forbidding. It is one of the reasons why humans need to name the land, and why, if Gaelic should ever cease to be spoken, Scotland would become in a way alien to its inhabitants, or its inhabitants alien to it. Even now the general massacring of a name like Bidean nam Bian indicates a common loss of intimacy with the mountain that bears it, and a loss of respect for it too. And yet, at the same time, the need to make contact with the land is why walkers are so often guilty of reciting a litany of mountain names, and I suspect the same need lies at the root of the desire to make lists of Munros, Corbetts and Donalds – all those species of Scottish hills – and tick them off. Names *signify*, and when you know what they signify – have been among these names and *on* them – they evoke the very best of days, and sometimes, in weather terms at least, the very worst.

I know, whenever the time comes that I cannot or do not wish to go to the hills, that my own litany will offer a certain compensation. Some folk sneer at the practice of Munro-bagging, but I defend it, because climbing those Munros that I have – along with many other smaller, though not always lesser, hills – has taught me more about the topography of my country, its extraordinarily complex physical composition, its vastness which is also a compact and detailed connectedness, than any lesson or book. And it has given me my own litany, with its own instant mental and emotional associations: simply naming Beinn Dotaidh, for example, calls to mind the weird, creeping sculptures of ice and grass I trudged past on a windy, snowy climb there; I remember the way rock gripped me and I gripped rock on the Aonach Eagach, *the notched ridge*, in Glencoe, as if we had made a pact (one which, of course, existed only in my imagination) that if I was not foolish it would not throw me to my death; I remember Beinn a' Bheithir above Ballachulish mainly because the rain and mist were so heavy I never saw more than thirty yards of mountain at any one time; I remember bold sunshine slanting through falling snow on Beinn Udlamain, and a huge herd of deer moving like a dun-coloured shadow below me in the corrie of A'Mharconaich; I remember the long stretch to Beinn Dearg in Atholl, and the ridiculously easy stroll up Meall Buidhe in Glen Lyon; I remember the spectral hares on Ben-y-Hone, the ptarmigan, snow buntings and dotterels that have shared other cloud-thick summits with me; I remember, on the lower slopes of Creag Meagaidh, picking blaeberries so fat and sweet I was, for a while, oblivious to the rain and midges; I remember the arête that snakes like an airy bridge between Carn Mor Dearg up to Ben Nevis, and how I crawled over its narrowest sections because the drops on either side took the courage from my legs, and how I had that vastness of mountain to myself for hours until finally, reaching the top of 'the Ben', I found myself among dozens of walkers who had plodded up the so-called 'tourist route'; I remember seeing the snow-covered Cairngorms, black and white and mysterious and beckoning, from the empty broad back of An Socach above Glen Ey; I remember my first venture into the Cairngorms, a few months later, and how from Beinn a' Chaorainn I saw the outline of northern Scotland laid out before me, the Moray Firth glinting and grey forty miles to the north. All these and more are in my mind, and will be, like moments from old love affairs, until the mind ceases to function.

In a poem called 'One of the many days', Norman MacCaig once wrote of the multitude of frogs he saw at the back of Ben Dorain – a mountain more famously and expansively praised by the 18th-century Gaelic poet Duncan Ban MacIntyre. MacCaig catalogues how the whole long day released a series of miracles: the river like glass in the sun, wading in Loch Lyon, a herd of hinds that gave the V-sign with their ears before cantering off, and the Joseph-coated frogs amiably ambling and jumping around. That's what days in the hills always do: release miracles, often small, even insignificant, but always memorable.

I have my own story of a miracle in the form of a plague of frogs. On this occasion I was with a friend, and we were climbing Stob a' Choire Odhar and Stob Ghabhar on the western edge of Rannoch Moor. It was a beautiful, blue, cloudless July day when we set out. The ground was dry –

parched, even – and when, halfway up Stob a' Choire Odhar, we came across a single yellow frog panting in the heat, we thought he was in quite the wrong location and that his circumstances could only deteriorate. But by the time we were on the ridge approaching the top of Stob Ghabhar we were reconsidering: a great black canopy of water-laden cloud had formed across the entire sky, and it was clear we were in for a soaking. The canopy ripped apart as we began our descent: the rain fell like tropical rain, hot, solid and unrelenting, as if from a power-shower. Not a centimetre of us remained dry. Later, I wrote,

> We stood beneath the downpour
> and our boots filled up and overflowed.
> Paths became burns; burns boiled to rivers;
> we were like ghosts of sailors
> adrift on a mountainous sea.

And then, as if this were not transformation enough, the entire hillside erupted: frogs, thousands of them, yellow, brown, green, so many we could not avoid stepping on them. They had been waiting and now they were in the right place at the right time while we, delirious and absurd, trudged and slid, jumping and wading torrents that hadn't existed ten minutes earlier, back to the day's starting-point.

What does this story mean? It means nothing except what it says: that it happened, that we were there, that it will never happen again in quite the same way, and yet that it happens all the time. The story is my story about a particular mountain, but the mountain does not know it, does not give a damn about it. I love the mountain for what it gave me, but the mountain does not love me. I find myself grappling again for other people's words to explain what I mean. Only this time I am caught between two sets of thoughts: those of the naturalist John Muir, who *really* loved mountains, *really* understood them, and those of the poet Hugh MacDiarmid, who knew the futility of such love and understanding. What are we to stones, MacDiarmid asked insistently. What are we to stones? We are nothing. We must be humble, because the stones are one with the stars, however stone-like they may appear to us. It makes no difference to them where they are, on top of a mountain or at the bottom of the sea, in a palace or a pigsty. There are plenty of ruined buildings in the world, MacDiarmid reminds us, but no ruined stones.

This is from the long poem of 1933, 'On A Raised Beach', constructed, as the title suggests, nowhere near mountains but on a stony shoreline in Shetland, but the poem transcends its particular place and time. It is so bleakly beautiful and so true that there seems to be nothing else worth saying, although MacDiarmid remorselessly exposes our fragility further: what happens to us, he says, is of no relevance to the world's geology; what happens to the world's geology is of utmost relevance to us. It is not the stones who must be reconciled to us, but we to them.

What then is the point? What point is there in my going to the mountains if all they throw back at me is my irrelevance and transience? On the February day on which I began this letter, I did get to the top of Beinn a' Chreachain and then Beinn Achaladair. I spent six hours on them, alone and happy, and when I came down the muddy track through the corrie and back to where I'd parked the car, I caught up with another man who had done exactly the same. We exchanged a few words about the absence of deep snow and climate change, and established that we were kindred spirits, but I doubt he really wanted to talk to me any more than I wanted to talk to him. We were rivals in some obscure sense, as well as allies, and the silences between us spoke at least as eloquently and profoundly as the words we uttered. Each of us was equally aware, after our long hard day alone, of our own irrelevance and transience, and the immovability of the mountains we had been on, and we knew that in the face of these truths our words were meaningless, mere stour in the wind.

And yet, now, I must try to make them mean something. I think of John Muir, born at Dunbar on the East Lothian coast, an emigrant to North America who became the great protector of that continent's wild places, and in particular of the mountains of California. You can open, almost at random, any of his books and find a good reason for going to the mountains. More than half a century before MacDiarmid, Muir recognised the same things in himself and in the world's geology that MacDiarmid recognised, but he made something different and holy from them. For Muir there was relief and redemption, where MacDiarmid found stones without mercy. 'The tendency nowadays to wander in wildernesses is delightful to see,' Muir wrote. 'Thousands of tired, nerve-shaken, over-civilised people are beginning to find that going to the mountains is going home . . .'

Ah, yes, going home. The journey I make into you, mountains of Scotland, is just that: a homeward journey. I go, I disappear for a while, I come back, having climbed or not climbed this hill or those – and I have both been, and am still to go, home. I have left a note to my wife on the kitchen table, saying where I am going, and she trusts me to come back. She loves me so much that she lets me go to you even though it fills her with worry, in case one day you should keep me. So I take off my boots, start the car and drive till there is a phone signal, and then I pull over and call her. We are reconnected, in touch again. When I get home I'll tell her the details of my day; whether or not I have seen another soul, and any small or medium-sized miracles I may have witnessed. And in return I will hear the details of her day. Ten, maybe twelve times a year – enough, but not nearly enough – I will make this journey, and it is indeed a journey of love in both directions. But no matter how often I make it, no matter the quickening beat of my heart as I set off, no matter all these words I have put down here, I know this journey means absolutely nothing to you. To me, on the other hand, driving home in the light of a big yellow moon, beneath the emerging stars that you and your stones are one with, back to her with whom I am one, it means everything.

ETGAR KERET

Translated by Miriam Shlesinger

Happy Birthday to You

The bus stops, the driver smiles at you, the windows are gleaming, and there's plenty of small change. In the row of single seats on the left, the last one is vacant as if it has your name on it, your favourite one. The bus pulls out, the lights turn green as it approaches and the guy cracking sunflower seeds gathers up the peels in a brown paper bag.

The elderly inspector doesn't ask to see your ticket, just tips his hat and in a very pleasant voice, wishes you a nice day.

And it will be a nice day. Because it's your birthday. You're bright, you're pretty, and you have your whole life ahead of you. Four more stops and you'll pull the cord, and the driver will stop, just for you.

You'll get off the bus, no one will jostle you, and the door won't close till you've stepped away. And the bus will leave, the passengers will be happy for you, and the guy with the sunflower seeds will keep waving goodbye till he's out of sight, for no reason at all.

Who needs a reason, it's a birthday, and on birthdays nice things happen. And the puppy running towards you now will wag its tail when you touch it. When there's a special date, even dogs can tell.

In your apartment, people will be waiting in the dark, behind the beautiful furniture the two of you chose yourselves. When you open the door, they'll jump out and surprise you. Just the way it should be at surprise parties.

They'll all be there, the people you've loved. Those closest to you, and the ones who mean the most. And they'll bring presents that they bought or dreamt up themselves. Inspired presents, and useful things too.

The funny ones will entertain, the smart ones will enlighten, even the melancholy ones will give a genuine smile. The food will be amazing, then they'll serve strawberries and top it off with a vanilla milkshake from the best place in town.

They'll play a Keith Jarrett disc and everyone will listen, they'll play a Satie record and nobody will feel sad. And the ones who are on their own won't feel alone tonight, and nobody will ask 'Milk or cream?' because they all know one another by now.

In the end they'll leave, and the ones you wanted to kiss you will kiss you, and the ones you didn't will just shake your hand. And he'll be the only one who'll stay behind, the man you live with, kinder and gentler than ever.

If you want to, you'll make love or he'll massage your body with oil, specially bought in an old bedouin shop. You only have to ask and he'll dim the halogen light, and you'll sit there embraced, waiting for dawn.

And on that magical night, I'll be there too, drinking my vanilla milkshake, and smiling a genuine smile. And before I go, if you want – I'll kiss you. And if not, I'll just shake your hand.

MANDY SAYER

Dear miss starling

You havent seen me this month because my dad is keeping me home to look after my baby sister. I miss my friends and the footy after school. My handwriting is getting better. At home we don't have a dicksionary so I cant look the words up like you told us to. I live out of town on the old ghost gum road the grey house with the broke down truck out the front. Mum said I was borned hear because I came out to quickly but my sister was borned in town. Its not so far from wear you live. We dont have a fone. Mum used to say its like in the olden days. People must be poor in the olden days like in the movies but for real. You could visit us one day miss starling and I could show you my rabbits. We eat them but never Charlie. He is all mine and his fur is brown like your hair and real soft. He sleeps with me in bed and never poos when he sleeps with me. If you visit us I coold show you the house I made out the back its in a tree mum used to call a weeping fig. I dont know why the fig is called that because trees dont cry but mum did a lot. Somtimes she went away to town to the hostipal the one wear my sister was borned. You told us in class to discribe things in writing to paint a picture that you can see. We have lots of other trees but they are to high for a house gum trees youcaliptus and the willow bye the creek and I like to swing on the branches. My house is made from things I found down the creek bits of wood and sheet metal and this rusty car door when you turn the handel the window still goes down. I pretend its a real house I have shelvs for my rocks and cars and a cup I have water and packets of chips on the shelvs. I have a blancket and a pillow and Charlie likes it up hear. You can look out the window and see for a long way. You can see purrple mountins and the waterfall and you can see the fruit bats in the sky when the sun goes down. You can see cows and sheep chooing grass. You can see the creek down the back wear they all dump there old cars. The top of the church in town the spire is what you call it. You can see the black stumps made by the bushfires on the next hill last summer. They look like little graves in a cematary. All of the animals were killed last summer the posums the bats the snakes the goanas I know I found them after the fire went out they were all black and smoky and I buryed them. From up hear you can see whose driving down the road towards your house and if its your fathers car you can even tell if hes drunk by the way he swerves all over the place and you can hide from him long before he gets home. Not in the tree house but. He knows to look hear. And down the back shed wear the chooks lay eggs. One day miss starling you dropped a hanky in the playground and I picked it up. It wasnt dirty but. It smelled like you like rarsberrys or cherries like the colour red. I have it hear in my pocket. If you come and visit us I could give it back to you. I could give you fresh eggs me and dad have lots. Dad shoots kangaroos and if you like the skins I could give you one of them to. He sells them to a man in brisbane and he says he makes a lot of money but I dont think so unless hes maybe saving up for something I dont know about like a fone maybe. Dad says there are to many roos anyway and thats why he shoots them. You look a bit like my mum before she stopped breathing. Her hair is brown like yours. All her dresses are still hear and I bet they would fit you. But your even more prettier than her. Like someone in a movie or on the tele. Like tracey on neighbours. When dad is out shooting roos I watch tele. When my baby sister cries I give her chips. She poos more than Charlie and dad makes me clean it up. Since mum went nobody comes to visit. At night the wind is really loud and makes me scared. Louder than when dad snores. Louder than when he punches the wall. The police came around three times but they never found out what really happend. I never said a word. My baby sister doesnt talk just baby ga ga and crying a lot. Dad told me if I told anyone the same thing woold happen to me and no one woold ever miss me. Woold you miss me Miss Starling. Woold you tell the police I was gone. My baby sister woold miss me but she cant talk. When you come to visit we can watch Oprah and you can learn how to loose ten pounds in two weeks and be normil like doctor phil. And how to live like a movie star even when you dont have any money. You can try on my mothers dresses and her shoes are size 9. They woold fit you miss starling and you can have them all. She has a fur coat but she told me it wasnt real but you can have that to if you want. Dad told me it was all my fault and thats why he did what he did to her. When the men from the school came around he told them I was sick and thats why I wasnt at school. I had to make out like I was sick and I had to coff a lot. If I didnt coff a lot in front of the men dad woold give me a big belting he told me. Miss starling your my favourite teacher in the hole world. When you were in the paper the other day for your prize I cut out your picture and stuck it on the wall of my treehouse you can see it when you come to visit. Sometimes I pretend the picture is real and you are hear already and you and me are talking to each other and where having a good time. Your wheering my mothers green dress and shoes and her real golden earings. Nobody is hear but us not even my baby sister. Where watching Oprah and eating chips. Where laughng at cartoons and then you put your arm around me and I start to feel all warm. I know wear you live miss starling its the pink house on mundeys farm I followd you home after school one day and climed a tree and watched you walk around in your nightie in the kitchen. You looked really pretty in your nightie it was a short one I coold see even more than your nees. You dont have a husband miss starling I know I never saw a man in there. Do you get lonly with no husband. Tomorow Ill push this inside your pink letterbox and wait until after school and watch you read it from the tree again and if I see you smile I know you woold come. Please please come soon miss starling. Where waiting for you. Its the grey house with the broke down truck out the front. The only one on ghost gum road. Come before dark before dad gets home he will get mad if he sees you hear. My mother now looks like a bad skinned rabbit and she is starting stink worst than before in the basement but please dont tell any one or else Im in big trouble.

see you soon
Ian Bromley

JEANETTE WINTERSON

Dearest,

Here are the photographs:

1) *Venice. The Lido. Hotel des Bains. March.*
Sun shining. Shoes and socks off. That's me, walking through the shallows. Tiny see-through fishes were warming themselves between the surface of the water and the shelled and ribbed sea floor. I am such a fish when the sun comes out, taking my chance, nearly at the top, but put out your hand, and I'm gone.

The Hotel des Bains, closed for renovation work, its clock stopped, its potted plants unwatered and brown. I like the seedy out-of-season feel of this photo.

You lay down, your body like a sun-sponge, gradually darkening. I walked on, thinking of Thomas Mann, and a book about a woman with webbed feet. This is an invented city, mercurial, unlikely, desired because it does not exist – or that what exists can be reworked, rewritten, scored over, and no one has ever found what it really is, its absolute self. There is no such thing.

Like love.

I turned round; the Hotel had vanished. A fisherman raised his hand to me. You were gone. There is no photo.

2) *Venice. Dorsoduro.*
Here we are, searching for a café with an empty table in an empty square. We found it, didn't we? Triumphant with ourselves. Here we are sitting down, sparrows coming to eat our bread, you pouring wine from a carafe cloudy with cold, the wine in it sparkling as the sun ran through it. These times hold my mind like a shell caught in a net.

3) *Venice. Fondamenta Nuova. Night.*
Here you are, in shadow, walking fast against the cold coming off the lagoon, cold forming into shapes like spirits. We came to a miniature osteria, just one room, serving purple wine from a vat, and tuna and onion on squares of bread. I gave some tuna to a cat slunk under a tarpaulin. I said to you, 'Will you stay with me?'

You didn't answer. You never do.

I took this photograph of you with your back turned.

4) *Pensione Seguso. Our room. Iron bedstead. Wardrobe. Basin.*
You were snoring in the iron bed while I lay awake watching the light from the boats bounce off the chrome taps in the washbasin. I got up, went down the corridor to the bathroom, big and old, iron radiators, iron bath. This place has never been refurbished. Everything is iron.

I sat on the loo in the dark, and thought of taking a bag, disappearing, getting the boat to Athens, changing my name, never coming back. What would be the difference, after all, after the first surprise?

In the bedroom you were asleep. I lay down and broached the boundary. You put out an arm, a peninsula from your island home to mine. I can sometimes believe that you are there, and that I am there with you, in the same place, but that is as tantalising and impossible as this city, which can be visited but not known, which is inhabited, but by others.

5) *The Zattere. Dawn.*
The city comes to life to the noise of outboard motors cutting out towards the jetties, and the voices of men unloading crates, and after that, sack truck wheels up and down the bridges, carrying aqua minerale and beer, pasta and tinned tomatoes.

I took this photo – very Venice – thinking about love.

If you loved me this moment wouldn't look any different. If you didn't love me, it would look the same, but I read the scene through your love of me or not, as though love were a translation of life.

Maybe it is. How else to read it? How else to write it? We're always reading what we see, and then rewriting it afterwards; perhaps it's better to acknowledge our inventions than to pretend otherwise.

Look, there's Aschenbach following Tadzio, feeling for the first time in his life what he has never been able to express. Look, there's a woman walking on water, which for her at least, is easier than being in love.

6) *Suitcases on the landing stage at the Ca' Rezzonico.*
Two Bellinis – not the paintings – then a ride by boat to the airport. At the other end, we go our separate ways, we always do. I am here on a Visitor's Visa.

And yet, and yet and yet, we are good together in many ways. Impermanence is human, and however we screen it over, all of what we do is temporary, so why do the words for ever and ever mean so much? Why not accept that I am a visitor here and never seek right of residency?

But I have to live somewhere.

6b) *Postcard of George Bush with an arrow through his head.* Outside, the world I cannot control is writing a dark fairy tale of white superman heroes and dusky-faced fanatics, comic-book grotesques.

This is the War on Terror, the battle for all that is fine and good, except that each believes in its own fine and good and will destroy everything else – everything, in its name.

The planes come over – the TV news is all destruction. The Pentagon is spending $650 billion a year on the military. Its African aid budget is $4.5 billion.

It's a lot of money to blow up a lot of homes. Pretty soon we'll all be homeless now.

And so, while they tell me that the small and the particular does not matter, and that this is the world stage we are playing on, I want to know where I can call home, if not with you?

I'm doing my best with the big questions, but I have a small one too:

'Do you love me?'

7) *Near the Hotel Accademia. Evening. Our favourite bar.* There's the man who asked to marry you. At least he bought us both a prosecco. In the shop next door a woman is buying slices of prosciutto crudo and black olives. A boy with a dog is running after his sister on a bike.

The lights come on, spilling yellow on to the canals and casting shadows on the pavements. People are walking arm in arm, arguing good-humouredly, stashing their supper into string bags, looking for a place to eat.

We drink up, walk on, always through the backs, always away from the known. We find bars big enough for eight and squash in to make ten. We eat where there are no menus.

8) *Still life with sprouts.*
The woman in the cucina told us that we must have artichokes with raddichio. We did; it turned out to be brussel sprouts, cut in half and covered in Parmesan and olive oil.

9) *Vaporetto stop – Saluti.*
We are in our coats huddled in the middle, waiting for the lurch towards the stop, and the slide of the metal gate, and the rope flung over the bollard.

You asked me to take this picture of the boatman because you said he looked like Jesus.

Two Americans are videoing the scene so that they can show it to their friends at home. But there will be nothing to show. Once left behind, there is only Disney Venice, a fake, a pretend, a tourist attraction. Be here, and it's still possible to find the city, but you can't take it home with you. Venice is a quantum city, a Schrödinger's cat of a map, simultaneously dead and alive, true and false, solid and watery, firm and disappeared.

Like us.

Like love.

10) *Fishmarket. Rialto. Night.*
Two boys beating drums with hands that move so fast they blur. A man sitting at a table selling tickets for a concert tonight. A mafioso on his mobile: camel-hair coat, straight Armani jeans, Berlutti shoes, shades. A water taxi purrs out of nowhere and collects him.

You turn back towards me, smiling. I like this photo.

11) *The Frari. The night of the eclipse.*
Already the moon is half covered by the sun that tints her chalky surface to copper like an etching plate. Night sky. Copper moon.

A Japanese person took this photo of us holding hands.

Your fingers are strong. You are good at opening jam jars. The portcullis our fingers make together is the way in to a private castle, the fortress we sometimes share, when the world is outside. But for us both it is a second home.

Look at the moon, serene and beautiful, untroubled by the flag planted on her surface. She will not be so easy to colonise, and I wonder why we are looking for new worlds to own when we have taken so little care of the one we have?

Perhaps I should ask myself that, and you too. When we have spoiled each other in each other's eyes, will we just go elsewhere? It's the fashion, it's almost the rule. Why look after what you have, when you can damage it and buy a new one?

But we can't live on the moon, and we can live here on earth. I don't want speculative space; I want to be with you.

It's late. Without speaking we get into bed and make love, deceiving ourselves that we are together – or do we deceive ourselves that we are apart?

12) *Venice. Various.*

This is an old city, built to last, not built to be endlessly torn down and redeveloped. I want to live in such a city, not too far from the forest and the sea, and I want to call it by your name.

Here's the cat we befriended – thin and sharp like a blade on four legs.

Here's you, standing outside Prada, looking pleased with yourself because you have bought a new skirt.

Here's the one of me buying prawns as long as my forearm.

Here's me again, wearing red. I look like a bottle of Campari Soda.

Here are those old postcards you wanted. I packed them in my luggage by mistake. *Venice – 1945.* In the Second World

War, it was agreed not to bomb Venice. It could not be replaced. Much else was bombed that could not be replaced, but we replaced it anyway. Since then, the preferred method, public and private, is bomb and replace.

Like us

Like love.

13) *The boat to Athens from our window.*

Here's our view, across to the Giudecca where ships the size of cities sail past on their way to fabulous unknown ports – Atlantis, Byzantium, Calcis.

Here's the ship, blocking out everything. Everything! Do you remember how we woke in the middle of the night – I suppose it was just before dawn, the small hours?

The room was shaking with vibration and noise, like under the footprint and bellow of some animal long extinct. I went to the window, and there was the ship slowly moving forward; deck lit, hull dark, blocking any sight except itself. It stopped on a slight turn, as it always does, to mark its farewell to the city.

I went back to bed, couldn't sleep, because all the sizeable ships that carry my nightmares trawl this channel, and stop for a moment so that the small figure in the small window can see them before they pass on, knowing that they will turn and return, some other small-hours night.

14) *The Guggenheim Museum.*

Our favourite museum. Photographs not allowed. I sneaked this from the garden, when you were standing in the long open windows, looking serious and happy. I wondered what I'd be thinking if I had seen you there, a stranger. This is a photograph of a stranger, taken unawares.

15) *You standing by the lion in the Arsenale.*
This is your impersonation of the lion, and it is surprisingly good. The mouth is right. After I had taken this photo, we sat down and ate pizza while you drew the lion on your paper napkin. We were happy that day, and close.

And if I say to you that I am glad of everything we have done together, and sorry that we will not be here together in forty years, laughing at a faded photo of you impersonating a lion, it having weathered well, you less so, as we stand fabulously old, in a city that understands what spirit it takes to be old, to be beautiful, to be much looked at, to be itself, to be never quite caught, to have a past, to be content, to have seen much, to have remained, to have continued . . .

Keep the photos.

MICHEL FABER

My most dear John,

The joy is not easy, with my poor English, to describe when a letter with your American postage stamps comes into my slot. It is a most happy and satisfied slot, I can promise you! And on the last few occasions, the joy has been made more deep by my knowledge that the time for us to meet gets closer with each passing day.

So many things I have told you about myself and so many things I have not! It is beyond conceiving how many mysteries remain even in the minds, souls and hearts of two persons who have tried with all effort to gain maximum intimacy. For example, you know already how I like a man to touch me, and on which pieces of my skin, and with what emphasis of pressure and softness, but do you know yet about my granny and grandpa? I believe not. They live in small village about ninety kilometres from Odessa. There I spent my childhood. Besides the village there is a forest with a great plenty of berries. We gather them and make jam and marinaded mushrooms. It's very tasty. Tell me more about your family and job, John. Do you like it? When we are embraced together, I don't wish to expend precious minutes on such ordinary things.

We have waited so long and I cannot wait to see you and I am so worried about everything. But I trust you with all the faith placed in me by God and by your own sweet words. My dearheart, I have excellent news for you! The ticket for the aeroplane has now been purchased and is safe in my home. A hundred times per day I must touch it, stroke it, in case it suddenly is not real! Only when I am finally united with you, will I be able to show my thankfulness for your sending of the money and the possibilities that have been opened by this act. You will learn how powerful can be the love of a woman who has been pulled out of the deep water! Because, before I met you, I was drowning in my troubled life. But now I am 'drowning' in love for you!

True to say, I have not been so healthy in the recent days. Weather here has been strongly freezing. I caught a fever and a grippe, and for some time I was weak and lacked mobility. But I am mending fast – because I am young, I guess! When I finish writing this letter I propose to have a hot bath containing medicinal salt. It will helps my health but also, as 'side-effect', it makes my skin very velvet and soft. Soft for you!

Now that the time approaches for us to be together, I understand that there are many things still lacking arrangement. I possess many clothes which are purposely selected to envelop my form, the exact measures of my body. You have seen pictures of me inside them, I know. You asked me how is it possible for a girl in a poor country like Ukraine to buy such beautiful clothes, and I informed you that, in this way, we show our pride of ourselves, even as we suffer the lack of other necessary things. But I have realised suddenly, my dear John, that I have not suitcases for bringing these clothes to our new home in the USA! Because I have never travelled beyond the borders of my country! So I must implore you please, to make it again possible for us to have the union that is smooth and without 'headaches'. Regrettably, you cannot, this time, use the bank account of my mother. She has become a little jealous of me, I think, for my good fortune in meeting a man as wonderful as you. A mother should wish the best outcomes always for her daughter, so this jealousness hurts me a small bit, but in defence of her I must say that it is difficult for a man from the West to imagine the burden upon females in countries such as ours. I recall that you discussed in one of your letters (please, PLEASE send me more letters, darling – they are to me like nectar in a dessert!), you said that it was remarkable that in our country it seems that all the young women are very shapely and beautiful, and all the middle-aged women are without shape and ugly. And you were confounded, when does it happen, this change? Because in America the women remain in good shape, and lose their beauty only slowly. Well, this is because life in our country is too bad. Only for a limited sum of years can a girl fight away the attacks of hard existence. It is like a siege that continues for ever. A time comes when the girl cannot fight longer and then the years of bad things fall upon her and she is destroyed. But I will not be destroyed, my darling, because you have come to my aid! Thank you, thank you, thank you, my most wonderful man! My hero!

But I was saying about my mother. She says that I must travel only with the clothes on my back, and not cry and make big fuss about leaving all my beautiful dresses and underwears and shoes that I have collected with so much love and sacrifice. So I discussed it with my uncle, who understands better my heart. He has proposed me to use his bank account, for you to send me some money for suitcases and other baggage. I am sure that $500 should be enough. My uncle's name is Dmitry Morozov. The bank details you require to use are these – BENEFICIARY: MOROZOV DMITRY GR 671134 ACCOUNT: 939011008837002 BANK OF BENEFICIARY: COMMERCIAL BANK 'PRIVATBANK' 9C, Serova-Naberezhnaya, 40907

Dnepropetrovsk, UKRAINE. All the other details will be the same as before.

I thank you for your support and kind words – I thank you for being YOU! I know that when we are together we will always take care of each other and help each other with all the life trials. I'm so excited, nervous, happy, amazed and worried in the threshold of meeting . . . You see, my feelings are very controversial! But the foremost and strongest feeling is excitement!! Again I must stroke the ticket! And my passport, which I am sorry cost so much money for you. Alas, there is in Ukraine unlimited corruption. It will be a blessed relief for me to leave behind a country with so much deceitfulness and greed, and come to the USA. I still have difficulty to believe it is true, this future of ours . . . It is a miracle and you are a maker of miracles. Each time I desire you, a star falls from the sky. So, if you look up at the sky and find it dark with no stars, it is all your fault. You made me desire you too much!

I had a wonderful dream about you last night, dearheart. We sat in front of a warm fireplace in a log cabin in the middle of a harsh snowfall. We had a sheep wool rug wrapped around us for the warmth. Your skin felt so tender and smelt so good, I looked into your eyes and saw Paradise within them. Then you fell asleep and I watched your sleeping, and I wrapped you very snug in the sheep wool and all night I sat by the fire, keeping its burning alive. My goal now is to transform that dream into a reality.

I send you my sweet kisses and tight embraces . . .

Svetlana (Sveta) (Sweetie)

HISHAM MATAR

Nori al-Alfi,
c/o Daleswick College,
Greystoke, England

Mona al-Alfi,
21 Fairouz Street,
Zamalek,
Cairo, Egypt

29 October 1978

Beautiful Mona,

Yesterday was my birthday. Today is the first day of my new fourteenth year. Strange to think I will only be thirteen once, as I was only twelve, eleven, ten, once and will never be again. I cannot say I feel any different, but I suspect I have grown even taller since the summer. You will be amazed now how fast I am growing. Soon I will be taller than you.

It has been six weeks since we were last together, 43 days exactly. I can still remember how my throat tightened as we approached Cairo airport early in the morning, trying to keep my promise of not crying. Why must all horrible things take place early in the morning? My feet are still browner around the strap marks of my summer sandals. Now it is so cold I must wear one pair of socks over another, and still my toes freeze. You are right; England is turning my skin the colour of garlic.

Alexei, the German boy I share my room with, is one year older than me and tells me he became a man midway through his thirteenth year. He told me about something called wet dreams. He says they are wonderful. When I asked him if girls have wet dreams he said he did not know but suspects they do not; so I have no idea if you know what wet dreams are and if you, too, think they are wonderful.

It was fantastic to see Father yesterday. He flew from Geneva just to spend the day with me. He managed to convince stubborn old Mr Galbraith, my housemaster, to let me skip school on account that I was 'Mr Birthday Boy'. That was how Father put it. You are right; he can convince anyone of anything. He is a fantastic talker. What a great surprise it was: in the middle of morning class Mr Galbraith walks in and who is behind him, wrapped in a coat and scarf, but Father. I almost cried. I know you keep telling me to stop being sad, that I must be careful of my sadness, but I do not know why such surprises make me sad, as sad as they make me happy. I could see the other boys squirm with envy as my father took me away. I was even permitted to skip the evening study hour, and so was exempt from handing in my prep the following day. I only had to be back by lights-out. What a treat it was to be driven away in Father's car. It was wonderful to sit in the soft warm leather upholstery all the way to London, particularly when I knew I should have still been sitting at that hard wooden desk facing the blackboard. When we drove away, I hoped that by some miracle I would never have to return to this cold place ever again. Father let me choose the music on the radio. It was wonderful, but it would have been paradise if you were there.

I hope you like your new coat. Did Father tell you that it was I who had spotted it first? I hope he did. But he might not have because when people buy someone a gift they like them to think it was all their idea. But, believe me, I saw it first in the window of Annabell's, the shop you like on South Molton Street, and it was also I who convinced him to buy it even though it was 'horrendously' expensive. I do not know how much, but Father's eyes bulged when he inspected the price tag and he said, 'It is horrendously expensive.' When I asked him what that word meant exactly, he said horrendously was similar to extremely. So I told him, 'You must buy it then because Mama Mona is extremely and horrendously beautiful.' (I called you Mama Mona because, as you know, he insists I do.) This made him laugh and he took the coat to the cashier. Anyway, I hope you like it. I cannot wait to see you in it, your hair rolled up in the usual way, like an actress in one of the old films.

It is almost 10.30 now, time for lights-out. I can hear Mr Galbraith's heavy footsteps coming up the long corridor, making sure that the two boys in every room are in their pyjamas and under the covers. It is so cold here. Which brings me to your beautiful gift. The pyjamas are perfect. Abu Muftah is the best tailor in Cairo, do you not agree? At least in pyjamas he is. Please tell him that they fit perfectly. The fabric is so soft and warm and comfortable that wearing it is almost like being in your arms. They are my favourite birthday gift ever. I am so thankful that God gave me such a beautiful stepmother. I have not looked at Mama's picture for at least a year now. Before you married Father, I used to keep her in my pocket. I was so happy when you finally married Father, not only because it meant you moving in with us, but also because now you and I share the same last name.

I have to stop. Mr Galbraith is about to open the door and switch off the light, say what he always says every night and morning: 'Good night, girls. Good morning, girls.' He thinks he is being funny. He is here, bye.

After Mr Galbraith left, Alexei and I lay in the dark talking, as sometimes we do. I asked him to tell me what I will see in a wet dream and he said I would see the woman of my dreams, the woman I will some day marry. I could not sleep after that. And long after we had stopped talking I had to wake him up to borrow his pen-size flashlight, which he and I call the James Bond pen, so as I could continue writing to you from beneath the covers. I must be careful because at this time Mr Galbraith takes his dog, Jackson, walking in the fields behind the house. He must not see a light.

Sometimes, like now, I miss you so much something in my chest hurts. When I cannot sleep, or if I am woken up in the dark by a bad dream, I say your name over and over in my head. I shut my eyes and try to see your eyes, hear your voice, smell your neck.

Let me return to my birthday with Father. He and I ate at your favourite restaurant, Clarisse's. I chose it because I knew you would have. You are right; they make the best cheese fondue in London. And you are also right that it is nowhere as good as the Cafe du Soleil in Geneva. I cannot wait for us to be there together in December. I am counting the days, 48 from today. But I was devastated when Father told me that I would only have one week with you. One week! He is taking you after that to visit his friends in Rome and I will have to return to Cairo alone and spend the holidays all on my own in that big flat in Zamalek with only Naima the maid to keep me company. I know Father loves me, but I think he hates it when you and I are together. This is why he sent me here after you got married. This is why he is taking you to Rome. This is why he asks me to call you Mama Mona. He is jealous. I wish we were Christians so as I could spend the entire Christmas holidays with you. God should have made us the same age.

He waited until we finished our meal at Clarisse's to tell me.

I of course ordered the cheese fondue. He ordered a large steak that bled every time he pressed it with his knife. Afterwards I ordered strawberry ice crème and he asked for a black coffee. When it arrived he lit a cigarette that kept smoking in my direction. As usual, we did not talk about much. He always seems bored when he and I are alone. His eyes looked beyond me and every time the waitress came, he seemed to come alive; whenever he has to speak to anyone else he comes alive. Sometimes I wish I can come to him as a stranger, to ask him things like if he ever misses Mama. She has been dead for over six years now and he never mentions her name. When someone would ask him about a plate or a piece of furniture she had bought, like you used to do, he would say, 'Nori's mother bought that.' Do not worry; I am not upset at him. Please, please, please do not mention any of this to him. I love him and I love him more for bringing you into my life. You know how some films switch from black-and-white to colour when the director wants us to know that time has moved on, or that things have become happier? The last year, since you married Father, has been like that. Anyway, just when I started eating the ice crème, he told me that you two would be spending Christmas and New Year in Rome without me. At that moment I wished he never came or took me to London; I wished it were not my birthday.

I have to stop now. I will try to wake up early to finish.

It is 6.40 in the morning. I am under the covers, but already dressed in my uniform. It seems even colder now. The sun might as well not be here. The clouds are as thick as blankets and their edges look bruised. The trees are leafless and dark. The whole thing looks like an ugly black drawing from a horror book. I remember, when you came here a year ago with Father, how you said that you love the English countryside, how romantic you find winter, how much you miss England. And when I said it was gloomy, you said it was exactly that gloominess that made it romantic and asked me to read *Wuthering Heights.* Well, I have read that book now and I still do not understand what you mean. I hate the cold and I hate Daleswick. There are boys here as old as eighteen; is that how long Father intends on keeping me here?

Summer is too far off to imagine. For a while all I could think of was December with you in Geneva, sitting beside you in the Cafe du Soleil, but ever since Father told me of his plan to take you to Rome I have been trying to imagine the summer months with you instead. Let's go to Alexandria again. Father will have no excuse then; we will spend the entire time together, swimming and getting as brown as we can.

I do not think it was a wet dream, but last night I dreamt I was kissing your shoulder. When I woke up I touched my underpants and they were dry. Alexei says that is the proof. But maybe they dried by the time I woke up. Anyway, it was a beautiful dream. You started laughing and snorting like you do when I tickle you.

I am keeping to my promise: praying all the five prayers and saying my dua every day. And I have already memorised the five suras you asked me to memorise. I cannot wait to recite them to you.

I have to go now or else I will miss breakfast. Today there will be no chance of Father turning up, and even less of you.

God protect you. I kiss your neck, the spot we agreed was mine and only mine. 48 days. No, I forgot, 47 now.

Forever yours,

Nori

GEOFF DYER

Letter to several possible recipients from the mid-1980s

To whom it may concern

Obviously I am writing to say sorry. I know this is meant to be a love letter but, as you will have guessed, I am one of those men for whom love – contrary to what the Ali McGraw/Ryan O'Neil film claimed – *always* means having to say you're sorry. At some point love letters become letters of apology. The thing separating the two is also the thing that makes the one blur into the other: a relationship.

To start at the beginning, I saw you at that party in wherever it was and you were beautiful. Is it superfluous to say that? Is there a man in the world who does – or at the very least *did* – not think his woman beautiful? (I fear that this is a paraphrase of something Arsène Wenger said, and back in the 1980s, when this letter purports to have been written, no one had heard of Arsène Wenger. But the thing about this letter is that while it's meant to be sort of written by me in my twenties it's a version of me in my twenties who benefits from all the wisdom and insight I've amassed – not much actually – since then. So, for the sake of clarity: as well as being a letter not to one but several exes it is also a letter from several versions of my previous self, some of them also exes. As such it was written both then and now and at various points between. Its tense, if it has one, is the present retrospective.) All else followed from seeing you at that party and thinking you were beautiful and that, somehow, I had to connive a way of talking to you.

You know those software statements? 'By opening this package you agree to abide etc . . .' I think you effectively sign a contract like that when you have your first kiss, and it's an agreement renewed and extended with every subsequent kiss: I agree that by participating in this kiss I am willing to have my heart smashed to pieces in return for this one moment of bliss. It's a version of the Faustus thing – 'O moment thou art fair, stay.' (I'll come back to this too.) I'm happy with the terms of that contract. It would be a dull life otherwise. The important thing is that we had some great times together, some great moments, most of which, if we're being utterly frank, I can no longer remember. Life is all and only about those moments. (So when I say this is a letter of apology I mean the opposite; it's a letter of non-apology.) 'You say yes to a single joy and you say yes to all woes' – that whole trip. As you know I was – in this context I am simply too embarrassed to use the word 'am' – somewhat of a Nietzschean. Sorry about that, about the way I was always quoting Nietzsche. In fact, while we're at it, I'm sorry about the way I was always *quoting*, period. All that Rilke and Dylan too . . . Well, honey, what can I say? That's what young guys *do*. They quote Nietzsche and Dylan and Rilke. Ditto the music, the relentless torrent of late Coltrane I inflicted on your ears. Sorry about that too. More specifically, I'm sorry that, after listening to *First Meditations (for Quartet)*, at top volume you said 'I guess I'm just too mellow for this.' Yes, that's right, I'm sorry *you* said that because that left *me* no choice but to say, 'Right, that's it.' After which you said, 'What do you mean?' After which I said, 'It's over. We're splitting up.' That may seem like rather an extreme reaction to your reaction but, even now, looking back, I think: fair enough, good for you (me, I mean). Frankly, anyone who doesn't swoon at the moment of transition between the first track, 'Love', and the second, 'Compassion', when the aftermath of the tenor is hanging over everything and there's almost silence, just the faintest residue of a pulse, before Elvin and Trane bring the whole suite swelling back to life again – frankly, even though we're dealing, literally, with the movement from 'Love' to 'Compassion', that person deserves to get booted out on their arse! After all, it's not like we'd been listening to *Ascension*. Now that really is a racket. For what it's worth I never listen to free jazz now. I'd rather put my head in a metal dustbin and have someone bang it very hard with a big hammer but when you're that age you just have to fill your head with this stuff. It calms you down at some level.

Another thing I'm sorry about is the way that I always wanted to go to that pub, the Effra. God I loved that pub! I loved all pubs but I loved that one even more than all the others. Now that I hardly ever set foot in pubs it seems hard to believe that I could have loved them so much. They strike me as horrible, smoky, violent places and they were probably smokier, more violent and even more horrible back then. It just seemed so implausible to me that you didn't like pubs. How could anyone not like *pubs*? Pubs weren't just where one had a good time; pubs were what one *did*. Especially the Effra. On a more general, beer-related note, it is a source of deep regret that you had the ill fortune to meet me in the depths of my real ale phase so that all our holidays (I know what you're going to say: we only had *two*) were organised around the CAMRA guide. Don't get me wrong. I'm not going to throw the baby out with the bathwater and de- (or re-)nounce real ale. I still love the stuff. Flat beer served at room temperature is one of England's great contributions to the sensual life of the world. But this I will concede: it seems a weird way to have spent one's twenties, always chucking pints of Dog Bolter down your – my – neck and searching out a boozer where they served Old Peculiar. This became especially clear in my late thirties and early forties – the Ecstasy years – when I ended up leading a life that was in some ways more youthful than the pubby one I led in my mid-twenties but, as with Arsène Wenger, the alternative just wasn't available back then.

I'm really sorry, as well, that you were such a headbanging feminist nutcase. Honestly. What a waste. There you were, twenty-five, slinky as a cat, and I never saw you in stockings or a G-string (I still remember the fury that the 'Underneath they're all lovable' advert induced in you, in me, in us), never even saw you in a dress in fact, only in dungarees and (a concession to glamour) that Simone de Beauvoir headscarf. Poor you, poor me, poor us. Hey, the sex was great though, wasn't it? In spite of all the political prohibitions about penetration and patriarchy and the dread figure of Andrea Dworkin hanging over us like a curse it turned out that, at some timeless level, naturally enough, we liked doing all the stuff that people have always liked doing. Those moments when you'd say, 'Do *anything* to me.' Well, call me an opportunist but I took that as meaning, in so many words, 'Do it in my arse.' Turns out that's exactly what you did mean, of course, but to have actually said so would have been craving your own oppression, like choosing to read Norman Mailer (at least I never quoted that tosspot!) instead of Toni Cade Bambara. All of which, of course, was part of the thrill. Ah, good times. Or great moments anyway.

Anyway, what I've been leading up to saying, basically, is that I'm sorry I was such a jerk. I'm sorry I thought the way to seduce someone – yourself, I hardly need remind you, included – was to undermine their politics, that the way to demonstrate that I was an alpha male of the mind was to quote Nietzsche and generally let it be known that I had read more Adorno and Lukacs than whichever rival male was also trying to do exactly the same thing. So, to show how genuinely contrite I am, I'm going to make a confession – a double confession, actually, the first part of which, if we're being entirely honest, is actually a boast: I *did* sleep with M that time, after that party in Bonnington Square when I said I'd ended up crashing at Pete Johnson's place in Oval Mansions. Guilty as charged (I'm trying to wipe that smile off my face but it's not really a smile, more of a smirk). That's part one. And the second part, I realise now, is also a sort of boast: I never actually read *History and Class Consciousness.* It was just too complicated and boring. The days when I could even contemplate reading such a thing are long gone – the brain is not what it was – but back then I was, theoretically, capable of doing so. The funny thing is that of all the stuff that didn't happen back then, that's something I really don't regret.

Love

MATTHEW ZAPRUDER

Dear X,

It's late at night, and I begin this letter by slipping into those moments right before I knew you. Thus I experience once again the mysterious shock of first seeing you. Later I will see the envelope and imagine its destination. It's so rare to hold a letter these days! I hope you find the news important and good.

Earlier tonight I stood annually in C.'s kitchen, already dreading the solstice ritual where we're supposed to read and then burn little scraps of paper on which we have written either the things we want or things we no longer need, I can never remember. Until this year it had never seemed to matter.

Last year I ended up standing before the fireplace holding two little pieces of napkin on which I had written these phrases: 'stop subletting' and 'regulate feeling like panda feeling'. As my moment came closer I watched several people hold in their trembling hands the little bits of what they hoped for or hoped would no longer return before throwing them into the fire and crying.

Have you ever felt like an awful blue tuxedo someone rented because it seemed so hilarious at the time? How sad, now they have nothing else but you to wear to the celebration. That's just one of the many feelings I'd like to be able to throw not into the fire but someplace just far enough from myself to forget it, and just close enough to instantly retrieve.

This year I found myself before the shelf upon which rests a collection of porcelain elves about the size of my thumb. Idly picking up one particular chipped figure I saw how eerily it resembled my high school geometry teacher. With a feeling of great excitement I turned, felt the sharp disappointment there was no one anywhere near me who cared, and caught or was caught by the sight of you sitting on a couch, holding a glass with a face painted on it.

I'm not what people would call a 'visual person'. In fact, I'm one of those people who likes the names of flowers so much he can't remember which ones they actually are. You were talking to someone who seemed to be but was not wearing a hat pulled down around his eyes, and as you turned slightly, below your short dark hair one side of your face was no longer shaded but lit pretty clearly by a lamp. I saw one tiny freckle just above the side of your mouth, which turned up just the slightest bit, I wouldn't call it a smile.

I could see it so clearly. All last year I was an artificial lake! Sure I had the occasional requisite live electrical cable dropped into me, but mostly I sat in the sun, full of little nameless waves and cheerful paddle-boats. So many missed chances to blunder. My father told me the problem with us is we are in love with being in love with love. My sister insisted I will just like she and my brother one day eventually learn to follow that feeling of doubt wherever it leads. It's a miracle our people have procreated at all. Yet we persist.

Then it was time to move into the living room. I kept pretending to look for something to write with, trying hard not to watch you laughing and passing a pen back and forth among your friends. When I looked down I saw one of those scraps of paper someone must have dropped. When my turn came I unfolded it and saw someone had written 'I wish I could draw'; without thinking I said 'I see need is no longer only for children' and threw it into the fire.

Many things happened until we met, sort of, finally at the end of the night. You may remember me as tallish by the door. I made a vague motion with my hands like I had either released and immediately begun trying to retrieve something invisible and weightless, or had started to help you with your coat, which I did, clumsily looking down at you from what seemed like an exciting and terrifying altitude. You said your name and turned and did not see me write it on my hand.

A girl just walked down my hallway, singing. The radio mutters along about the president. Do you think he will for once at last defy his advisors and decide against the next war? Maybe by the time you have read and put down this letter we will already know, and we will attend instead of a demonstration a calm victory celebration that almost exactly resembles an ordinary evening, just a little more full of the great unguarded anonymous affection even the most selfish of us remain unexpectedly capable of.

Someone once said to give a gift is the most selfish act of all. That person was wise but not a great house guest. In the spirit of great beginnings I'd like to bring you something you never will need. Not even a potion that does nothing, nor a translucent umbrella you can carry to work on overcast days to protect your freckles from the clouds, nor a tiny golden talking boat, no bigger than the palm of your hand.

So besides the paper on which these words are written I humbly enclose nothing at all. Not even my great desire to see you. Just the feeling that remains after you are given the pleasure of being given nothing, along with the beautiful electric fear of choosing your own particular way of locating someone you so far know only a few things about, and of deciding those reasons are more than enough.

CARL-JOHAN VALLGREN

Translated by Sarah Death

Stockholm, 25 February 2007

Dear Mamma,

Two months ago, I invented a photograph of you, taken in 1942. I was one track short for the album I was recording; the working title of the record was *Family Life* and my idea was to use pop music to tell the story of the most recent period in my life: divorce from my previous wife; moving back to Sweden from Berlin after twelve years in voluntary exile; how I met my current partner; falling in love once more, against all the odds, in spite of all my bitterness, in spite of all the ingrained cynicism that afflicts divorced men of my age; and then the little miracle of becoming a father for the first time, at forty.

I had written songs about being in love again, about the pregnancy, about my daughter's birth, about my relapse into doubt; I had written a bitter farewell ballad to my ex-wife, taken my leave of Berlin (which had given me so much, not least in artistic terms) but I was still missing a song that could plumb the family depths, cut across chronology to put me and my little family in our historical context. And that was how I came to create the song 'The Photograph', based on your tragic fate.

The lyrics have you standing on the quayside in Åbo harbour. You're three years old, and there's an address label hanging on a string round your neck. There are vague figures, Red Cross staff, in the background. Doctors, nurses. And children everywhere: thousands of Finnish refugee children waiting to be shipped across the Baltic. You're amazingly like my daughter, your granddaughter. You're both the same age. Both raven haired, with the same sensitive mouth. But in your look there is something I have never seen in hers: deep, existential terror.

There are appalling accounts of the transportation of refugee children from Finland to Sweden during the 'Continuation War' of 1941–44. Russian planes pursued the convoys out over the sea and attacked them with machine-guns. The children, many never to return to their families (you were one of them), were desperate. Your sister Ritva ought to have been with you. But she was two years older and realised intuitively that catastrophe lay ahead. Poor Ritva. She was supposed to be looking after you. Your father was at the front, your mother was seriously ill. The idea was for you both to be sent to the same host family in Sweden and then return safe and sound to Finland as soon as the war was over.

But it didn't turn out that way. Minutes before the ship sailed, she wriggled out of a nurse's grip and rushed back to the quay where your aunt was standing; she got down on her knees, they say, and begged to be allowed to stay. People have told me that the last they saw of you was a small figure, hand in hand with a Red Cross worker, swallowed up in a tide of children who were swarming like lemmings up the gangplank; you were too little to understand what was happening.

In one of my earliest memories, you are showing me some medals that you keep in a kitchen cupboard. 'These are your grandpa's bravery medals from the war,' you say. I'm maybe seven. There are about fifteen metal plaques, fixed to a board; if I were to believe the evidence of my own eyes, my biological grandfather on my mother's side must have been awarded every honour that had existed in the Finnish army since the days of Runeberg. But when I ask to have a closer look, you put them back up in the cupboard with an expression as if to say: they're not intended for children to look at. It's only in adulthood that it begins to dawn on me: you were showing me your old sprinting medals from local athletics tournaments . . .

There was another time, during the summer holidays when I was about ten, when Swedish Television showed an old feature film about the Finnish Winter War. I think it must have been based on some of Väinö Linna's novels, maybe *The Unknown Soldier*. In one key scene, Russian tanks advanced through a forest on the Karelian Isthmus; one incredibly brave Finnish soldier attacked a tank completely unaided, and managed to knock it out with a Molotov cocktail.

'That character is based on my Pappa's exploits,' you said. 'He stopped a tank like that, all on his own.'

As a child, of course, I felt mightily proud that my biological grandfather was a decorated Finnish war hero who had stopped tanks single-handed in the forests of Karelia; I told anyone who would listen about his martial prowess, oblivious in those days to the in-built racism of the Swedes towards their former colonial subjects to the east. The only thing this episode brought me was a new nickname: *bloody Finn*.

I don't think any of your lies have been deliberately misleading. I know they spring from an old habit of trying to make life a little more beautiful, a little more adventurous, a little more bearable. I believe you started inventing life right from the age of three, as a survival strategy . . .

It's not easy for me to write that I love you, Mamma. I have never said those words. Something stopped me when I was little, maybe that unreliability, those remarkable stories that later turned out to be fabricated, your wildly fluctuating moods and the recurrent crises in your life, your uncertainty about who you were and where you really belonged.

Your biological parents wanted you to go back after the war, but your step-parents refused; legal proceedings were begun, and in the end the authorities gave permission for adoption. On grounds of language, they said. By that time you had forgotten all your Finnish. Finnish and Swedish are two entirely different idioms, with entirely different roots: Swedish is Germanic; Finnish is Finno-Ugric, and thus not even related to Indo-European. You were said to have been fluent when you reached your new country at the age of three: perfect Finnish pronunciation and a wide vocabulary. In Sweden you became virtually deaf mute: you understood nothing, nor could you make yourself understood. Three years later, the situation was reversed.

I wish I could say I love you. But I can't. It's not that I don't love you, because I genuinely do, in a way that's so natural there's no need even to formulate the feeling. I have no choice, so to speak: unlike you, I've never had two mothers to be torn between. The biological one, forced by the war to give you up, thinking you had better chances of survival in Sweden and would soon come back – and your step-mother, who became so attached to you that she insisted on adopting you.

It's strange – or perhaps not so strange – that since I became the father of a daughter myself, you have triggered emotions in me that I didn't know I was capable of. Terrible attacks of separation anxiety; manic retrospective looks at my own history and at your fate, which in a sense has moulded mine. And imagining myself in your biological parents' situation plunges me into what I can only describe as clinical depression.

You were thirteen when you finally saw them again, very

briefly. That was in 1952, during the Olympic Games in Helsinki. Your adoptive parents took you there so you could meet the two people who brought you into the world, but on neutral territory. They lived in the middle of Finland, in Jyväskylä I think. I'm told your adoptive parents wouldn't let you stray more than a few metres from their side: they were petrified you might be kidnapped.

It may have been after this trip that you came up with the story of being related to the Romanov family. You told me on quite a few occasions, even when I was well into my teens, that an ancestor on your father's side had supposedly been in service at the court at St Petersburg and become pregnant by one of the Tsars. When I double-checked the story with my father, he explained in a pitying tone that it was a story you had made up when you were a girl, to help you feel you were a cut above the average abandoned Finnish war child.

It all fits together, Mamma. 'And I understand you much better now,' as I sing in the chorus of my song. It's all about blood, about blood being thicker than water. I really do love you. And that's why, finally, I'm writing this, in a love letter you will never read. Paradoxically enough, doing it this way makes it all the more 'true', because I have nothing to gain.

So I write those incomparable words and let my readers bear witness: I love you, Mamma.

Your son, C-J

JOSEPH BOYDEN

New Orleans Times Picayune – Missing Persons Section Online

September 1, 2005

If you have seen or know the whereabouts of Mrs. Geraldine Solomon, age 52, of 3682 S. Desire St., please contact NOPD, Times Picayune Missing Persons Bureau, or any official of Department of Homeland Security, New Orleans Bureau. Mrs. Solomon was last seen by her husband, Fred Solomon, August 30, approximately 7 a.m., during the levee breech. Mrs. Geraldine Solomon is African American female, 5′2″, 145 pounds, light complexion, freckled nose and forehead.

September 2, 2005

Missing, Mrs. Geraldine Solomon, age 52, of 3682 S. Desire St. since August 30, 2005, lower Ninth Ward. 5′2″ in height, approximately 145 pounds. Light complexion. Not a strong swimmer. If you know the whereabouts of this person, please contact NOPD, Times Picayune Missing Persons Bureau, or any official of Department of Homeland Security, New

Orleans Bureau. Her husband, Fred Solomon, remains in New Orleans searching for her. *I'm still here, Geraldine.*

September 3, 2005

Mrs. Geraldine Solomon, last seen on the roof of her house on the morning of August 30, 2005, before being swept away by surging waters at approximately 7 a.m. in the lower Ninth Ward near the intersection of S. Desire and Marigny. Geraldine Solomon is approximately 5′2″ and 145 pounds, light complexion, green eyes, freckled nose and forehead. She is not a strong swimmer and is diabetic. Her husband Fred Solomon can be reached through NOPD, Times Picayune Missing Persons Bureau, or through any official with the Department of Homeland Security, New Orleans Bureau. *I'm still here, Geraldine. I didn't want to let go of your hand. I lost you, but I'm still here, baby. I know you're still alive.*

September 4, 2005

Missing: Mrs. Geraldine Solomon, age 52, 5′2″, 145 pounds. Heavyset woman. Last seen at 3682 S. Desire St, Lower Ninth Ward on the morning of August 30 by her *loving* husband Fred, who lost contact with her on the roof of their home during a flood surge at approximately 7 a.m. She has green eyes and freckles on her nose and forehead. Scar on her left arm. Geraldine is diabetic and not a strong swimmer. She needs insulin once daily. *Baby, I'm still here. Why'd you tell me to let you go? Please tell me where you at. I need you. Your children need you. Your grandbabies need you.*

September 5, 2005

If you know the whereabouts of Geraldine Solomon, age 52, 145 pound African American female, light complexion, heavyset, green eyes, last seen in Lower Ninth Ward at the intersection of S. Desire and Marigny, please contact NOPD, Times Picayune Missing Persons Bureau, or any official of Department of Homeland Security, New Orleans Bureau. Geraldine Solomon is a diabetic and needs daily insulin injections. Her husband, Fred Solomon, has been evacuated to Houston. *National Guard made me go at gunpoint. They forced me to, Geraldine. I am in the Astrodome with Keysha and her two and we need you. Why'd you tell me to let go? Your man needs you. Your children and grandbabies need you. I couldn't hold your hand longer.* Her family searches for their mother/grandmother. She has *beautiful* green eyes *that light up when she smiles and her* freckles *make her stand out in a crowd. She needs daily insulin injections and can't swim a stroke.*

September 6, 2005

Geraldine Solomon. Your family needs you. Missing, Geraldine Solomon. S*hort and heavy-bodied.* She has a *freckled nose and* light complexion with *startling* green eyes. She needs insulin once a day. She was swept away from the roof of her house on the morning of August 30. *The Homeland Security and the NOPD say they know she is missing and they are doing everything they can to find her.* Geraldine has three daughters, one son, and six grandchildren. *Grandkids OK, Geraldine, but they need their grandma. Baby, I know you're sick with your diabetes. Tell me someone's helping you. Please, if you see her give her an insulin injection.* If you know of the whereabouts of Geraldine Solomon please contact her husband Fred Solomon. *Red Cross lady here* *tells me I can be reached at* http//www.nolamissingpersons/katrina/houstonastrodome.gov.org

September 7, 2005

Missing person named Geraldine Solomon is *desperately needed. She can read but doesn't have her glasses and so if you found* a black woman, age 52, short and heavy build, *freckle nose and forehead, beautiful green eyes.* Please contact Fred Solomon at http//www.nolamissingpersons/katrina/houstonastrodome.gov.org. *She needs insulin and might be very delirious at this point, but she goes by Geraldine. Fred needs you, Geraldine. The grandkids need their mama. If you read this and found Geraldine, please give her some insulin. Department of Homeland Security says they know she is missing and is looking for her. But they won't let me go back to look for her. So if you have come across Geraldine, please let her know that her husband Fred is coming soon as he can so please if you have found her, report her to a police officer or official. We are in Houston, Geraldine. I tried to keep looking for you but they made me go. Please let her know this.* She is diabetic. *Eyes no good without glasses. Freckle nose and light complexion for a black woman. Beautiful eyes.*

September 8, 2005

We are missing our wife/mother/grandmother, Geraldine Solomon, age 52, light-skinned African American female, *freckle nose*, green eyes, heavyset. *They forced me to go to Houston.* Father, daughters and grandchildren in Houston at Astrodome. *If you found her please read this to her as she lost her glasses.* Geraldine's family can be reached at http//www.nolamissingpersons/katrina/houstonastrodome.gov.org. She requires daily insulin injections. *Authorities say they know she is missing and say they're looking for her, so please let them know if you found her. She might be sick from her diabetes but will answer to the name Geraldine if she is conscious.* Last seen by her husband Fred on morning of August 30 on the roof of their home before high water and winds swept her away. *You told me I had to let go or we would both drown. You need insulin and some food and water now. Lord, please look out for her.*

September 9, 2005

We're praying for you wife/mother/grandmother. Department of Homeland Security/NOPD looking for Geraldine Solomon. If you have seen her or know her whereabouts, *even if she is dead,* please contact Fred Solomon at http//www.nolamissingpersons/katrina/houstonastrodome.gov.org. *We believe she is still alive as she is a very strong woman but might be weak now and needs insulin once a day. Her glasses are missing so please read this to her.* Her family is at the Houston Astrodome. *We were forced to go there but Fred is trying to get back to New Orleans and will be looking for you soon as police let me go home. I am trying, Geraldine, so hold on baby. We miss you and the grandkids need their mama.* Geraldine is short and heavyset *and has a big laugh and smiles a lot. Very kind woman, and if she is delirious will still answer to her name.* 52 years old. *Neighbors know her as Miss Geraldine. Please read this to her if you found her, and please get her some insulin.*

September 10, 2005

We're praying that Missing, Geraldine Solomon, married to Fred Solomon at New Orleans Courthouse, May 8, 1972, *is found by her loving family. Geraldine's born and raised in the Ninth Ward and neighbors know her as Miss Geraldine.* She is short and heavyset and has a light complexion with freckles on her nose and forehead and *beautiful* green eyes. *You will know her by her eyes.* Fred Solomon lost his wife from the roof of their house in the early morning hours of August 30 in high winds and water. Geraldine can't swim, *but I heard a Coast Guard helicopter nearby shortly after she got swept away from me and I pray to the Lord that they found her. If you have come across Geraldine, please let her know that her husband Fred is coming soon as he can. Hold on. Please get her to a hospital. She is diabetic and needs insulin shots every day. She can read but lost her glasses, so please read this to her, even if she is delirious or unconscious. She will understand you. I'm in Houston, baby, but I will come back soon as I can find a way back.* Her family has been evacuated to Houston. *Geraldine likes the music of Bobby Blue Bland and Fats Domino and she particularly likes gospel music. She also will listen to rap that is not offensive. If you know of her or found her she will respond to gospel even if not awake. Your grandbabies need you. Your children need their mama. I need you. Hold on.* Scar on her right arm. Wedding ring on left hand. *We are in Houston.* Her family can be reached at http//www.nolamissingpersons/katrina/houstonastrodome.gov.org.

September 11, 2005

Geraldine Solomon of 3682 S. Desire, Ninth Ward is still missing *and her family fears the worst.* She is a short, heavyset black woman with light complexion and green eyes *you can't miss.* She has freckles. *When she's in the sun the freckles become more noticeable. She'll be hungry and tired and might not be herself. Play her some gospel music. She'll respond to it.* If you have seen her or know her whereabouts please contact her husband Fred at http//www.nolamissingpersons/Katrina/houstonastrodome.gov.org or Homeland Security or NOPD.

Geraldine's missing 12 days but her family prays and hopes for the best. She loves music. Can dance like a teenager. Sometimes in the right mood she'll sing and can sing like an angel. If you have seen her please contact us. *Where are you, baby? Please. I'm coming. They won't let me go, but I'm coming.*

September 12, 2005

Missing: Mrs. Geraldine Solomon, age 52, of 3682 S. Desire St. Please contact NOPD, Times Picayune Missing Persons Bureau, or any official of Department of Homeland Security, New Orleans Bureau. *My wife. I can't go on without you.* Mrs. Solomon was swept from the roof of her home on August 30, approximately 7 a.m., during the levee breech. *Why, baby? I should never have let go.* Mrs. Geraldine Solomon is African American female, 5′2″, 145 pounds, light complexion, freckled nose and forehead. *Pray for Geraldine.*

September 13, 2005

If you have seen or know the whereabouts of Mrs. Geraldine Solomon, age 52, of 3682 S. Desire St., please contact NOPD, Times Picayune Missing Persons Bureau, or any official of Department of Homeland Security, New Orleans Bureau. Mrs. Solomon was last seen by her husband, Fred Solomon, August 30, approximately 7 a.m., during the levee breech. Mrs. Geraldine Solomon is African American female, 5′2″, 145 pounds, light complexion, freckled nose and forehead.

NEIL GAIMAN

My darling,
Let us begin this letter, this prelude to an encounter, formally, as a declaration, in the old-fashioned way: I love you. You do not know me (although you have seen me, smiled at me, placed coins in the palm of my hand). I know you (although not so well as I would like. I want to be there when your eyes flutter open in the morning, and you see me, and you smile. Surely this would be paradise enough?). So I do declare myself to you now, with pen set to paper. I declare it again: I love you.

I write this in English, your language, a language I also speak. My English is good. I was some years ago in England and in Scotland. I spent a whole summer standing in Covent Garden, except for the month of Edinburgh Festival, when I am in Edinburgh. People who put money in my box in Edinburgh included Mr Kevin Spacey the actor, and Mr Jerry Springer the American television star who was in Edinburgh for an Opera about his life.

I have put off writing this for so long, although I have wanted to, although I have composed it many times in my head. Shall I write about you? About me?

First you.

I love your hair, long and red. The first time I saw you I believed you to be a dancer, and I still believe that you have a dancer's body. The legs, and the posture, head up and back. It was your smile that told me you were a foreigner, before ever I heard you speak. In my country we smile in bursts, like the sun coming out and illuminating the fields and then retreating again behind a cloud too soon. Smiles are valuable here, and rare. But you smiled all the time, as if everything you saw delighted you. You smiled the first time you saw me, even wider than before. You smiled and I was lost, like a small child in a great forest never to find its way home again.

I learned when young that the eyes give too much away. Some in my profession adopt dark spectacles, or even (and these I scorn with bitter laughter as amateurs) masks that cover the whole face. What good is a mask? My solution is that of full-sclera theatrical contact lenses, purchased from an American website for a little under 500 euros, which cover the whole eye. They are dark grey, of course, and look like stone. They have made me more than 500 euros, paid for themselves over and over. You may think, given my profession, that I must be poor, but you would be wrong. Indeed, I fancy that you must be surprised by how much I have collected. My needs have been small and my earnings always very good.

Except when it rains.

Sometimes even when it rains. The others as perhaps you have observed, my love, retreat when it rains, put up the umbrellas, run away. I remain where I am. Always. I simply wait, unmoving. It all adds to the conviction of the performance.

And it is a performance, as much as when I was a theatrical actor, a magician's assistant, even when I myself was a dancer. (That is how I am so familiar with the bodies of dancers.) Always, I was aware of the audience as individuals. I have found this with all actors and all dancers, except the short-sighted ones for whom the audience is a blur. My eyesight is good, even through the contact lenses.

'Did you see the man with the moustache in the third row?' we would say. 'He is staring at Minou with lustful glances.'

And Minou would reply, 'Ah yes. But the woman on the aisle, who looks like the German Chancellor, she is now fighting to stay awake.' If one person falls asleep, you can lose the whole audience, so we would play the rest of the evening to a middle-aged woman who wished only to succumb to drowsiness.

The second time you stood near me you were so close I could smell your shampoo. It smelt like flowers and fruit. I imagine America as being a whole continent full of women who smell of flowers and fruit. You were talking to a young man from the university. You were complaining about the difficulties of our language for an American. 'I understand what gives a man or a woman gender,' you were saying. 'But what makes a chair masculine or a pigeon feminine? Why should a statue have a feminine ending?'

The young man, he laughed and pointed straight at me, then. But truly, if you are walking through the square, you can tell nothing about me. The robes look like old marble, water-stained and time-worn and lichened. The skin could be granite. Until I move I am stone and old bronze, and I do not move if I do not want to. I simply stand.

Some people wait in the square for much too long, even in the rain, to see what I will do. They are uncomfortable not knowing, only happy once they have assured themselves that I am a natural, not an artificial. It is the uncertainty that traps people, like a mouse in a glue-trap.

I am writing about myself perhaps too much. I know that this is a letter of introduction as much as it is a love letter. I should write about you. Your smile. Your eyes so green. (You do not know the true colour of my eyes. I will tell you. They are brown.) You like classical music, but you have also ABBA and Kid Loco on your iPod Nano. You wear no perfume. Your underwear is, for the most part, faded and comfortable, although you have a single set of red-lace brassière and panties which you wear for special occasions.

People watch me in the square, but the eye is only attracted by motion. I have perfected the tiny movement, so tiny that the passer can scarcely tell if it is something he saw or not. Yes? Too often people will not see what does not move. The eyes see it but do not see it, they discount it. I am human-shaped, but I am not human. So in order to make them see me, to make them look at me, to stop their eyes from sliding off me and paying me no attention, I am forced to make the tiniest motions, to draw their eyes to me. Then, and only then, do they see me. But they do not always know what they have seen.

I think of you as a code to be broken, or as a puzzle to be cracked. Or a jigsaw puzzle, to be put together. I walk through your life, and I stand motionless at the edge of my own. My gestures – statuesque, precise – are too often misinterpreted. I want you. I do not doubt this.

You have a younger sister. She has a MySpace account, and a Facebook account. We talk sometimes on Messenger. All too often people assume that a medieval statue exists only in the fifteenth century. This is not so true: I have a room, I have a laptop. My computer is passworded. I practise safe computing. Your password is your first name. That is not safe. Anyone could read your email, look at your photographs, reconstruct your interests from your web history. Someone who was interested and who cared could spend endless hours building up a complex schematic of your life, matching the people in the photographs to the names in the emails, for example. It would not be hard reconstructing a life from a computer, or from cellphone messages. It would be like filling a crossword puzzle.

I remember when I actually admitted to myself that you had

taken to watching me, and only me, on your way across the square. You paused. You admired me. You saw me move once, for a child, and you told a woman with you, loud enough to be heard, that I might be a real statue. I take it as the highest compliment. I have many different styles of movement, of course – I can move like clockwork, in a set of tiny jerks and stutters, I can move like a robot or an automaton. I can move like a statue coming to life after hundreds of years of being stone.

Within my hearing you have spoken many times of the beauty of this small city. How, for you, to be standing inside the stained-glass confection of the old church was like being imprisoned inside a kaleidoscope of jewels. It was like being in the heart of the sun. Also, you are concerned about your mother's illness.

When you were an undergraduate you worked as a cook, and your fingertips are covered with the scar marks of a thousand tiny knife-cuts.

I love you, and it is my love for you that drives me to know all about you. The more I know, the closer I am to you. You were to come to my country with a young man, but he broke your heart, and still you came here to spite him, and still you smiled. I close my eyes and I can see you smiling. I close my eyes and I see you striding across the town square in a clatter of pigeons. The women of this country do not stride. They move diffidently, unless they are dancers. And when you sleep your eyelashes flutter. The way your cheek touches the pillow. The way you dream.

I dream of dragons. When I was a small child, at the home, they told me that there was a dragon beneath the old city. I pictured the dragon wreathing like black smoke beneath the buildings, inhabiting the cracks between the cellars, insubstantial and yet always present. That is how I think of the dragon, and how I think of the past, now. A black dragon made of smoke. When I perform I have been eaten by the dragon and have become part of the past. I am, truly, seven hundred years old. Kings come and kings go. Armies arrive and are absorbed or return home again, leaving only damaged buildings, widows and bastard children behind them, but the statues remain, and the dragon of smoke, and the past.

I say this, although the statue that I emulate is not from this town at all. It stands in front of a church in southern Italy, where it is believed either to represent the sister of John the Baptist, or a local lord who endowed the church to celebrate that he had not died of the plague, or the angel of death.

I had imagined you perfectly pure, my love, pure as I am, yet one time I found that the red lace panties were pushed to the bottom of your laundry hamper, and upon close examination I was able to assure myself that you had, unquestionably, been unchaste the previous evening. Only you know who with, for you did not talk of the incident in your letters home, or allude to it in your online journal.

A small girl looked up at me once, and turned to her mother, and said, 'Why is she so unhappy?' (I translate into English for you, obviously. The girl was referring to me as a statue and thus she used the feminine ending.)

'Why do you believe her to be unhappy?'

'Why else would people make themselves into statues?'

Her mother smiled. 'Perhaps she is unhappy in love,' she said.

I was not unhappy in love. I was prepared to wait until everything was right, something very different.

There is time. There is always time. It is the gift I took from being a statue – one of the gifts, I should say.

You have walked past me and looked at me and smiled, and you have walked past me and other times you barely noticed me as anything other than an object. Truly, it is remarkable how little regard you, or any human, give to something that remains completely motionless. You have woken in the night, got up, walked to the little toilet, micturated, walked back to your bed, slept once more, peacefully. You would not notice something perfectly still, would you? Something in the shadows?

If I could, I would have made the paper for this letter for you out of my body. I thought about mixing in with the ink my blood or spittle, but no. There is such a thing as overstatement, yet great loves demand grand gestures, yes? I am unused to grand gestures. I am more practised in the tiny gestures. I made a small boy scream once, simply by smiling at him when he had convinced himself that I was made of marble. It is the smallest of gestures that will never be forgotten.

I love you, I want you, I need you. I am yours just as you are mine. There. I have declared my love for you.

Soon, I hope, you will know this for yourself. And then we will never part. It will be time, in a moment, to turn around, put down the letter. I am with you, even now, in these old apartments with the Iranian carpets on the walls.

You have walked past me too many times.

No more.

I am here with you. I am here now.

When you put down this letter. When you turn and look across this old room, your eyes sweeping it with relief or with joy or even with terror . . .

Then I will move. Move, just a fraction. And, finally, you will see me.

VALERIE MARTIN

My Darling,

The train was an hour late out of Penn Station; there was a fire on a platform in Newark, or so they told us, and then there was a further delay while they switched tracks; it was almost three hours to Philly. Normally this would have made me livid but I was in such a daze of euphoria and so hopeful about the future, our future, that I scarcely minded. I got to the apartment around eight and there he was, unwashed, unshaven, sitting on the couch with the remote between his legs, flipping through the stations. The volume was deafening and I had the sense that he heard me coming from the hall and turned it up just to annoy me.

'I'm back,' I said, standing behind him.

'How did it go?' he asked. I didn't want him to see my face because I knew it was suffused with joy and it's hard on him when good things happen to me. 'It went really well,' I said. 'I got a part.'

'What?' he said.

I pitched my voice very low, barely audible. 'I got a part,' I said. He flicked off the TV and turned around to look at me, not certain himself, I thought, how he was going to react.

'What part did you get?'

'Elena.'

'I think Sonya has more lines,' he said. Not for the first time, I was grateful we don't have children.

'Guy,' I said, 'Elena is a great role and I'm perfect for her.'

'Why? Because she's beautiful and useless?'

I laughed. 'Perhaps.'

'And because she married a man she despises.'

'That's ridiculous. Elena doesn't despise Serebryakov.'

'Was Papp there?'

'He was.'

'Is he a big guy?'

'No, small.'

Then he smiled. 'So you're going to play Elena at the Public,' he said.

'I can hardly believe it.'

'Who's playing Vanya?'

'Max Brokoff.'

'That's good. Who's playing Astrov?' He stood up and put the remote on top of the set, then, because I hadn't answered, he turned a cold, suspicious eye on me and repeated the question.

'Edward Day,' I said.

'Oh, really,' he said.

'I knew you'd be upset,' I said. 'But it's not important. It just happened and there's nothing any of us can do about it.'

He paced around in front of me, looking for something. 'Uncle Vanya, Uncle Vanya,' he said. 'Ah, here they are.' It was his cigarettes. He lit one up and blew a ring in my direction, very contemptuous and cool. 'If I remember correctly, Astrov and Elena kiss twice,' he said.

'Yes,' I agreed. 'Once very briefly; Vanya interrupts them, and then near the end, as she's leaving.'

'So you'll be kissing Ed Day twice a night for what, six weeks?'

'I won't be me and Ed won't be him, we'll be Russians, for God's sake. It's a play. We kiss in front of two hundred people. If you want to see it, I'll get you a ticket. I'm married now, the past is over. We're professionals. He knows it, I know it and you know it.'

'He knows it. How does he know it?'

'I told him,' I said. 'We had coffee and I told him.'

Which is true, darling, I wasn't lying. We did have coffee and I did tell you we would have to be professional and forget the past. But my hand was shaking so badly I couldn't lift the cup without rattling it in the saucer, and you rested your hand on my arm and you said, 'It's been nearly eight years. It will be eight years next Thursday.'

'You had coffee?' Guy said.

'Yes. At Dante's.'

'And after that?'

And here of course I did lie. I said I came straight home.

He went to his desk and pushed a few pages around. 'When do rehearsals start?' he asked.

'April 15.'

'Opening?'

I couldn't answer him. I stared at him and I felt my blood thinning in my veins. I knew exactly what he meant to do, and I knew I couldn't stop him. He's going to shadow me like a body double through the whole production. My darling, we'll never be alone!

He looked up from his calendar with his chilly smile. 'About the end of May?' he said.

'That's right,' I said. I gave myself over to loathing him. Why, I asked myself, am I bound to this wretch. I had the paradoxical wish that he hadn't saved you that night, so long ago, when we were all so innocent – or at least you and I were innocent – I sometimes think Guy was born cruel. If he hadn't saved you, we would have no debt to him and we could tell him to go to the devil, but of course, there would be no we because you wouldn't be here. Because he saved your life, I can't entirely despise him, and I know now, as I've never understood before, that I am not entirely myself when I'm away from you, that your life is as dear to me as my own.

As if he was reading my mind – I sometimes think he can – he said, 'I save his life, he fucks my wife. Does that strike you as fair, Madeleine?'

'It's over,' I said. 'It was over long ago.'

'Really?' he said. 'Well, in that case I know how pleased you'll be that I can go with you. As it happens, my calendar is completely clear.'

Two kisses, my love. Two kisses in front of two hundred strangers, six nights a week and twice on Saturdays. That's what we are to have, that's what will be allowed. My Elena will be the most ensnared, frustrated, beaten-down Elena the stage has yet seen, and those stolen kisses with Astrov so charged with burning passion and cruel restraint the audience will think that Anton Chekhov sat down at his desk a hundred years ago with Madeleine Delavergne in his mind's eye, pleading for the right to live free of family, duty, and the indifferent tyranny of her tiresome husband, free to live only for love. How we will astound them as our lips meet and our hearts race, our senses yearning towards each other – just as we did this afternoon at the door to that marvelous hotel room – and Guy Margate will be there, in the front row, night after night, powerless to do anything but look on. It will be our secret triumph over him, and no one will know what it cost us and why we must pay and pay and pay the price.

But know this, my dearest love, the day you say we've paid enough, Anton Chekhov and Guy Margate be damned, this time I'll find my courage, bid good riddance to my conscience, and be forever and

Entirely yours,
Madeleine

PETER BEHRENS

with First Canadian Army in France
August 10 1944

Margo *ma chère*,

The letter is to be the wings of a dove and somehow fly between us but it's no bird, this letter. My pen is almost dry so is my mouth I can't speak. Haven't had a decent thought in days.

I'm trying to shake myself out like the sheets we stripped from the bed that morning in Maine. Shook them, left in a bundle for the charwoman to wash and wring and hang where the sun and the clean breeze would cure them.

You'll never get me clean, Margo, I'm afraid.

Let me tell you this. The sun here is the same sun as in Maine or Canada. I would not believe it, but know it's true.

There is a rifleman in Lt. Trudeau's platoon, Pvt. Blais, a farmer – no, a farmer's son. From Arthabaska.

I'll tell you about him later.

Right now there are planes humming overhead. Our planes always. The Germans possess none, apparently.

They say we own the sky.

What can I tell you, that will kill the frenzy of distance between us?

The people from Brigade say that we have beaten the Germans only they do not know they are beaten, and therefore we, the infantry, will have to walk to Germany and remind them again every mile, every farm, every village, on each street corner.

Where are you reading this? What clothes do you wear? Do your fingers really touch this paper? Does the ink speak to you? Are the leaves fat and soft on shade maples outside your papa's house in Westmount? Does sunlight filter slowly? Pale green light in early afternoon when you lie down for your nap. And when you awaken and draw the water in your bath and your underclothes fall on the tiles, what do you have to do with me then? How are we connected exactly, Margo? I feel more of a connection to certain bullets than to you. And you lie in the tub, gorgeous. You step outside in the late afternoon wearing a silk dress and the black straw on your head, your heels tap-tapping along the stone path out to the garage. Does your father's garage smell of rubber and gasoline still, and grassblades, fermenting on each blade of the mower? The air is always cool in there, isn't it. The air plays with you.

The rasp of silk upon your legs, Margo.

I'm thinking of your wrists now.

I once knew my wife, down to her bones.

Do you have a sweet tan this summer? *Comme une huronne*?

I have no appetite for adjectives.

Whatever sense I once had, whatever solidity I inherited from my Norman ancestors, has been beaten out of me, I think, in this growling ground. This summer of things bursting.

My father's people, the Taschereaus, came out of Normandy to New France, did you know?

Let me dispose of my adjectives, please. In your arms, please let me release them.

bloody,
silly,
faecal,
loud,
beaten,
red,
terror.

You see I have slipped into nouns, so let me deliver a few more. You don't have to unwrap these, Margo. Just sign for them, then you can put them away.

Child,
children,
machine-gun,
antitank,
.303,
88,
tree-burst,
counterattack,
head wound,
prisoner,
neck wound,
aorta,
femoral artery,
battle.

And men of good cheer are singing now. In this little 'rest area' the men of the *Regiment de Maisonneuve* are being fed hamburgers and *fèves au lard* and a bottle each of Black Horse beer.

P'tit Canada dans un pâturage normande.

Are your thighs still your thighs?

I'm sorry. I apologise.

O ma femme.

Is the little boy . . . no I shall not think of him. No I shall not. I don't want him to appear in this place.

Your cunt.

I'm sorry. I apologise. *Je vous en prie.*

The whitest *peau* the softest skin the tissue of yourself, Margo. Your grey eyes fix me.

In the last letter you announced that you are now living in your parents' house. You say that you have gone home, because you were lonely – you and the boy.

Your father, that *maudit Irlandais.* He has you.

Me, I want you on your back.

I want your belly sweet and warm like sugar pie.

Anti-tank.

Howitzer.

Tiger.

Bocage.

Tell your father he can cover me. Tell him that to lose your head out here, *c'est tellement facile.* The 88s do come cracking through the forest at dawn, high velocity, very flat trajectory, dismembering trees. What kills is often not the shell itself but spinning bits of riflemen, and splinters of rocks and trees. The thing comes at you like a girl you want, like a cunt, so sweet and so indirect.

Soldiers in rifle companies are killed by pieces of other soldiers in rifle companies. Arms, boots, knees. I tell my platoon leaders, it's another reason to keep the men from bunching up which is what they will always do at first, like cattle, no matter their training.

Think of your men, I say, as sources of shrapnel, dangerous. Watch out for those flying steel helmets. A splinter of leg bone can do astonishing damage.

My Sergeant Major, on the beach.

There.

I want you to cover me.

Three young German boys in a staff car on the road through the woods. As little Lieutenant Duclos reported, he fully intended to offer them a chance of surrender. Only Corporal Dextraxe offered them a lively burst instead. And the young lieutenant, the jesuitical prig, straight out of Brébeuf, was quite cool delivering his report. He'll lose no sleep over dead Boches. It was the corporal, one of our best, a rugged forester from Megantic, who was trembling and cursing.

Their company commander, this is who I am. Their confessor. I am not your husband any more, Margo. I don't belong to anyone but the tree-bursts and right now the greasy floating of air from the hamburger tent where our survivors gorge.

Replacements are due up tomorrow: for my company, seventeen fresh men.

Everyone is tired.

The riflemen assure me there are beautiful, famished girls alive in the basements of Caen who will do it with vigour for a piece of cheese. And afterwards they'll offer you a bottle of apple brandy for one lousy Sweet Caps cigarette.

I don't want to tell you the stories Margo. I must find someplace else to put them as soon as I get home.

I don't want you to think the less of me.

Your papa, the old banshee, he would have me anaesthetised with his Irish religion, not so different from mine really. The French and the Irish. He would have my balls off, wouldn't he? An exorcism. Doesn't want me returning from this filth to touch a cool, clean daughter. He wishes she had married a snowman, with a carrot for a nose and instead of a prick, an icicle.

That Pvt. Blais, the rifleman I mentioned. The imbecile got

his girl pregnant last year just before shipping for England. Her old man put her off to the Grey Nuns in Montreal where she had the child and was forced to give it up and is now a slavey, scrubbing floors for the Sisters, and very miserable. Her letter which he showed me is pathetic, do they send girls in the country to school at all? This one hardly makes herself understood. In any case. Will you go to the convent and perhaps see the Mother Superior to determine what can be done, you may drop the name of my uncle, the bishop. The girl's name is Lucie something or other, from Tingwick, fifteen or sixteen of age. Blais is a good chap and insists they will marry if he survives. Perhaps you can find her a maid's position. With the wages they're paying at Vickers these days I expect you are short of slaves in Westmount.

Oh my dear. Oh *mon dieu.* I am shook up and no one but you knows it.

Forgive what you can. I give you my blood, my heart, my kisses for our son.

Johnny

10 Sydenham Avenue,
Westmount, P.Q.

August 10 1944

Dear Jean,

Still no word from you will you please drop a line, we're all terribly worried.

Are you in France? We think you must be.

As I wrote in my last, Henry and I are back at No.10, and here very happily. I know you wanted us to keep up the flat but it was just too bleak there, Jean, you really wouldn't have wanted me to stay. We couldn't get anyone to clean the place and Dornal Avenue is not my cup of tea. Never was, never will be. After the war we'll find something much nicer. Patty and Frankie are such a help with p'tit Henri. At this very moment Frankie is giving him his bath, I can hear him splashing. He's a lucky boy to have doting aunts and grandparents while his papa is overseas. This morning at breakfast Daddy was feeding H scrambled eggs off his plate. Sweet! I only wish you could have been there.

I hope you're safe wherever you are, dearest.

Daddy says the war is practically over.

The things you put in your letters . . .

I understand how hard it is for you to be separated from the people you love.

You're a passionate man.

When this is over and we're together once more I'll be able to show you that I love you.

All you expect of me, all you want – I'll try to be all those things but I don't know if I am able. If I fail your expectations, what will you do then? In some ways my life is easier now that you are so far away. Wartime. A perfectly good excuse not to bother each other.

Our boy is good and sweet. He is in love with balls, any sort – balloons, tennis balls, golf balls, baseballs, rubber bouncing balls. He saw the globe in Daddy's study and reached out shouting ba, ba, ba.

Listen Jean I'm cold without you. Whatever it is in you that throws me out of whack, I need that now. The days are the days are the days.

Sometimes I want to scream at this letter paper, or lick it, chew it. I'd like to destroy my own weakness. I want to snap the pen in half and throw it out the window.

Will we ever travel? I want to see Rome. France. I want to see Paris with my husband, who was an officer in the war.

You were always complaining that I was not affectionate enough, that you were made to feel unsure of my love, that my feelings for you were small and inaccessible. And I remember you saying any number of times that I did not understand myself.

As if you did, Jean.

It made me angry to hear you say those things and I was afraid you could be right. But now I know I must have you in a life of trouble. And lately I feel inside a sense of luck about everything, and an openness, Johnny, that wasn't there before.

Before you went away I felt this way only once or twice, when you were inside me. I tried to tell you but you weren't prepared to listen because you were a man going off to the war. Now it's with me almost all the time, this feeling, the very opposite of foreboding. I don't know where it comes from, Johnny. Joy. All the things the nuns said about you, most of the warnings were true, but I still don't care. I know now that you are going to survive and come home. I have seen in dreams, don't laugh, you and me and Henry together. I'll be everything for you and we'll make more babies won't we. When the war is over and you've come home we'll go away for a good long time. We'll go down to Maine, or up north. I'll want you to tell me everything you have seen and felt. And then we'll leave the war behind us and walk into the rest of our lives.

I think you have to keep yourself within yourself and not give too much to your men and when you are feeling very low, get some sleep.

Everyone here sends their love and best wishes,

yours xxx Margo

URSULA K. LE GUIN

The Kalends of June, 766 BCE

To Aeneas the Trojan, King of Latium, visiting at the court of the Lord Tarchon of Caere in Etruria, greetings!

I hardly know how to write to you, my dear husband, since we are both probably illiterate. In fact even the Etruscans may not have figured out how to write yet. But I miss you very much, and I believe a love letter can be sent even if it can't be written or read, so long as the love is strong enough. People are always making insuperable obstacles out of the most trivial things. After all, the fact that you fought in the Trojan War in the thirteenth century BCE and I live in Italy in the eighth, which seems to present a considerable obstacle to our union, made no difference at all. You crossed the centuries to come to me, and it only took you seven years. And, thanks to the oracle, my father chose you for his son-in-law before he even met you. You had to get poor Turnus out of the way first, but then we got married, and fell in love – the proper order of events, I think – and since then our happiness together has only grown.

You are a serious, conscientious man, my dear, and I know that even in happiness you worry about the past, accusing yourself of deep wrongdoing. You are also tender-hearted; you worry about me, because I'm so young and you fear to hurt me. I want to tell you something that might ease your mind somewhat. It is the kind of thing that is easier to bring up in a letter than face to face – which is why we really must learn to write.

I want to tell you that I know what happened in Africa.

Please don't blame Achates for telling me about it. It was the green wine – he was a little drunk. He is such a dear! If he thought he'd been disloyal to you he'd be utterly miserable. You may blame me for listening, though, and you may blame me for wheedling more of the story out of your charming son Ascanius. He's only too happy to go on and on about Queen Dido, and how pretty she was, and how nice she was to him, and how she let him ride the finest horses in her stable and go out on hunting parties with her, and even told him he could clamber around on the scaffolding of the buildings she was having built in Carthage – which you had strictly forbidden. 'Oh, Dido was terrific,' he says. 'I wish we could have stayed there for ever!' I know he finds Latium backward and boring. And of course he misses his real mother, and I'm not enough older than him to be much of a replacement.

But anyhow, through his chatter, and good Achates' sympathetic maunderings, I gathered a good idea of what happened. And all I want to say about it is that it breaks my heart. That poor queen! Of course she loved you. She was crazy about you – any woman would be who had the chance. You're not only a gallant, romantic figure, a king in exile driven by inexorable fate across the seas, you're also a very nice man. And handsome. Really handsome. You take after your mother in looks, though not altogether, I am glad to say, in personality.

Dido must have seen you as the answer not only to her loneliness as a widow but to her need for a consort, a defender to keep the local kings from trying to annex her city by forcing her into their bed. You were godsent.

And how could you have resisted her? You'd been widowed too, you were lonely too. Your father had just died. All your people depended on you and looked to you for every decision. And you had this mandate laid on you to go to someplace called Italy and found a huge empire – and it wasn't working out at all. After seven years you'd only got as far as Sicily, and now here you were shipwrecked back in eastern Africa. You were at a low point. And Dido was offering you a haven, a kingdom, her love, everything. Of course you took what she offered. What kind of man wouldn't?

But the trouble was, you weren't godsent. You were god-driven. And she couldn't see that, she couldn't accept it. What kind of woman would? She tried to keep you, to hold you back from where you had to go. But she couldn't do it, because you weren't just a romantic hero – you were a tragic one. And so she had to discover the same thing about herself. The hard way.

Oh, when I thought about it, I felt so sorry for you both. I didn't cry when you left last week, Aeneas, you told me not to; but I cried that night after Achates went home.

I wonder, when you went to the Underworld, by the gateway in Cumae, did you meet either of your wives down there – Creusa, or Dido? Could you talk with them? I'd dearly like to know, but I dare not ask you. I only know you went there, and will not speak of what you saw.

If I should die before you – don't laugh, I'm much younger than you but nobody knows when death may come – if I do, I'll wait for you down there by the dark rivers, in the sunless woods. When you come I'll hold out my hands to you and I'll cry out in all the voice a shadow can have, here I am, come to me, my dear, my love!

But this is morbid. Forgive me. Let me tell you about the baby. Silvius thrives, suckles like a piglet, sleeps like a puppy.

When I was sweeping the Vestal hearth and setting out the sacred meal this morning, he watched me and the fire for a long time, with such an attentive, intelligent look. You see, he's pious, just like you! Seriously, the older he gets, the more certain I am that he's going to look like you and be like you. Only perhaps he won't have all the troubles you've had. What a good thought.

Come home soon so that we can make a girl baby.

Give my regards to Lord Tarchon. Be well, my dear husband. Come home soon, soon, soon!

Please excuse errors in writing.

Lavinia, Queen of Latium

NICK LAIRD

Belfast
3 February 1987

Father,

You might have been surprised at my reaction.

I was drying the dishes and listening to some farming programme on Radio Ulster; then I was sitting on the floor-tiles next to the fridge, hearing David's voice on the phone repeating that it was over, that it was all over at last. He was crying – quietly, like everything he does – and that set me off. I shouted through to Jane who was doing her sums in the living-room and she helped me get up from the floor. I told her what had happened, then went over to the writing desk and got my phone book, and rang round the cousins. I finished the dishes later that evening and went to bed. Three large gin and tonics and one of the prescription sleeping pills I've been hoarding meant I passed out almost immediately.

I missed the flurry of snow that fell in the small hours. Jane woke me with a cup of tea at eight the next morning and I went downstairs. I stood in my nightie in the living room, leaning against the sofa and looking out. The whole place had turned white. An occasional car would glide silently past, synthetically bright.

It's been several weeks now. We buried you in your church-yard, and I have talked to you more in these past two months than I had in the last twenty years.

The day after – the day of the snow – I drove over to David's with tray-bakes from the freezer and umpteen sandwiches. I'd sent Jane to the shop for two loaves and stood in the kitchen making rounds of ham and tuna and egg and cheese, unable to stop. There is a refuge in small acts of the domestic. Jane packed the sandwiches in Tupperware boxes, and kept making pots of tea. Jane knew enough to know your death was something very serious, and she became a little darling, docile, obedient, her anti-self. You know about children and death of course. We were always meek and invisible when you came in from taking a funeral. At your key-scrape and boot-stamp we'd stop talking or laughing or messing around and scurry off to our rooms to read or whisper.

I began talking to you on the drive to David's. I wanted to tell you what I was thinking. I was remembering the story of how you first came here, to the north, on the train up from Cork when you were eleven. It was in 1920 or '21. Your father had started getting letters – telling him and all the other Protestants to get out of Ballydehob. He'd sold up the farm and taken all twelve children, most of his livestock – the horses and long-horned cattle – on the train up to Armagh. It was night when you reached the county. There was some confusion – at Hamiltonsbawn, was it, or Poyntzpass – and the family had disembarked quickly, unloaded boxes and furniture frantically, dropped the ramps from the cattle-cars and led the animals down onto the platform. The train pulled away and your father realised they'd got off too soon, several stops too soon, and were not in Mountnorris but the middle of nowhere. A farmer, who happened to be passing, took the whole lot of you in. I grew up best friends with that farmer's granddaughter Mary.

You liked her. She teaches physics at a university in Seattle now, and lives there with her third husband.

To be honest, I prefer talking to you dead. I couldn't have mentioned to the living you that Mary has been married three times; you would have frowned and talked of absolutes, of sanctity, of the perverted mind of man, of the enemies of the Gospel.

Oh, the enemies of the Gospel! That glamorous list could go on for ever. Ireland, Britain, America, Muslims, Papists, Dancing, Liquor, Sodomites, Drugs, Disrespect, The Government, The Television, Portrush, Literature, Mum, David, Me.

The funeral was, as you would have expected, gigantic. The church couldn't take everyone. Your entire flock and most of the town huddled in pews or outside in great coats and scarfs and gloves. The church doors were kept open so the service could be heard in the car park; the draught blew straight up the aisle to your coffin.

And you may be gladdened to know I wore a hat in the church: I had to borrow one of mother's. Throughout, she was calm. She seemed to drift into the rooms of the manse: she had somehow straightened up, and looked taller.

Grief is a strange thing. It's sudden, localised in pockets like the snow I'd come upon weeks after, out walking the back lanes. Something always survives the thaw, lying out of reach in a hedgerow's ditch or the divot left by a wind-felled tree. The sudden whiteness was wounding.

I was pulling warm clothes from the tumble dryer yesterday, and I thought about you. Last week when they came to deliver the coal, the same thing happened. The lorry driver had pomade in his fine grey hair, and you could see the tracks of the comb still in it, just like in yours.

It's not that I've forgiven you. Don't, for heaven's sake,

think that. It's just I understand a little now how you were shaped by everything you met.

You were so full of anger. It crackled from you in static electricity. Half the time you flicked on the big light in the living-room, the bulb would pop. Once I watched you press your hand on a man's forehead in a revival tent near Garvaghy. He had come to the front to be saved and after he got off his knees the white imprint of your fingers remained on his temples.

We didn't speak for five years. I don't know what that did to you. Jane will be twelve in three months. You missed her first five years completely. I haven't told her that of course. I almost told you about her father before you died, but in the end you didn't ask, and it seemed too much like dredging up some unexploded shell from an old, a superseded war. For the last few months all you did was lie in bed smiling weakly if someone arrived or held your hand or moved your pillow.

It was the most relaxed I've ever felt with you, sitting there. I wanted to ask you about *your* life, your father, your youth, your faith. I sat there thinking that I had no idea who you were. Not that you knew David and me. You were irritated and bemused by us. You watched us much as Jane and I watch Penny now, the border collie, with some interest and concern but unsure that she's even in the same reality we are.

One day a month or so ago, after Jane had gone to school, I picked up a book she'd left on the arm of the sofa. It was an old St. John's Ambulance manual, and listed the appearances that generally accompany death: breathing and the heart's action cease; the eyelids are half closed, the pupils dilated; the tongue approaches to the under edges of the lips, and these are covered with a frothy mucus; coldness and pallor of surface increase. I couldn't square any of those things with you. There was no way to begin.

I've spent weeks reading around the old religions to try and find some means of imagining what happened to you, where you are or what you're doing. I've found something in the Upanishads about that moment, the moment we leave. You wouldn't approve. *When the person in the eye turns away, and become non-knowing of forms.*

I think again of the snow that fell. There is an idea that we go back, when we die, to being part of one thing. Death is a catch being released. I'd like to have talked with you about this. I can imagine the look on your face, a defensive, lipless smile, as if to say, *You already know what I think.*

Will you do me a favour, father? If you are there, somewhere, go out and find a bit of solitude, in a garden or an empty corridor, and read a fragment of the Upanishads aloud.

He is becoming one, he does not see, they say; he is becoming one, he does not smell, they say; he is becoming one, he does not taste, they say; he is becoming one, he does not speak, they say; he is becoming one, he does not hear, they say; he is becoming one, he does not think, they say; he is becoming one, he does not touch, they say; he is becoming one, he does not know, they say.

When I was a child and would tell you something your first reaction was a kind of wariness. Your responses were judgements. I would like to make you listen now to other ways we've dealt with being human.

How about the Tao, Father, how about that? There, the knowledge of the ancients was perfect, since they were not aware that there were things and so nothing can be added. There, the Fall you preached is different, gradual, a slow taking on of knowledge. The ancients became aware that there are things but not aware there are distinctions, then some became aware that there were distinctions but not aware that there was right and wrong. When right and wrong became manifest the Tao thereby declined. Now, isn't that something? *The Tao thereby declined.*

A lot of wishy-washy rubbish. You were far too taken with Jesus Christ to think about the other paths. You were in love only once, and not with my mother. With Him. I remember the Sunday Margaret McConnell came to church without her hat. You opened the address by saying, very quietly and sadly, that it was a direct insult to Christ for a woman to come to the House of the Lord without a hat. You quoted St Paul: *a woman should wear a veil on her head because of the angels*, and then looked straight at Mrs McConnell. She was smiling, unperturbed. I was so shocked – shocked that someone would defy Christ, in his own house, and that someone would defy *you*, and in *your* church! The devil could choose any instrument he liked, even this silver-haired widow in lilac.

She was my hero.

As it turned out, she was also in the early stages of Alzheimer's; she thought she *was* wearing a hat. She cried in the car park afterwards, when a church elder took her aside and explained.

You thought you were another John the Baptist, sent here to prepare the people for the return. You talked as if Christ might be arriving for dinner. When I was very young, a freckled nervous thing with pigtails, I thought every knock at the door might be Jesus himself.

And what else? I never told you but back in 1975 Jane's father and I drove to Birmingham, for my interview for a research fellowship. It was just after the IRA bombings and I was heavily pregnant with Jane. We couldn't find anywhere that would let us stay. *No Blacks, No Irish, No Dogs.*

Well, you know which one of those Jane's father was. And which one was me.

We slept in the car.

You were an idol to me when I was a child. When you fell, you fell completely. You betrayed yourself. There's you on the UTV news, sharing that platform, shaking hands with a loyalist terrorist, endorsing him, smiling. There is more than the fall of the Latin, *cadere,* between the cadaver and cadence.

And now what? Are you looking down on us? Has your soul been whipped up like a kite into the sun? Are you floating along above, sitting up as in a rowing boat? I think everyone should have to live an afterlife very different from whatever they believed in. That's how it should work.

The Toradja set the dead one's body in a hollowed-out tree trunk. They have a litany for taking leave of a corpse. They say, 'O father, we have put everything for you down here. Stay here. Your dead relatives are coming to keep you company, and among them is also so-and-so, who will tell you what you must do and must not do. As for us, whom you have left, we too have someone whose orders we obey. This is the end of our relationship. This far you have a claim on us as your children but we are making the steps of your house black. Do not come back to us.'

Jane is upstairs on the computer, and Penny is asleep at my feet, stirring inside her separate dream. I hope your hollowed-out boat is passing above, on this bright cold afternoon, and you are trailing a hand in the water. Do not come back to us. Do not come back.

Ruth

SAM LIPSYTE

Dear Miss Primatologist Lady in the Bushes Sometimes,

Shhhh. Do not be afraid, my sweet. Please just read this. Try to glimpse my heart through the awful ape-ish scrawl.

Thing is, I shouldn't be telling you this, literally shouldn't, as I haven't acquired the capacity for language, let alone writing, none of us have, but to hell with language. I must speak. I may never return to this little patch of forest again. I may never find occasion to lope over to your moss-soft blind beside the river, to feign wariness and a creeping hard-won trust, to let you cradle me and pick burrs from my scalp and call me by the name you have apparently bestowed on me, 'Ari'.

If such is the case, if I do not return, I want you to know how much I, your faithful Ari, will miss our afternoons by the river. Who cares that my name is actually Mike?

Oddly enough, I once worried you would be the one to go, that after you'd come to understand our ways, or thought you had, you'd pack up your cameras, your notebooks and laptops and camp chairs, leave for ever, maybe to study those ridiculous bonobos. (We are well aware of the bonobo craze among you humans, though none of us can guess what knowledge you hope to glean from those fucked-out party monkeys.)

But, as fate would have it, I am the one who must go, who's

getting, as they say, or, I guess, you say, shipped out. Worse, I know that the reason I am leaving will horrify you, so that even if I do return (and, as they say, or, I guess, we say, nothing's certain under the canopy), you might not be able to look at me the same way again.

You see, Miss Primatologist Lady in the Bushes Sometimes, word has come down from the Big Branch. We're off to kill a chimp named Mingo. We don't need language to liquidate. We've got opposable thumbs, a complex system of screeches. We're incredibly strong. So's Mingo. He's one tough bastard, or so our intel would have us believe, and our intel is pretty decent as far as simian networks are concerned, or so I've been told. I'm not sure how we'll handle Mingo once we cross into his territory and find him. Maybe we'll do a bait-and-pummel. Maybe we'll just beat him with a log. We'll definitely bite his balls off. Our raid leader, Gilbert, will make sure of that. You know Gilbert. He's the one you call Pushkin. He loves to bite off balls.

Please don't ask why we are going to kill Mingo. Probably even Gilbert doesn't know. I'm sure there is a good reason. The Big Branch wouldn't send us off without a good reason. Why do chimps kill chimps? Somehow Mingo must be threatening our way of life, not to mention our balls, and the balls of our children. But ours is not to wonder why. Ours is to bite Mingo's balls off first, and maybe also beat him repeatedly with a log.

Such is the nature of a raid, I guess. The Big Branch makes the call and we get ready. We eat bushbaby meat, rape some females in our troop. The bushbaby meat and the raping saps us a little, but so what? We might not be back for a while. Is this shocking you? I don't want to shock you. I just want to be honest about who I am and what I've done in the service of my troop, and not just my troop, but other troops as well, done, in fact, for every chimp who yearns for true forest freedom but suffers under the yoke of Mingo and his Mingo-ish ideology.

God, listen to me. I sound like one of those fat chimps in the Big Branch, the ones who drove my father to the other side of the river all those years ago. Doubtless as a scientist you've also witnessed your share of nature being cruel and indifferent and just plain not giving a shit about anything but itself, because that's the nature of nature, or so Gilbert says, but I also know, from conversations I've overheard near your campsite, that unlike some of your colleagues, including your husband, you cannot accept the premiss that chimps are as sick and calculating as men.

This is partly what makes me love you so much, along with your smooth, lightly freckled arms and your soft auburn hair, not to mention the dainty way you pluck burrs and bugs and things from my scalp fur, and it's why telling you the truth about why I won't be coming by the river for a while is so painful, so, I don't know, is *fraught* the word? I'm still pretty shaky with this language stuff, but I think *fraught* might be the word. You see, my dear sweet beautiful primatologist lady, I want you to love me as I love you, but I fear you could never love me as I truly am, that Mike will never find a place in your heart as 'Ari' has. And so my great ape heart is breaking.

So be it then. I will learn to 'accept' this fact, just as I heard you say to your husband the other night while I crouched beside your tent that you would learn to 'accept' his dalliances with Cindy the Grad Student. (Though if you'd seen them behind the generator the other night, doing things that even your average kink-drunk pornobo would find distasteful, you might not be so accepting.) But please know that I would swing through every tree in every forest to find the perfect banana leaf for you to wear in your beautiful hair, or use as a platter for a delectable selection of termites I would also be thrilled to provide, or, if you preferred, you could use the leaf to scrape the fragrant lady poop from your sumptuous rump. It's all the same to me, though you should know I've never been a real tree-chimp. I'm better on the ground, biting, pummeling. Pummeling's my specialty. I love to pummel. Clubbing with logs, or stones, that's okay. But pummeling, or any situation calling for pummeling, that's where this chimp comes alive. Anyway, that's not my point. My point is I love you and would do anything for you, including pummel your prick of a spouse into forest mulch, though I know you are too gentle a soul to wish that on him. I love you, Miss Primatologist Lady in the Bushes Sometimes, and I'm scared. I'm scared I will never see you again. I'm scared that Mingo will prove too tough. We lost my best friend Lychee to poachers on the last raid, and always we live in fear of the bullet, or fist, or tooth, with our name on it (even though we technically would not be able to read our name on it, of course).

I'm scared I'm losing faith, too. I never used to question my orders from Gilbert and the Big Branch, but I'm beginning to see the bigger picture. Hell, maybe I don't have to pummel. Maybe those little orgy fiends the bonobos have the right idea. Maybe it's better to fuck your fights out.What I know for sure is that it's frightening to suddenly have thoughts that are my thoughts and not Gilbert's or the Big Branch's. All those afternoons we groomed and played you must have been growing a new chimp deep inside of me.

Remember that time you cradled me and picked burrs from my scalp and stroked my head and told me all about the human world, the one you fled because everything was too fake and murderous and shiny, the one where you couldn't find any kinds of creatures you could stand, and said, 'My little Ari,' you said, 'what kind of creature are you?' If I could have answered you then, if I'd known I could, I would have told you I was the kind of creature who was never happier than during that moment with you, even as I felt this vague ripple of sadness under my fur, the sense that everything was already too late, that nature always got the head start, that nurture never had a shot. Or remember that time you picked more burrs and maybe some twigs out of my scalp, and said, 'Oh, my Ari, deep in your heart you are a kind, loving chimp, aren't you?' Well, I didn't quite have the language yet, but if I had, I would have said, 'Yes! Or, no, not yet! But I want to be! I really do!'

Still, maybe wanting is not enough. Maybe I'll never be more than what the Big Branch made me: a machine for turning living, breathing brothers into heaps of hair and bone. I don't want your pity, save your pity for the hair heaps, but I guess I am mostly afraid that since now you know the truth, 'Mike' has forever destroyed your feelings for 'Ari'. Even as I nibble on some post-rape bushbaby meat, I feel a teardrop nestling in my cheek fuzz. It is a tear for you, my darling, but maybe more a tear for me. I cannot deny my chimphood. You could never love a chimp that would. But still I pray we meet again, that the braver, better ape inside me gets another chance to grow.

Yours truly,
Mike 'Ari'

[The following letter, folded into a small square, was found affixed to the first with an unidentified animal hide glue, possibly primate.]

Dear Bush Bitch,

Goddamn you, data-collecting whore of Babylon. How dare you come here and head-hump one of my best pummellers! That's right, this ain't your lover ape, this is Gilbert. Or should

I say Pushkin? (Pushkin! I did a tour at the Language Research Center in Georgia, America so don't try to hoity-toit me. Have you even read *Eugene Onegin*?)

Good thing I found this note before you did, because I really think it's time I made my two-cent deposit. By the time you read this Mike and I and the rest of the ol' death squad will have already set out to do what we were put in this freaking forest to do, namely de-Mingoise our buffer zones. I respect my chimps so I'll let the kid's words stand, but I do believe a little addendum is in order. You see, we may all seem alike to you, but the fact remains that Mingo represents a grave threat to our freedom (and don't give me any of that seditious conspiracy jive about the Big Branch's plans for mussanga fruit access.) Furthermore, I hate to shatter your theories, but sometimes we kill just for the thrill of it, or to maintain our murder chops. As we like to put it: One chimp rusted, the whole troop dusted.

Well, do with *that* intel what you will. I trust you'll bury it. If chimps are as bad as people, then maybe people aren't bad or good. That'll throw your precious moral system out of whack. But what I really want to talk about is Mike. Look, he's just a dumbass youngster. It's me you want. A chimp with experience, a rough-knuckled hard-swinging ape's ape that knows how to stick his dick in the anthill of life. Listen, honey, I know I scare you. But I know I excite you, too. You can't hide that. And you can't hide from me. I'll be home soon, but I have a weird feeling in my gut that your love monkey Ari might not make it back. I worry that 'fraught' will indeed be the word for his furry ass. The fog of war, etc. Don't get me wrong, we'll all be sad. And after I take care of your two-timing husband, you and I will be sad together, beside the river. We'll get our sad on like you can't believe.

'Til then,

Push

PANOS KARNEZIS

When I first saw you, I have to admit, I mistook you for a stranger, perhaps because I had been living on my own for such a long time, a voluntary isolation that was beginning to affect my speech as well as my vision. But then I had a better look at your reflection on the water, rippled by the swan gliding across the pond, and I saw clearly the short hair, the long nose, the familiar coat: we knew each other from somewhere. After a futile year, I had begun to take daily afternoon walks in the park to lessen the torment of loneliness, which was devised to punish the weak of this world, along a route that took me past the pond, where I fed the ducks, past the Hill, past the Edwardian Pergola, stopping to sit briefly on one of the benches dedicated to the dead.

It was a brief encounter. Then I did not see you again for several months, and I was beginning to convince myself that, after all, you were one of the accidental ghosts that roam the park at any time of the day, mystifying the dogs by their ethereal presence, surprising the sleeping anglers and angering the gardeners by trampling all over the flowerbeds, until we bumped into each other again the following spring. Christmas had passed without escape from the despair, watching cartoons and merciless repeats of comedy on television that could not even make amnesiacs laugh. January had not been better either. Work had been slow, and the joy of writing had given way to a routine that was beginning to resemble the life of a pearl diver. Nothing happened in February either, a month invented only to delay the coming of spring, but then in March I had the providential idea to come into town for a matinee. After the play, being too early to return home, I mixed with the twilight crowd, walking with their umbrellas in the rain, going in and out of shops, restaurants, amusement arcades. Then, suddenly, there you were again, splendid and palpable in a shop window, among the sinister mannequins, the clouds of exhaust fumes and the stalls of the street vendors.

At the time I lived on the first floor of a red-brick house in north London, in a small flat where the bath was in the kitchen, so that I did the laundry, bathed and washed the dishes in the same water in order to save on expenses. Late every afternoon, the landlady came to inspect the property, going from floor to floor in her army general's walk, sniffing the air because smoking was strictly forbidden, before paying a visit to her daughter and son-in-law, who stayed in the garden flat. A well-built Frenchwoman, my landlady had been stranded in England after marrying an English wine merchant who died of cirrhosis five years later, leaving her with a daughter and the freehold of the big house. She converted it into flats and since then had rented them out to young professionals. Once a month, when she came to collect the rent, she warned me, in her precise French accent that tolerated no dissent, that I am a guest, even though I always paid on time and put the rubbish out every Sunday night, as she had instructed me, the black bin bag tied with a silk ribbon and a thank-you note addressed to the dustmen, who would otherwise not collect it.

This was the world before I met you, and if I had not gone insane I owed it to my tenacity. I had come to London with the intention of becoming a writer, without a contract, without a plan, without even a plot for a book, on the strength of a good word about my stories from someone who soon proved to be more courteous than sincere. I had saved enough money to last me six months and given up a good job, an easy decision because that job meant nothing to me. Convinced I was destined for greater things, I had shaken hands with my boss, a thin man with tired eyes, a captain's beard and a northern accent, who had sent me away with his blessing: 'You're fucking crazy.' I moved into the flat in north London and shut myself off from the world, hoping that inspiration would save me from the foretold fate of aspiring writers. A year later my optimism had all but run out, and I had been left with a growing fear that I was wasting my time. I was making ends meet by working a few hours a week in an old bookshop where people seeking shelter from the rain and innocent tourists were cowed into buying first editions of the classics and rare prints made in China a few weeks earlier.

The second time I came across you, that evening in town, I tried speaking to you, but as soon as I turned round you vanished. I stood in the middle of the torrent of Saturday shoppers, listening to the honking of cars and the blood-curdling shouts of cabbies telling me, *inter alia*, to get out of the way, and for the first time I experienced an oppressive loneliness that I had not felt since my coming to London. After that I looked for you from the moment I stepped out of the door until I returned home late in the evening, in the park, in the street, at the shops, and kept a diary of unconfirmed sightings, which was soon filled with details of the date, the time and place I thought I saw you. I ate little, just enough to sustain my hope but not my body, and soon I was losing weight. I slept badly, waiting all night for morning to come, when I could leave the house and roam the streets in the rain, without an umbrella, walking for miles, further and further from home each day, and coming back in the evening, tired, disappointed and wet through. I was stopped by the police, dogs barked at me and I earned the reputation of a man one should stay clear of: the Stranger.

Weeks went by and the weather improved. The branches of the trees on either side of the streets spread out, and the leaves formed dense canopies lit up from above by the early-evening light. Peace reigned over the neighbourhood that was disrupted only by the purring of lawnmowers. At weekends happy crowds poured into the park, lost their way through the meadows, where the grass had grown several feet tall, and were never seen again, the place echoing with their heart-rending cries. I had stopped changing my clothes, bathing or shaving. If I could have afforded to, I would have taken a holiday in order to soothe my grief and take a break from the eternal search, but instead I stayed home, where I suffered the ordeal of a heat wave the like of which had not been seen before. In August, when my landlady knocked on my door to collect the rent, she wrinkled up her nose and gave me a look of disapproval. I decided that I had to spruce myself up. That evening I sat in the scalding water of the big bath in the kitchen, perfumed with oils of lavender, peppermint and jasmine, and fell asleep while thinking of you. When I woke up, the water had turned cold and my teeth were chattering. I dried myself off and went to shave. I have a cut-throat razor, bought on a sentimental impulse, a beautiful antique with a whalebone handle and a Sheffield-steel blade I sharpen once a week. I lathered my face and began to shave. Then, as soon as I finished, washed the razor under the tap and raised my head, lo and behold, I saw you in the mirror, looking back at me.

I do not know how you found me, an unimportant man in a city that has no time for insignificance, but however you did it, it was the happiest surprise of my life. I looked in the mirror with admiration and as much satisfaction as if I had drawn you there myself. Then I put on cologne and ironed clothes, polished my shoes, combed my hair and carried my old clothes to the bottom of the garden, where I burned them in a ceremony that felt like an immolation, the only witness my landlady's son-in-law, watching me with his sad slave's eyes from inside his flat.

I knew what else I had to do. The following morning I went to the bank, where I withdrew the last of my savings and spent them all on mirrors, big and small, square, round and rectangular. After I had them framed in gold, like portraits by the Old Masters, I hung them round my flat: in the kitchen, the bedroom, the living-room, the toilet, from the ceiling, everywhere, so that I could see you in any direction I turned to.

Autumn brought relief from the heat. The traffic wardens, doomed to walk eternally the streets of the borough, ploughed through the dry leaves and were still giving tickets. I rarely went to the park any more, preferring to stay at home with you instead. In the morning I had coffee, listening to the news on the radio for a while, and then I sat at my desk. Suddenly work was going well. I was writing non-stop, without having to wait for inspiration, without self-doubt, without effort, the pen flowing like a boat caught in a tail wind. At one o'clock, I stopped for a light snack and a brief afternoon nap, a Mediterranean habit that no amount of coffee could exorcise. I left the windows open, so that I could fall asleep listening to the wind carrying the melodies of songbirds and the learned discourses of parrots which had escaped their cages and lived in the park. One day, in the middle of my nap, a gust of wind blew through the flat, and a heavy mirror fell to the floor and broke into pieces. I woke with a start. The noise alarmed my landlady too, doing the rounds of the house at the time, and a moment later she banged on my door. 'Open up!' she demanded. 'In the name of the Housing Act.'

I had no choice but to comply. I tiptoed to the door, dressed in my best gown, and opened the door, forcing a big smile. My landlady frowned and tried to see behind me. When she finally saw the mirrors that covered the walls from floor to ceiling, she let out a scream: '*Mon Dieu!*' Then she recovered herself and added: 'I want you out by Friday. This is a reputable house.'

I tried to convince her that she was wrong, that there was nothing sinister or immoral about the mirrors, but I did not dare to tell her about you in case she thought I was subletting the flat, a terrible crime punishable by death. The mirrors, I said, were a simple way to brighten up the place in a country where light was brought over from Africa to be sold by the bucket load. She did not believe me. 'Out! Out!' she kept repeating in her precise voice, incensed and resolute, even after I shut the door in her face. When it was quiet again, I heaved a sigh of relief. I took the dustpan and brushed the broken glass, I made coffee, I sat at my desk, and it was some time before I looked in a mirror and saw that you were not there. I tried another mirror, then another until I had looked in all of them. To my horror, all I could see was my reflection multiplied countless times: you were gone.

There was no point searching for you. I knew by then that you would only be found if you wanted to be found, and what I had to do was simply to wait. The following Friday I moved out of the red-brick house, watched over by my landlady, who withheld my deposit without an explanation, and found a basement bedsit. Then I sold my mirrors to a travelling funfair to build a house of mirrors, which some time later the police shut down because it was too terrifying for children. I kept only one mirror, out of hope as well as necessity, which I hung above the bathroom sink in order to shave. Every time I lather my face, I look deep in it, hoping one day you will again come up from the bottom of the glass.

I hope it will be soon. Do not try the patience of a man in love holding a razor to his throat.

JAN MORRIS

O fy nghariad, fy nghariad, carissima mia!

I am on my way home to you, my love, and my pulse is beating faster already, my head is awhirl with sweet memories, my mind alive with fancies! This is the condition the great poets were in, when they penned their immortal sonnets. The beauty in their imaginations was no more exquisite than the beauty in mine, as I speed through the twilight past Dolgellau. My passion is no less, my thirst as demanding, my longing – so soon to be fulfilled! – just as urgent.

Well, almost as urgent. It is true, my dear, that neither of us is as robust as once we were, but to my mind that has only enhanced the grace of you. I love you the more for your laughter-lines, as it were. When I first knew you long ago there was something melancholy about your beauty – as though nobody had possessed you for years, and you had been waiting, waiting for me to come! Am I right, dear heart? When I arrived that evening at your front door, did you feel, as I did, a magical sense of fulfilment, even of reconciliation?

Just over the bridge at Llanelltyd now, with a rising moon shining in the water, downstream from Abaty Cymer – the same moon, as lovers always tell themselves, that is shining now on your own roof, not so far away. For me the rush of the river below is the music of our own sweet Dwyfor, and I can almost smell the scent of the woodsmoke drifting from your kitchen – just as evocative to me as Proust's madeleine. And you yourself, I can almost see you there in the half-light, clad in Beauty, 'like the night . . .'

The sounds of the river, the scent of the woodsmoke, the pale suggestion of you there in the dusk, in the shadow of the sycamore – all these triggers of the memory are there for me always, whenever I want to summon them, but they are more immediate than ever, and more sensual, driving now through the empty moorland in the gathering dark. Of course they are essences of you, but they are also essences of Wales itself.

You don't think, do you, that one can love a whole country in the way I love you? You are right really. Wales is too wide for my embrace! But still in my mind the pair of you are one. I see you in the hills of Wales. I hear you in the sweet language. When the sun shines I see the laughter of your eyes in the ripples of Bae Abertawe, and when it rains or drizzles, when all Wales seems to be in tears, my love, my love, I know you are crying too.

But not tonight! The moon shines bright tonight, and I know that you are happy, as I leave Trawsfynydd behind me and can see the mass of the Moelwyns looming ahead. Past the turn to Gellilydan now, and soon I'll be in Penrhyndeudraeth. I love the old familiar names – for me they are part of you too! Does it show I'm getting old, *cariad*, that I like the familiar best?

For yes, I suppose – don't laugh, don't be sad! – but yes, I must count you among the old familiars. In a way you always were. When I first found you – when we found each other – you seemed to me curiously like an old acquaintance. You were younger then of course (but no more beautiful), but somehow you were not new to me. I was instantly at home with you. Were you at home with me? Did we perhaps know each other in a previous life? Or is it just that, after our half-century together, the emotions of the present have become blurred with the emotions of the past?

Or perhaps, once again, it is just the Wales in you. Wales grows older too, and not always gracefully either, but there is to its very presence something always young. Call it romantic, call it foolish, but the Wales I have cherished for so long remains changeless in my mind, always young like you, impervious to the creeping assault of caravans and executive homes all around us. *Aros mae y mynyddau mawr*, the poet sang long ago, and he didn't simply mean that the mountains were eternal, but that the idea of them, the idea of Wales – the idea of you too, my darling! – would never alter.

But now I'm almost there, and this love letter in the mind must soon end. I'm just crossing the Cob causeway into Porthmadog, and the traffic is thickening. Here are the desolate High Street shops, here the rival supermarkets, youths loitering, a smell of fish and chips, some lout leaning on his horn behind me – English, you can bet your life.

Yes, my dear one, I know, a letter of love should not dwell upon the squalid, or even the ordinary, let alone the prejudiced. Love one, love all, one ought to feel, I suppose – love a cottage, love an executive home! But in a moment or two I am out of the streetlights anyway, the town is behind me, the moon rides gloriously high above and I am scudding along the coast road towards Llanystumdwy. Ah, I feel the ecstasy rising! That light beyond the woods up there? Can it be your light? Is the breeze from the sea stirring your heart at this moment as it stirs mine? Is your kitchen door open for me, with a flicker of your firelight brightening the yard?

Oh my love, my light, my glory! I am coming! You are waiting! Up the bumpy lane (my heart bumping too), round the last corner – there's the cat Ibsen, his eyes like little embers, there's the gate open for me, and there you stand before me, with all the welcome of Wales in your stance – dear heart, *fy nghariad*, *carissima mia*, my one and only house.

HARI KUNZRU

Dear Aisha

I suppose this letter will come as a shock. It's so long since we met. You're probably surprised I even know how to contact you: we never swapped addresses and the way we left things I can't believe you'd expect – or want – to hear from me again. Blame the Internet. In the digital age, none of us can hide forever.

I need to tell you how it was for me, why I behaved like I did. And why, when you rang me in London, I hung up. By doing that I probably confirmed all your worst suspicions – of the foreigner who only wanted one thing, who used you for a night and then threw you away. When I heard your voice, the atmosphere of my time in Jordan came rushing back and I was seized by what I can only call a blind panic. Not an adult reaction. Not a compassionate one. I told myself you'd ring back, but you never did. I've always been ashamed I didn't speak to you, and this letter is an attempt to rid myself of that feeling. Maybe it will make things better for you too, hearing my side of the story. I don't know.

When I first saw you, swimming in that hotel pool, I thought I'd never seen a more beautiful girl. You and your friend Maryam were sitting on the side, dangling your feet into the water. I tried not to stare, but I found myself taking in every detail of your face – the long black hair plastered against your cheek so that one strand curled into your mouth, your brown eyes, the long straight nose, marred by a little pink patch of sunburn. And I noticed your body too. How could I not? Droplets of water clung to your brown skin, running between your breasts, whose nipples were clearly visible through the fabric of your yellow bikini. I swear when you saw me swimming towards you, you opened your legs a little, showing me the dark ruck of fabric between your thighs, a gesture I found so shockingly sensual I had to turn away, treading water and feigning interest in some point in the middle distance while I tried to compose myself. I wanted you so much, Aisha, I didn't think about the consequences.

And of course, in that moment – and everything that came afterwards – we gave ammunition to all the bearded moralists, all the angry ascetics and woman-haters who would have wanted to beat and burn us for displaying our bodies to one another so shamelessly. Only in that place, that five star hotel, was such an encounter possible in your country. Outside on the street, most of the women were veiled, escorted by male relatives as they shopped or took their children to school. Behind the high white walls, where the staff were paid to keep their opinions to themselves, the mores of international tourism prevailed. Money breeds pragmatism, but only among those who get to spend it: that was one of the lessons I learned from meeting you, under the disapproving eyes of all those barmen and pool boys and waiters. In the years that have passed since then, pragmatism has fallen out of fashion. I wonder how you've fared, as the religious battle lines have hardened, you who were already feeling torn apart by the pressures of your life.

The trip was supposed to be a perk, a reward for late nights and weekends in the office. In the three years since leaving university, I'd been working for an events management company, organising corporate junkets and meetings. The job bored me senseless, but there was nothing else going on in my life, no girlfriend, no big dreams or ambitions. I worked like a dog because it distracted me, stopped me feeling so hollow and scared. In retrospect, I think my boss was worried. You should have more fun, he said. We were planning a conference in Amman for a software company and he announced that, although I was very junior, I could research what was quaintly termed the 'wives programme', day trips and excursions to run in parallel with the formal events. The Jordanian tourist board had supplied a guide and a driver, two middle-aged men with paunches and heavy moustaches, with whom I'd just spent a week tearing round 'highlights' in a large air-conditioned Mercedes. Mr Mansour and Mr Hussein were unfailingly polite, but after sharing breakfast, lunch and dinner with them every day since my arrival, conversational topics (soccer, makes of car) had dried up and the parade of resorts, rug factories, luxury spas and ancient ruins had begun to pall. People stared when we walked into restaurants, trying to work out why I was accompanied by what looked like two bodyguards. I felt stifled. I wanted to go out on my own, to lie on a sun lounger without them smoking cigarettes and talking into their mobile phones beside me. You and Maryam looked like heaven, giggling and whispering to one another, shooting flirtatious glances in my direction.

I swam over and said hello.

When I told Mr Mansour that I had other plans for dinner, I was surprised by his reaction. Who are these girls, he asked abruptly. Are they Jordanian? Yes, I said, you were students from Amman, in Aqaba visiting relatives. He wrinkled his moustache and frowned. And these girls are making dates with you? Tell me, what are their surnames? Suddenly I felt I was being interrogated. I looked at him, his narrowed eyes, his pursed imperious lips, and decided he could fuck off. It was none of his business who I chose to spend my time with. I shrugged and said I'd see him in the morning. Six-thirty, he said, petulantly. We had a long drive ahead of us. I suspected the early start was a punishment.

Mansour and Hussein were watching, sitting on a sofa in the far corner of the lobby when you and Maryam arrived to pick me up. You were wearing a cotton print dress which exposed your shoulders. Your eyes and mouth were heavily made up and you smelt, even at a distance, of some strong, musky perfume. You had an air of expectancy, a nervous tension which mirrored and heightened my own. Maryam, also dressed up, looked worried. Maybe she knew what was coming, how obstinate you were, how desperate and confused.

We decided to go for a drink, an activity which in my ignorance I assumed was acceptable for young people in that tourist town. We sat upstairs on a restaurant terrace and I ordered a beer. You asked for one too. The waiter, a sullen young tough with an adolescent moustache, shook his head and tutted. You and Maryam spoke sharply to him in Arabic. Reluctantly he brought bottles and glasses. See how we are living, you said. Even this guy thinks he can tell us what to do, how we should behave.

I noticed other patrons staring coldly at us. I didn't feel we were doing anything wrong, but I began to feel nervous, as if I were walking through customs or talking to a policeman. We chatted a little, finding out about each other. You told me you were twenty-one, studying literature. You wrote poetry. Your parents wanted you to get married to a banker, the son of family friends. Reading between the lines I realised you were a rich girl. Rich and bored. Then it all tumbled out, how you were sick of living in Amman, sick of being told who you could speak to and what to wear, sick of being called a prostitute just because you were having a conversation with a man. Is that what the waiter said? I asked. You shook your head angrily. He didn't like it that Arab girls were with a foreigner. He didn't like it that we were drinking alcohol. What did his honour have to do with anything? What business was it of his?

I noticed Maryam was trying to soothe you. Don't take it so personally, she said. Forget about that guy and enjoy your evening. You snapped that it was all right for her. She was living abroad. She had a boyfriend in Germany. She could go out late. She could wear a miniskirt and get drunk and walk down the street if she chose. In Germany no one would say a word. Maryam shrugged. Soon, she said. Soon you'll be able to leave.

We sipped beer and you asked about my life. I said there wasn't much to tell. You pressed your leg against mine, looking fiercely at me, as if you wanted to gobble me up, squeeze me dry. I couldn't tell whether you were hungry for me or the freedom I represented, my stories of living in a flat on my own, travelling in foreign countries. There was something wild, even a little insane in your look, but you took my hand and twisted my fingers in yours and it was all I could do to stop myself leaning forward and kissing you there and then. Maryam looked balefully at us across the table. We have a curfew, she told me. Aisha's aunt wants us back by ten. Well, I said, then we should eat. No, you insisted, waving your empty bottle at the waiter. Why eat? Let's drink more. Then you grinned wolfishly and started talking about sex. Did I think all Arab girls were innocent? I said I didn't know. Did I realise I was sexy? By the way, you said, I wasn't to think I was dealing with some fool who didn't know about the world. You'd had a boyfriend, the previous year in Amman. He was good to begin with, but then he started acting like an asshole. Casually, you let your hand stray under the table, on to my lap. Maryam stared into space and smoked. When I offered to pour her more beer she shook her head.

The sun set. We drank. Maryam finished a packet of Marlboros and sent the waiter for another. Finally, she pointed out that ten o'clock had come and gone. Well, I said, I was going to be in Amman in a couple of days, just before I flew out. We could meet again. I was a little drunk and was trying to be sensible, which was difficult, because your hand had found its way into my trouser fly. I had the sensation of being on the edge of a precipice. I kept meeting the scrutinising eyes of men at other tables. I felt that everyone was aware of what was happening, the erection you were massaging between your thumb and forefinger. I knew Maryam was only pretending she couldn't see.

To tell the truth, I was out of my depth. I wasn't sure where the boundaries lay. I'd never been in an Arab country before, but even in London what we were doing would have been risky. Besides, I was beginning to think that you seemed very young, perhaps even younger than twenty-one. Something about your forwardness, which might have come across as a sign of experience, felt gauche, the clumsiness of a teenager clutching at pleasure, heedless of what other people were thinking. But you were turning me on, Aisha, making me stupid. I had my hand on your thigh, one finger pressed into your sex, moist and slippery through what felt like a pair of silk panties.

Finally Maryam insisted you had to go. When we got outside, you pulled me into a fetid alley where you kissed me, your tongue darting in and out of my mouth like a little dagger. As I crammed my fingers between your legs, you clawed at my back, digging in your nails as if you were trying to draw blood, all the time making little anguished movements with your pelvis. You seemed so angry, overflowing with rage and frustration. Finally Maryam dragged you into a taxi. I told you the name of my hotel in Amman and said I'd see you there. As I stood on the corner, watching you go, I felt excited, relieved and scared all at once. I wondered if I'd just had a narrow escape.

Half an hour later, as I sat on the edge of my bed at the hotel, flicking through satellite channels looking for an English movie, the phone went. It's me, you said. We're in the lobby. They won't let us come up to your room. The man says it's not decent. I asked why you'd come back. We've run away, you said.

Then I was really scared, Aisha. I was a long way from home and things seemed to be getting out of control. I went down to the lobby and under the suspicious gaze of the concierge, tried to find out what was going on. Maryam was with you, looking glum and apologetic. I was having too much fun, you said, gripping my hands. I don't want tonight to end. Let's go somewhere we can be together, now.

I was at a loss. It was too much for me, what was happening, too intense, too strange. With nowhere else to go, we took a walk along the hotel beach and sat down on a plastic sun lounger. You kissed me and cried about your horrible parents, about your brother who was only interested in his computers and his Koran, about all the men who wanted to put you in a prison cell because they were old and jealous and stupid. Maryam sat a couple of loungers away, the orange tip of her cigarette flaring in the darkness. Every couple of minutes, one of the porters would walk past, peering at us. I realised the concierge was sending them, checking in case we were committing acts of immorality. It made me angry. Who were these people? What was it to them if we wanted to be together? Let's go dancing, you said, clapping your hands together. All right, I thought, let's go bloody dancing.

After midnight there was only one place in Aqaba to dance, and that was the hotel nightclub. We walked down a flight of stairs into a dark thickly carpeted basement, lit only by a glitterball, which turned forlornly over a little circular dance floor. This empty space was surrounded by tables, at which sat groups of men, smoking water pipes and watching a middle-aged singer perform on a tiny stage. She was plump and garishly made up, dressed in a skimpy belly-dancer's outfit. Her love songs (Habibi! Habibi!) were backed by the plink-plonk rhythm of an electric keyboard, played by a sallow man in a red sequined waistcoat. We were shown to a table, but at once you stepped out into the light and abandoned yourself as if you were in the middle of a rave, twirling your arms in the air, thrashing your hair from side to side. Instantly all eyes were on you. And on Maryam too. I knew what those men were thinking. One was even beckoning to me, wanting to open negotiations. Apart from you and the singer, the only other women in the place were two prostitutes, Thais or Filipinas, who sat with their European clients, big brick-red men in floral-patterned shirts. I got up to join you. Maryam did the same. We had no alternative, really. The three of us danced together, swinging our arms and shaking our hips. Sometimes you stepped forward and draped yourself around me, hanging from my neck so that I staggered and had to hold you tight to stop you falling. All the time we were watched by dozens of intent, hostile, appraising eyes. Go on, I thought. Watch, you bastards. Watch and weep. I'm with two girls, who've come here out of friendship, not because I've paid them. I don't hate them for being beautiful, or for showing off their beauty. Not like you. In my world, this happens. My world isn't like this place, so seedy and repressed and full of shame.

After a while we sat down and Maryam started talking to you

in low rapid tones, beseeching you to go home. I didn't care what happened any more, but I knew there was nowhere we could be alone: that hole of a nightclub was a dead end. Amman, I said, squeezing your hand. We'll see each other in Amman. There were tears in your eyes. I want you, you said. I swear I'll die if I don't have you. Yet finally you agreed to leave. Though it was very late, you could still patch things up with your aunt. She wouldn't tell your parents. We'd see each other in two days' time.

The next morning, bleary-eyed, I met Mansour and Hussein in the lobby. They were sullen and uncommunicative, which suited me fine. They didn't ask how I'd spent my evening and I didn't volunteer any information. We drove for hours through the desert, then walked round a dusty crusader castle, a bleak place, the site of a siege and a massacre. Mr Mansour pointed out architectural features. I nodded and grunted, unable even to simulate interest: my head was too full of you, Aisha. I was disturbed, jumbled up. I didn't think I'd done anything wrong, but at the same time nothing felt quite right. Eventually Mansour asked if I was ill. We drove back to Amman, arriving after dark. I checked into my hotel, a mausoleum of marble and cut glass, ate a room-service dinner and fell into a fitful sleep, unable to get comfortable, irritated by the rattle of the fridge and the asthmatic hum of the air conditioning.

The next afternoon you and Maryam picked me up in an enormous boat-like Mercedes. You were the worst driver I'd ever seen, changing lanes without warning, tail-gating other cars, oblivious to what was going on around you. Once you almost killed us, swerving on to an exit ramp at the very last moment, narrowly missing a crash barrier. I've always been a bad passenger, and by the time we reached our destination, a hilltop viewpoint where we could watch the sunset, my nerves were in shreds. Once again, Maryam sat apart and smoked, while we groped one another in the back seat. I felt self-conscious, and asked you whether you didn't think it was awkward for your friend. She understands, you said. She doesn't mind. Then we drove back into the city to go to a bar. When you said I had to hide under a blanket, I laughed. We're getting close to my family's house, you told me. People know this car. If anyone sees us, they'll tell my father. At first I didn't believe you, but your expression was deadly serious, so I swapped places with Maryam and lay down on the back seat, covered with a tartan travel rug. You swerved your way through the busy shopping streets. Whenever you braked sharply, which was often, I was thrown into the footwell. This is insane, I thought. This is the dumbest thing I've ever done.

I felt as if I were in an altered state of consciousness. I knew what reality looked like, the reality in which I got out of the car and walked away. But we arrived at the bar and you put the palm of my hand against your breast and soon we were going through the same routine, kissing and groping in a back booth until once again my brain was so fogged up with sex that I forgot everything else but your body. And so, inevitably, I ended up sneaking you and Maryam into my hotel room. Maryam stoically watched TV with the sound turned up high, while you and I undressed one another on the bed. As you wriggled out of your dress she abruptly stood up and told us she'd wait in the lobby. Sorry, I said. Come back in fifteen minutes, you told her. Then, at last, it was just the two of us. I slid off your underwear and marvelled at what I'd just uncovered, the dark nipples and the little mat of pubic hair, framed in bikini-shaped triangles of milk-white skin. You were beautiful, Aisha. Mesmerising. I certainly didn't take you for granted. Please understand that, if nothing else. I felt like the luckiest man in the world. But there was a bad atmosphere in that room, a cloud of guilt and tension hanging over our caresses.

Things started to fall apart when I mentioned condoms. I had some in my washbag and went to get them. When I came back I found you hunched up on the bed, clutching a pillow and staring at me suspiciously. Why do you carry such things? you asked. You must expect to pick up girls when you travel. I shrugged and you called me a seducer, using that odd, old-fashioned word. A seducer with many girls. I promised that wasn't the case, which was true enough, but I knew as I spoke that disaster was looming. Maybe, I said, we shouldn't do this. I don't want to hurt you. I think we should just get dressed. But you shook your head and wagged your finger like a schoolmistress ticking off a naughty class. You hadn't finished with me. The interrogation went on. How many other girls had I had? I said it didn't matter, not so many. Did I love you? I said I'd only just met you, so, no, I couldn't say I loved you. You appeared to consider this for a minute, then lay down and opened your legs. OK, you said. Fuck me.

That was too clinical for my taste, Aisha. Too cold. I told you to put your clothes on. You refused and pulled me down on top of you. You clawed and bit my neck like a cat and I felt alarmed and my head was aching but your skin was soft and your legs were wrapped round my hips and you were sopping wet so of course that was it, because I'd been imagining nothing else since I met you, but I kept thinking that any minute Maryam would knock on the door, or Mansour or the people from the front desk, and I worried you might have lied about your old boyfriend, that you might be a virgin, and when I came it was intense and far too soon and all my worst fears were realised as you started to cry, swearing at me, calling me a pig, a bastard. Your old boyfriend had been gentle and kind. He took his time. He was respectful, unlike me. I made you feel dirty. All I could say was sorry, and I said it again and again. We struggled into our clothes and sat dejectedly beside one another. That was how Maryam found us. Her face too was streaked with tears. Five times, she said. Five different men had approached her and asked her price as she sat in the lobby. She couldn't stand the place another moment. She wanted to go home. So did I.

I walked you down to your car and gave you my phone number in London and you pecked me on the cheek and got in and Maryam drove you away. Early the next morning I flew out. I hadn't slept. I'd spent the night going over everything that had happened, trying to work out when I should have stopped, at what point I should have pushed you away. I was appalled at myself. I'd really thought I was inured to the sexual guilt all around me. I considered myself innocent. But perhaps I wasn't. Perhaps I was everything I appeared to be. Exploiter. Abuser of your body, destroyer of your family honour. Perhaps I was the kind of pig you should have been protected from by your father, your brother, the waiter at the restaurant, by my driver and my tour guide and the concierge at the hotel. It suddenly occurred to me that you might report me to the police, tell them I'd raped you. I wondered how I'd explain myself, what treatment I could expect. When the plane took off I almost wept with relief, until the stewardess came round with hot towels and soft drinks.

Then I got home and put you from my mind. I buried you deep, Aisha, deep as I could, until my phone rang and a voice asked, accusingly, do you know who this is? In that moment it was all too much. I couldn't bear to go back into that midden of guilt and shame and I put the receiver down to make it go away. I'm so sorry, Aisha. You didn't deserve that. You weren't ready, even though you said you were. I hope you escaped – from Jordan and from me. I hope so with all my heart. I didn't mean to hurt you. It's just you were so beautiful. Forgive me, Aisha. Write back and let me know you're all right. It would mean a lot, even after all these years.

ANONYMOUS

Hi Fi and Tobe,

I know, I know this must be weird getting a letter from me as I've not returned your emails or calls since I got back. Sorry about that and the handwriting (Eek). Must be a decade since I've even tried to write something by hand – other than signing cheques – hope you can make out my scrawls! I've been attempting to email you but every time I start I end up deleting bits and starting again and it all comes out like an 'I'm fine' newsletter thing and the truth is I'm not fine. I don't know how I feel. Just very confused and finding it hard to eat and sleep. Don't worry Fi, it's not the old eating thing coming back.

Where do I start? It's late on Friday night and I'm sitting in our flat and Mike's just moved all of his stuff out today (I hadn't realised how little I'd actually bought over the years, couldn't believe that the TV and stereo and all of 'our CDs' turned out to be his.) Anyway, I'm drinking our Duty-Free ouzo thinking about you both on our beautiful holiday and it's given me the guts to get this letter done. I'm just going to keep twittering on and get it all said and not even read it back, then stick it in the envelope and drop it in the postbox before bed (if I can still walk straight!). Don't worry about me. I'm actually very happy, quite ecstatic in fact. Maybe it's the ouzo.

The fact is I can't stop thinking about you. Both of you and our little chalet in Naxos. You were so kind and loving to me in those two weeks. To hell with Mike as you said, Fi. He was a coward and a bully over the abortion. In fact I think the last year he's just spent trying to be nice to me so he could leave without seeming like a total cunt. Which he is, I see that now.

But first the news LOL! (Isn't it funny how we use email talk even in letters.) So Mike's said he's going to reimburse me for his half of the chalet rent and car hire – gee thanks! The last week has been an awful round of predictable excuses about why he stood me up at the airport and his fear of commitment and how he thought the holiday seemed almost like a marriage proposal – the two-couples-together-thing seemed so middle class and middle aged, he said (so him), and since time was pushing on he was worried (again) about the baby question (because you'd both been talking about it and trying so hard to have a child) and he really wasn't ready, he said. He's done now what I sensed he would for the last year. Run off to 'be alone and think things over'. I just know that he's got a bit on-the-side but to be honest, it's like you said, Tobe – Mike will never be ready. And you were right, Fi. I have to move on, because I am worth more.

Anyway, I don't want to talk about Mike. And I don't think what I'm feeling right now is some kind of rebound trauma because I'm just so damned fucking happy. I was crying today thinking about us on the beach, playing in the water together like kids. All these images coming back to me. Even when Mike was lifting out his last box I was thinking about that night we walked miles as the sun went down . . . The skinny-dipping.

Those little things in the water, the sparkly thingies, what did you call them, Tobe?

I'm sorry, this is as unexpected to me as it must be to you. It's taken me two weeks to admit that this is the situation and to scrape together enough courage to try to do this. So the ouzo! To hell with it all as you say, Fi – 'Another round!'

Sorry, I should have said before. I want you to read this letter together, even if one of you gets it first. I want you to read it together, in bed. I want you to cuddle up with the letter between you (like a kind of me) like we did on that first night when I was crying.

Algae – that's what they're called! Yeah? Swimming so far out, treading water, and the stars in the sky and the flashing algae in the water, splashing each other with sparkles. And you both kissing, and Fi, you reaching to hold my hand under the water as you guys were circling tongues. Anyway, that was what I was thinking of when Mike was waiting at the door for his guilt-free goodbye. He said 'See you around, then.' And I really didn't give a shit because I was thinking about us in the water and how he never kissed me like that and how he's scared of going any deeper than paddling.

Anyway, this feels great. I'm not even reading back what I've written. Do you think this is maybe the problem with technology these days? That everything we write and do and think and feel can be saved and edited and deleted. Anyway (isn't it funny how that word seems the only way to start a sentence?). Anyway, maybe I'm drunk. Must be, because I'm laughing and crying. Weird, for days now it's been these flashbacks. At work and with Mike and his boxes and I get these flashes of you both.

That time we went to the farmers' market, all those old sun-ripened faces, you said Tobe, and Fi, you took my hand and then, Tobe, you took my other. And we were walking around, hand in hand, pigged out on goat's cheese and olives and the locals were staring and we didn't give a damn. Like being kids again. Naughty kids. Did you feel that too?

You both said so many times, 'We understand, you're going through a hard time, but just know that we love you.'

And Fi, that night when Tobe went out for more retsina and you confessed you'd both been going through a hard time recently too, with all the pregnancy tests and the blame and seeing the pain I was going through had brought you and Tobe closer cos sex had become this thing, almost medical, for you both.

I'm sorry but I have to say it. You must have known I heard you in the night. Fi, the beautiful noises you make. Sorry, maybe you thought I was asleep. But the walls were so thin – Tobe, you said that. And Tobe, you groan like a bull. And that look you both gave me the next morning, every morning (because you guys really went at it, every damn night!). The way you were so tactile with each other in front of me in the kitchen. You fondled each other at the breakfast bar. Tobe, you were kissing Fi's breasts as I tried to pour the muesli. Remember?

Oops! Have I gone too far? I've never been good at boundaries as you know, Fi. Mike did all that for me.

These flashes, like they're trying to tell me something.

It must be the ouzo, this philosophical me. Fi, you always said I should put my 'great mind' to better use. OK, what I'm thinking now is that the problem is, was, still is – it's all about couples and that's what the problem is. You know, couples are together, what? Maybe three, four years then it gets suffocating, so then it's talk of babies or maybe a pet (like Sharon and Susan and Sooty). What I mean is when it's one-on-one then maybe people try to turn each other into each other and it becomes this battle to see who wins. And dogs and cats and kids are maybe good because they stop couples from tearing each other apart. Fi, it was you that gave me this idea. Was it Sartre? Maybe you just said it to make me feel better about Mike, but it has played on my thoughts. Who fucking said that couples were the ideal model anyway – who? The Church?

And my parents were about to divorce but then my granny came to live with us and suddenly they were both caring for her and they started getting along. And Shaz and Suse were about to split up until they got Sooty and they even joke about how a cat saved their relationship. You know that line of theirs: 'So good to have pussy again.'

No, but I was, and you must have known, every night listening to your creaking bed and your voices and your breath, trying to time it so when I came my gasps would be drowned by yours. You must have known.

I'm beating about the bush. (Hey Fi, remember those lesbians we met at that Anti-Iraq War demo with a hand-painted placard that read 'Lick Bush', or was it 'Fuck Bush'?)

I should calm down on the ouzo, methinks. God, I miss you both. And the sun and the sand and the sky.

But these flashbacks. Tobe, you gave me that back massage and Fi, you were there in the bedroom and you must have seen as Tobe straddled my back. You must have seen. And Tobe you must have known, that night we ate lobster, that Fi was stroking my thigh as she played footsy with you. You must have because you started touching my other thigh and you both held hands and kissed me on either cheek.

Were you both playing with me? Maybe you were just trying to be nice to me because of Mike.

I can't help thinking about all the things you each said to me separately. Fi, about our drunken fumblings in college and you thought that maybe that barely explored side of yourself would come back to haunt you and maybe wreck your marriage if you never managed to have a child. And Tobe, how you were worried, about if you could stay with one woman all your life if there wasn't another life in your life, how the more it came down to mortgages and retirement plans, without the hope of a child, you felt your eye wander. And Fi, how you said that my name was like a full stop in your life and you'd never really got over me.

I'm sorry. Maybe you think I'm just trying to cause conflict. No. No. Please. All I'm trying to do is tell you both what you each told me separately. I hope you're reading this in bed together. I hope you're holding each other as you read it, and Fi, that Tobe's hand is over your shoulder and reaching down to stroke your nipples, your sensitive nipples (mine are dead to the world, as you know) as you both take turns reading.

I didn't plan this. Sorry. Tear this up and tomorrow forget about it. Fine, do that. In fact, yes. Do that before you read another line. This message will self-destruct in one minute! Maybe I've already destroyed what we have. (Fi, you always told me that I had too much love and that it turned to hate when it wasn't reciprocated.)

I'm sorry. I don't even know what this means or how we could go about doing what has been plaguing my thoughts every day. To be together. How can we? Can we?

All I know is I love you. Am in love with you. Both of you. Mad drunken ouzo fuelled love for you both. Fi, please tell Tobe of that night in college, of Vodka Specials, the night before you left. How we kissed and kissed as we touched ourselves, each alone, how we came together then sucked and kissed each other's fingers, how we slept so well that night after three years of aching confusion as room-mates, and how we never spoke of it again and wrote it off as drunkenness. Tobe please tell Fi, truthfully, how you felt when you gave me that massage . . . your hand moving up my thigh as we ate lobster, of how your eyes looked into mine every time you touched Fi, those eyes that told me she'd told you of that one night she and I spent together.

I don't want to come between you. I'm sorry, drunk and stupid and sorry. But these flashes. I'm staring out at the city sky through my little window and I'm walking hand in hand with you both as we sample virgin olive oil and the way you both kiss, your mouths wet and laughing as, each on either side of me, you reach for my hands.

I don't know. I don't know what to do. I've been running it through my head all week as Mike packed. Maybe it's me thinking I can't be a couple again, can't risk so much on one person. Maybe I need two lovers not one. Maybe I'm invading and wanting the love you have for each other for myself. Blackmailing you into it. I don't know. How could it even happen? Could we live together? Should I take you at your word, both of your many words? 'We love you so much,' you said together. 'I love you,' you both said to me, separately, secretly.

'You terrify me,' you said, Tobe, in a whisper as you bit my neck when Fi was in the shower.

And Fi, the way you held my waist as I tried on your bikini. The way you, your fingers lingered.

I worry though that our time together may have pushed you both apart. Maybe you have been fighting like me and Mike did over 'the other woman'. Please don't make me that. Please.

This phrase going round and round in my head.

It's something you said but it seems contradictory.

'We love you.' Not 'I'.

And it scares me.

I want you both. I am too much, I want it all. I want to take that moment further. For Tobe to massage my shoulders and to look up at you, my love, my delicate Fi while he enters me, I want to kiss your neck, your cheek and hold that long kiss that we broke from ten years ago.

I want us to make a life. Together. To give you both that child that you want so much. Just ask me, please.

Please tear this up. I'm so stupid. I'm crying and so happy

and I know I've destroyed everything. Can we still be friends?

I'm not going to read this over. I don't know where we go from here. I can't bear to think of the days and weeks waiting for your response. I hope I've not forced you apart. Maybe, Fi, you should call me first, if any of this has made sense to you. If not then I'll take your silence as a 'No'. Please, please know I love you both, that I want and need your love, that I want to share your pain and laughter as we did in Naxos. To just have you both on either side of me. I want this letter to bring you closer, my loves. I so hope you're reading it together.

I'll understand if you never reply to me. I love you both so much that I'm willing to take this risk.

On second thoughts please don't call or email or text me. I'm spending the next week with the phone turned off. Please, the only way we can deal with this is if you write me a letter. If there's no letter after a week then I'll understand.

I love you.

I love you.

Dot

MARGARET ATWOOD

You don't need to know my name. Let's just say I've been around for a long time, and after my years – my decades – my centuries of immersion in the trade, I know my stuff.

Some people call me Anon., but that can be confusing, as there are a lot of Anons around and the quality varies. Anons write on washroom walls quite a lot – *Call me, I'll surprise you,* with a phone number – and they do a roaring business in the Personal Classifieds: *Morose MWM seeks afternoon dalliance with well-built SBW, 25–35, non-smoker, spanking.* No skill to it, merely the crude particulars. I hate being confused with that sort of riff-raff.

So don't call me Anon. Don't call me anything. We'll just skip the formalities, shall we? When we meet, that is. As we will.

How then will you recognise me?

I used to be well known. I'd go about from city to city, on horseback if times were flush, on foot if the pickings had been slim. I carried a carved staff and wore a pair of sturdy sandals. My garments were a bit eldritch – made the customers believe I was versed in ancient wisdom, which I was, and that I had a pipeline to the invisible forces, which I did. I shouldn't have had to emphasise these features, but if you've got it and you don't flaunt it who can tell? So I wore the eldritch outfit as a kind of signage. I'd set up shop in the main square, tucked discreetly into a corner, quill and papyrus at my elbow, or later, vellum, or later still, pen and paper. The desperate would know where to find me.

Things changed. They always do. History shunted me here and there, from one prime game park of love to another. A clientele with time on their hands – romance needs that – and a little spare cash, which never hurts either, and an interest in appearing stylish. Nowadays I hang out in Toronto, once a desert for my kind of enterprise, now an oasis. Where there are tapas bars, there are love letters.

You can usually spot me at the Bar Mercurio, an establishment I've singled out in tribute to my patron god, Mercury, alias Hermes. He's the ruler of communication and charm – you can see why I'd want those attributes – and also of trickery and lies, which can come in handy as well. My other patron is Aphrodite, goddess of Looove. That can be sticky, as the two of them don't get on very well. For Hermes, a roll in the hay is a roll in the hay, after which he's on his way with no tears shed. If he has to do a cunning imitation of being lost in love, he'll do it, but that's all it will be – a cunning imitation. Description, for him, is an end in itself: not for nothing has he been called the Dancing King of the Adjective.

Whereas Aphrodite's a purist. For her, love is serious to the point of tedium. She'll push her devotees all the way to the funeral pyre if need be. Your heart really does have to beat triple-time, your longing and despair must be genuine, or she'll give you what for by making you fall in love with a donkey next time around.

I can draw on either one of them, depending on the wishes of the client: a quick seduction, an in-depth life-altering emotional experience complete with threats of suicide. Your choice.

(Don't make the mistake of believing that I'm scornful of love. I make jokes about it, yes, but it is after all the most powerful force in the world, and in any case I wouldn't want to offend my goddess. I have dedicated myself to its service, at least on Wednesdays and Fridays. Essentially I worship it, like everyone else.

It's only that nowadays its manifestations have become so tawdry, so paltry, so venal, so shrivelled . . . but enough of that.)

I used to do most of my work at night, but the music has become too loud for me, so I've taken to the mornings. The Bar Mercurio is near the Bata Shoe Museum, so I can nip in there when I'm feeling homesick for the old days and ways, and gaze at my outworn shoes – fifteen pairs of them at least, from the aforementioned Roman leather numbers to the pointy toes of Renaissance Florence to the stacked red heels of the eighteenth century French monarchy.

These days I wear comfortable trainers, and the aqua and lilac leisurewear of a plump matron out for a slenderising morning jog. Or, in my male avatar, some good-quality jeans, an admittedly ridiculous though sincere baseball cap – *I (heart) The LEAFS* – and a black T-shirt, with a gold chain around my neck. Only one gold chain, mind you; I don't want to stand out.

I sit there with my latte, reading the newspaper – the horoscopes add a touch of comic nostalgia to my day – and wait for customers. If you require my services, just sidle up to me and introduce yourself in the following manner:

'Hot enough for you?'

(For which Cold, Wet, Foggy, Sunny, Cloudy, Smoggy or Snowy may be substituted as appropriate.) After I have given the standard reply – 'We'll suffer for it later' – you should give the password:

'*O lente, lente currite noctis equi!*'

If I like the look of you and feel that we can work together, and that you aren't likely to stiff me for the fee – I wouldn't recommend doing that, by the way – I will answer, 'The stars move still, time runs, the clock will strike.'

But if you don't come up to my standards, I will say, 'I'm sorry, I only speak English.' If you persist, and start shouting that you know who I really am and you absolutely have to avail yourself of the essential services only I can provide – if you fall on your knees and start kissing the hems of whatever it is I have on – I will call the manager. I can't handle complete lunatics, but he can.

You see, although you have to trust me, I must be able to trust you as well. Our enterprise requires teamwork. You've got to feed me the emotional raw material. You can't just sit back and do nothing. That's why I'm so choosy.

But I'm not turning down as many applicants as I'd like, these days. My stock in trade has always been the graceful and effective manipulation of the written word, directed towards a desired end – copulation at midnight, long-drawn-out sweet'n'sour flirtation, full-throttle white satin wedding bells – but grace seems to be flying out the window. Now a young man can text-message his target on her cellphone – I WON 2 FKU – and she might actually turn up at the video arcade and go through with it. The decline of modesty has not been a plus, from my point of view. It's bad for trade.

Once there was a heavy demand for well-turned sonnets – *Love is not love which alters when it alteration finds*, that sort of thing – or even for lighter verse – *Gather ye rosebuds while ye may*, and so forth. It showed a girl – however erroneously – that a man or woman had more on his or her mind than her or his body. Now it's just URAHOTTEE. Where's the art in that?

So I've had to hustle a bit to keep myself going. I've come

up with what I think is a subtle yet convincing pitch. Here's what's on offer:

SCRIBE OF AGELESS LOVE!
THE MENU OF DESIRE!

- Wide experience of both main genders, plus gaiety, cross-dressing, paedophilia, fetishism, animal husbandry, and more!
- Melt her/his/its heart with a splendiferous bouquet of customised verbiage!
- Candy's dandy, say it with flowers, liquor's quicker, but an expert letter is way, way better!
- What modern woman wants: Great abs, an agile and persistent member, total adoration, but, more than that, a sense of humour! Woo her with drooling drollery!
- All girls are curious: Let me turn you into a purple package of dark mystery she longs to open!
- Arouse her pity! Allow me to hint at your secret wounds – those only the poultice of Love can heal!
- Choice of 100 openers: My sweet darling, My beloved pumpkin, My sinful but organic chocolate, My Venus in furors, My leather whiplet, My surreal fur-lined teacup, My jugular vein of passion, My voluptuous and odoriferous onion, I kiss your tattooed triceps, I want your Size 12 stiletto denting my neck, You unbelievable shit, many more!
- Optional: Disappearing ink! Vanishes after a week/month/year, to avoid embarrassment at a later date!
- Dignified letters of rebuke for dumped Misses. Win him back with a cool/hot note!
- *Odi et amo*, updated!

- No job too small, no heart too fractured!
- Braille at no extra charge!
- I can do for you what Viagra can't!

TORTURED BY THE PANGS OF LOVE?
THINK YOU CAN'T AFFORD ME?
YOU CAN'T NOT AFFORD ME!

So there you have it.

With each order I can offer a month's supply of scented notepaper, with tasteful monogram in a rose design – for the gals – and, for the men, a genuine snakeskin card case, with several false names on the cards. Handy when you're in a hurry.

And here you are, at last! Look into my eyes. You have my full attention. Tell me your love problem. Propose your favoured solution. Don't be shy: remember, anything you've fantasised about, I've already done. More than once. Oh, so much more.

Leave it with me overnight. Payment in advance, please: you'll soon be in such raptures you'll forget to write the cheque.

Don't worry. It's money well spent. I always get results.

Thank you.

You won't be sorry.

DAMON GALGUT

My dear Wouter

I should confess straight off that I've been hitting the gin again. Mostly it's under control, but I've lurched off the straight and narrow lately. Never before sunset, of course, or at least the middle of the afternoon. But everybody needs their anaesthetic, my dear, as you of all people should know, blissed out with religious ecstasy in your little cell. But let me not sound bitter, so early on.

Wouter, I'm going to come right out and say it – I WANT YOU TO COME BACK. I've tried to be understanding and supportive and all that, but the truth is that this set-up is just bloody awful. I mean, what are you doing there, actually? Well, I know *what* you're doing, the praying and meditating and fasting and the rest of it, which I have to say sounds diabolical, by the way – all that *deprivation* – but what are you hoping to achieve? You've tried to explain it to me, the oneness with the universe etc. etc., but deep down you know it's twaddle. You're too sensible to fall for such hollow consolations. Of course, you've always had a tendency towards, what's the right term, spiritual fads, you know what I mean, your yoga phase, for example, until you put your hip out, and that dreadful retreat you dragged me on, no speaking or eye contact and the gurgly chanting by that shiny fat man. I know you accused me of running away that time because the food was bad, but really it was the chanting that did it. There's something so egotistical about people trying to lose their ego, I can't bear the self-indulgence, and even you admitted afterwards that the organic gruel they served us was unspeakable. But what you're doing now sounds just like that retreat, bad food and silence and stupid chanting, except that it never comes to an end. I hope you won't take it personally when I say that I can't imagine anything more hellish.

Wouter, nothing, NOTHING in my whole life, has hurt me as badly as your last letter. Even now it stabs me to the core when I think of it. Because you made it sound like it was, in fact, the very last time that any of us would be hearing from you. It's cruel, darling, to play with people like that. That rubbish about dying to the world in order to be reborn, having no family or friends or possessions . . . It's all very well if you're a monk, but you're not. Well, yes, you *are* now, I suppose, in a technical sense, but not *really*, not deep down. Let's be honest about this and admit that what you're doing is a reaction to being caught in bed with me by Renata and your mother. It was terrible, of course, I'd be the first to admit it. I was just as ashamed and humiliated as you were. Or maybe I was a *teeny* bit less traumatised, because, well, it wasn't *my* wife and mother, and thank God for that, I may add, especially with regard to your mother, and I wasn't hiding anything, sexually speaking, but I wasn't in the most flattering position at the time, as you know. But let's not dwell on that.

The point, darling, is that – bugger it, I've forgotten the point. It's always about this time of the evening that things start to get hazy. The plot disappears, only the characters remain. And this is about all the future has to offer me right now, a hangover in the morning and a long gin-slide into obscurity after lunch. But it could've been so different,

Wouter, and now I remember the point again. It's that, instead of being a calamity, Renata and the Mater Carnivora coming home early like that was actually an opportunity to turn this whole thing around. No more sham, no more acting and pretence. No more of those horrible weekends away, with you being all loud and over-jolly and me dragging along some colourless appendage as a cover. You were living a lie, you said it yourself many times, and all because your father was a Dutch Reformed minister who thrashed you senseless as a boy. But he's been dead many years, and we're not in the Middle Ages any more. For God's sake, my dear, gay marriage is legal here now, even the blacks are doing it. We could've just told the truth and been ourselves for a change. The truth is middle-aged and past its prime and not very pretty any more, if it ever was, but it's . . . well, it's the truth, I suppose.

I'm not sure what I was driving at, actually, in that last paragraph, but I know what your answer will be in any case. You'll say that you've found the real truth where you are now, in that awful cold monastery place. But you haven't, darling. The truth is me. The truth is what Renata found when she came stomping in unexpectedly that Wednesday afternoon. Better to face up to it than spend the rest of your life languishing in what, when you come down to it, is not very different to a common jail cell.

Wouter, I LOVE YOU! I want to scream it out like the death-bellow of a lung-shot buffalo. I speak metaphorically, of course, never having shot a buffalo, or anything else for that matter, but you get the point – anguish and desolation and loss. Not to mention a tank of gin, which I see needs replenishing. And this is a good moment for it, my darling, because I can feel myself going to pieces. Things have got to the point where I can't tell the difference between grief and alcoholic dementia any more.

All right. I've pulled myself together. You'd be astonished at the insights that come to a man on his lonely odyssey between the fridge and the booze cabinet. I had a very clear one, a moment ago – an insight, that is, except that I've lost track of what it was. Damn it, can't you see what I'm reduced to, after only three months without you? Do you know we've hardly spent a day without seeing each other since we met at the station eight years ago? All right, it was a relationship with inauspicious beginnings, I grant you that, but we went from strength to strength. We defied language and class and culture. Nobody has ever made me as wildly, dizzily happy as you did, even with all the lying. The only really tragic occasion was being best man at your wedding, and I can tell you I had to choke back a sob when you kissed the bride, though you made up for it with that sly pinch in the registry office. Blast and bugger, it was written in the stars, it was meant to be, all we had to do was follow the inevitable, and now look what's happened. After the big scene with Renata and the White Witch, all the screaming and crying and throwing of shoes, everybody knew the score. The divorce, well, it was gory and painful and all the rest, but it was FREEDOM, Wouter, don't you see it? You shouldn't have given her *everything*, for God's sake. The house, the car, the savings – what were you thinking? Not to mention the tattoo parlour, which was a real money-spinner in these parts, as you know. I mean, a *little* guilt might've been appropriate under the circumstances, but to reduce yourself to a snivelling, selfless heap like that – oh, it broke my heart. And then, of course, when you wanted to go off to Korea to *find* yourself, you couldn't even pay the air fare. And who did you come to . . . ?

Which reminds me. I gave you that money on the understanding that it was just a two-month trip, to get yourself together. You were supposed to be coming back to me afterwards, one month ago yesterday to be precise, to be my assistant, not that I need one or that you could tell a Louis-Quatorze armchair from a Woody Woodpecker tattoo, but it would be a way to share my *life*, for God's sake. It was never the plan to shave off your hair and join a monastery. Is that the thanks I get? I could sue you, if I wanted to, for the money *plus* interest, if I wanted to get vindictive. Which I don't, but I'm just saying.

Something else has just occurred to me. Do you have somebody over there? I've always wondered about those monkish types, all men together sharing showers and whatnot. There must be quite a lot of sidelong glances going on in the prayer sessions. Because I'll kill you if you are up to something, Wouter, and you know me, I *will* find out. Please, please, say it isn't so. Write to me one more time, just to ease my heart. For your information, you bastard, I'm not considered completely undesirable myself in certain quarters, in fact an undue amount of interest has been paid since your departure by that ginger-haired queen downstairs, the one with the two dachshunds. Not to mention the snaggle-toothed number who manages the local Pick 'n' Pay. But I don't care about them, I have eyes for only one man, his name is written on my soul, W, O, T, fuckitte I mean U but what am I doing you know how to spell your name. The point is, Wouter, no, I've lost the point again. The point is I'm broken. The point is I'm missing you terribly. The point is PLEASE COME BACK WOUTER what do you want me to do I'm down on my knees and pleading. If it's possible to lose all dignity long-distance by airmail darling there's not a shred of self-respect left. This morning I started weeping in front of a client, a very sweet woman who actually thought I was moved by her fake Biedermeier side-table. Truth is I started drinking around breakfast that's how it's been the last few days. Wouter if you don't answer I'm going to come and get you I promise you I'll fasten myself on to your foot and won't let go until you give in but to do that I'll have to close the office and fire Beauty and liquidate some assets money has been a little tight lately but what the hell I'll do it interior decorating has never been very big in this part of Germiston anyway. But what I'd prefer and I think you would too if you only knew it is if you came back here and lived with me and we just started our lives over the way they were supposed to be if I don't know what if things were different you weren't so afraid or your father hadn't been such a prick why can't it be simple. Actually it IS simple just the world that makes things complicated. But the world is all we've got my dear there is no spiritual truth no second chance just this one life with all its mess. Please answer me Wouter. And if you're wondering what these marks are on the page they're tears the real thing except for the big splotch in the corner where I spilled my drink.

Always –
Neville

AUDREY NIFFENEGGER

September 1, 2005

Dear Sylvie,

I'm writing you this letter because I don't know what else to do. Your cellphone is dead. All I get when I call you is a computer voice telling me to call back later. You haven't answered my emails. I've been watching the news for hours, days. Water everywhere, bodies floating down the streets, collapsed highways, abandoned pets. Where are you, Sylvie? I want to go to you, but I'm afraid that if I leave the apartment you'll show up and I won't be here. I know that you won't read this. There's nowhere to send it any more.

Last night I dreamt that we were together in your parents' house when the flood came. In my dream we crept up the stairs quietly, as though the water could hear us, as though it would find us – we were its prey, and we went upstairs so silently, holding hands like little kids. And the water rose just as silently. We were afraid to touch the water, or to let it touch us. It was formidable, evil. If it touched us we would die. You kept putting things into my hands, things you wanted to save. We went into the attic. It was full of your mother's clothes and I knew you were sad that the flood would ruin her extravagant dresses. The water kept rising and we climbed out the dormer window and on to the roof. We sat side by side on the roof, and the water washed everything away. We saw cars, trees, bodies in the water. All the birds were gone, there was no noise except the sound of the water lapping and swirling, now and then a dog would bark, but there were no other people there. It was an empty world. The water had taken everything. We sat on the roof and looked out at nothing. We made love up there because we had no food or water to drink. The roof was our island. Then I saw the rough green asphalt shingles of the roof through your hands. Your body gradually became transparent, and I was alone on the roof, watching the water invade, watching the city disappear. I looked at the things you had given me to save. I was holding your glasses and a tennis ball.

Sylvie, I hope you aren't in the city. I hope you evacuated. (Though how could you have left the city with no car? Did you ever find your mom? And why haven't you called?) The TV is showing horrible things. There are reports of killings, rapes, looting, old people dying in nursing homes because the staff left them behind. Why haven't you called? I don't know what to do, Sylvie.

Before you left last week I said *Please don't go.* And you said *She just wants me home for a few weeks, Nancy. I'll be back in Chicago when classes start.* I sit in front of the television looking past the reporters, trying to see your house in the wrecked scenes behind their freaked-out faces. I remember the garden in your mother's backyard, the yellow gladioli and the bright red canna lilies, the honeysuckle that engulfed the garage . . . I remember the scent of the garden at night, how it came in through your bedroom window, so strong I felt almost nauseated. You kissed me in the backyard; I worried that your neighbors might see. You laughed and printed your lipsticked mouth on my white blouse just over my left nipple . . . And in the afternoons, I remember how everyone sat on their porches in the heat, and they all waved at us when we walked to

Jimmy's to buy cigarettes and beer. All under water now. Whole blocks, whole neighborhoods. I stood on our front stoop this morning with the newspaper in my hand, looking at Hyde Park Boulevard, imagining it all under water.

Do you know how to swim, Sylvie? I never asked you. It's amazing to me how much I don't know. After two years you'd think we'd know everything there is about each other. But I guess you never can tell what will be important. Why would it matter if you could swim? We only talk about what we're reading. We eat and sleep and take baths and put on clothes and take them off again and fuck each other delirious and go to classes and all around us the air fills up with words about books. If New Orleans was flooded with words I would not be afraid for you, Sylvie. I know you can swim in words. But water . . . can you swim in water, Sylvie?

The apartment seems vacant without you, even though it's crammed with your stuff. Since you won't read this I'll admit that I've been crying over the stupidest things. Tonight I opened the junk drawer in the kitchen and found your old key ring with the little plastic Pink Panther and that set me off. I can't explain why. It was just pathetic, I guess. Your possessions seem like they're expecting you; they don't have the slightest doubt that you'll come home. I feel superstitious. If I close my eyes while the phone rings it will be you. If I take a shower, then the phone will ring, and it will be you. But when the phone rings it's always other people asking if I've heard from you yet. *No,* I say. *Not yet.* There's not much to say after that. We're all embarrassed by our own politeness. *Call me if there's anything I can do,* they say. *Sure, yeah, of course,* I say. I want to scream at them. I want to howl, like a baby, until you come to me. Oh, Sylvie. You have to be safe, because I am wrecked without you. My levees are breached, and you have flooded me, and I am a city under water now.

Ugh – I'm getting all metaphorical. Come home and make fun of my bad prose.

It's almost 5 a.m., Sylvie. I'm sitting at the kitchen table, looking towards the lake. It's funny how we think of the lake being there, a presence even though we can't see it because of all the tallish ugly buildings. The sky is getting lighter. I remember when I first met you, and you thought it was weird that I always knew what direction the lake was, no matter where we were, as though I had an internal compass that points east. How strange it would be if the lake rose up one day and came into the city. It would be like a fairy tale, as though an enchantment had caused the city and the lake to merge, silently, like a painting of a city in a lake. But that's not what I see on TV, Sylvie. On TV there are dead people slumped in folding chairs in the baking sun, and people spray-painting Xs on the houses, and everything is either in motion when it should be still or stranded, stopped.

It flooded here once, Sylvie. Someone knocked a hole in the bottom of the Chicago River, and it drained into all the basements in the skyscrapers, the deep basements below the basements. I'm not making this up. It was a flood no one could see, a sort of conceptual flood, except to the people who had to deal with it; for them it was probably pretty real.

The sun's up, Sylvie. I'm going to bed. Maybe when I wake up you'll call. Maybe you're on your way here. At least maybe I'll dream about you.

Nan

JULI ZEH

Translated by Judith Orban

First Chapter

We could have been happy if only we had met. The day on which we didn't meet was fine. Pouring rain at a time when only the rain was holding sky and earth together. You took refuge in a café, I too sat at a window in the warmth. It was the season of grog and gingerbread. We played at telling our future fortunes by pouring the molten wax of the candle on the table into water. The future consisted of flat red bloblets floating on the surface of a glass of mineral water. A woman crossed the room with small steps, holding a brimming cup with both hands. It was beautiful.

Second Chapter

Even as children we had similar interests. I gathered snails off paths so they wouldn't crack like hollow hazelnuts under the shoes of walkers. You rescued frogs into which neighbourhood kids had stuck straws to blow them up. We liked to stand in the corner, we liked the fashions of the decade just past, we were interested in big fat books, and particularly enjoyed saying things no one understood. So we both became objects of people's derision. That's the best prerequisite for lifelong happiness together.

Third Chapter

You were my type, I was yours. Both of us blue-eyed with dark hair, an unusual combination. Because we were shorter than average, we liked to take holidays in Asia. Birds of a feather flock together. We loved long walks and quiet evenings at home. Out of timidity we preferred most of all to be by ourselves. We had difficulties getting to know people, and it's particularly important to be in agreement on such a sensitive issue. But neither did we ignore the fact that opposites attract. That's why you were male and I was female. We didn't have any problems with that. We had been brought up to be tolerant.

Fourth Chapter

Like all true lovers we drew closer to each other in a round-about way. We were young and nervous. We didn't want to hang around waiting for life to begin. You slept with a bewitching peroxide-blonde hairdresser, I possessed a hearing-aid technician. Soon the blonde was merely a hairdresser, and my acoustic technician took deafness to be an economic blueprint. All the while we knew we were destined for something else. For being the knight in shining armour and the princess in the tower. For each other. For happiness. The days provided distraction, the nights consisted of waiting.

Longing taught us to believe in true love. We liked to think of each other, particularly while masturbating.

Fifth Chapter

We also had some hard times. I grew flabby around the hips, your hair turned grey. How were we to recognise each other in this condition? A long succession of days passed in bitter silence. When the sun shone brightly we cursed as we looked into the mirror. The weather should not be lovelier than the person, when everything else – as we all know – is so relative. But the hate faded away, I knew you so well. Your despair was the salt in my soup. My suffering was the sugar in your tea. Your thoughts were mine. We had learned it was inner values that mattered – and just how much they did.

Sixth Chapter

Once I almost lost you. It was winter yet again, the whole city was treading on thin ice. You were widowed, I was divorced, snow pelted us with light from all sides. You were crossing the street on which I was driving. I was singing a love song along with the eight o'clock news on the radio when a flash of light from your glasses hit my retina. My hearing aid stopped working, your cry was lost in silence. You bent down behind some parked cars to search for your cane. The road ahead of me was empty. By a hair's breadth – I tell you, my darling – I just missed hitting you by a hair's breadth. For years I couldn't shake off the feeling that something strange had happened.

Seventh Chapter

We grew old together. For a long time already sex had become irrelevant. We took pleasure in cake and falling leaves. Our rooms were pungent with the aroma of the past. The cleaning lady came once a week and mopped the floors. On her raised flowered buttocks I saw a hilly spring meadow, you didn't see anything any more. Together we were the lame, the blind, the dumb and the deaf rolled into one person. We understood each other without words. We fingered similar photos, we ate the same porridge. Outside our dingy windows migratory birds revealed the future in ever identical formations.

Eighth Chapter

A great love conquers all obstacles. Great love shies away from nothing. On that very day when we didn't meet each other we were sitting in different cafés. The future consisted of flat red bloblets floating on the surface of a glass of mineral water. A woman crossed the room with small steps, holding a brimming cup with both hands. As so often, my beloved, we had something in common. You remained alone, I remained alone. But I don't even care about that. For time and again, day after day, my whole life long, I shall forgive you.

LEONARD COHEN

You're going to leave me. I know you're going to leave me. Like you left Laporte. Like you left Arif. I'll be someone you call by his last name. Laporte didn't look too good tonight at the Alhambra when he limped over to say hello to you. He didn't want to give me his hand because it was so wet. He took the tips of my fingers and he smiled cheerlessly, as if to say: The greatest fuck you've ever had, the deepest love you've ever known, and she's going to leave you very soon, you poor stunned sonovabitch. In the car you told me that his hands always get that wet when he has to meet people. You know his terrors, don't you? As you know mine. We haven't seen too much from Laporte lately, film-maker of a certain period, when you were his juice, when he was allowed to tie you up, and you commanded him to treat you like a slave. Then you told me to look at the moon, so I looked through the windshield at the moon. Then you told me to be impressed by the colour of the sky, so I applied myself to a study of the royal blue Paris sky. The turbaned Sikh assigned you, as he always does, the most impossible space in the garage, and when we walked past his window, he said, as he always does, The Champion of Parking. In the room you did sail so sweetly into my arms. I'm yours. For tonight. Your big joke. And my heart still leaps up between the declaration and the punchline. Like you left Laporte. Like you left Arif, and then slept with his twin brother. I leave them just before they leave me. It's better that way, no? Not to have a crying girl on your hands. Okay, darling, you're sleeping, the night has come to an end, and I'm nervous as hell. You'll either read this by yourself one day, or we'll be reading it together.

1980

PHIL LaMARCHE

Baby,

When you reached inside the shower curtain when I didn't know and turned off the cold water and burned me terrible, JESUS, I still don't even know if you were pissed or did it for a laugh, but you know the hot water heater could boil eggs, you KNOW that, and when I punched in the wall and busted my hand, it wasn't you I swung at, I PROMISE I didn't even imagine your face on the square pink tile that cracked and caved in (and don't worry about that, I'll replace the whole wall when I do the remodel) but that night, when I tore down the shower curtain and came freaking into the hall, naked as an ape, it wasn't you I expected to see, and what I said, JESUS what I said, I didn't mean it for you at all, I thought I'd find some bastard friend of mine, or even your brother, that fuck and his jokes, but you took off and didn't give me the chance to explain and I couldn't follow, being naked, and you went and went to your parents and you KNOW how that makes me feel, I've told you, it's like you're on their team and not mine and when you wouldn't take my calls and I didn't stop calling and your father finally answered and told me QUIT IT and I told him to go to HELL and GET FUCKED and that I'd be over to get you, over his broken ass if need be, it was all only because I was so afraid of losing you and because I LOVE you so much. I know, I KNOW I'm no good at 'communication', you don't have to say it AGAIN, I get it, OKAY?

I can see how you didn't understand, but when I got to your parents' and the police were there, do you know how that FELT? And didn't it say something about how much I love you, that I didn't give up, even then? It took three of those PIGS to bring me down, that's got to mean SOMETHING, doesn't it? Sure the stun gun finally got me (it felt like someone set my blood on FIRE) but even then, on my knees, did I really seem beat? And the MACE? Of course it blinded me but still I could sense you, halfway up the stairs, in a crouch, your knees pulled to your chest with that beautiful look of a child you sometimes have when you get scared. I could feel you there, and as I rolled around blind, covered in my own spit and snot and tears, as they creamed me with their night sticks, it was YOU I was still reaching for.

Of course once I was out cold they did what they wanted with me and I can only imagine their scrawny arms struggling to get me off the ground, my ass or heel dragging on the concrete of your parents' walk as they hauled me to the rear door of their cruiser, tossing me to the back seat next to the puke stain of some highschooler brought in from a keg bender, and you, baby, forced to watch from the steps of that house, that place I once rescued you from, and that's what feels the worst, sending you back to THEM after all they did to you. I remember when you first told me, that night at Frazier's brother's with the rum punch (remember the back porch, the two of us with the stars so bright they were reflected in the pond and you told me you felt safe and I said you should because I'd fucking pummel anyone who even looked at you wrong and then you smiled?). It KILLS me to think I ruined all that, to think that now I seem worse than them, worse than your mom constantly telling you she's prettier and your father silent forever. I haven't forgotten, I remember everything you said that night and I'd do anything to get that back, to have you feel safe again. ANYTHING.

I know what you're saying, you're saying it's more than the night in the shower, you're saying what about when you punched the shit out of the brand new microwave and we had to bring it back and lie and say it came that way in the box? What about the time you threw the mug through the window in the back door? And what about the hole in the bedroom door or the hole in the mudroom wall or the radio you shot with a RIFLE? I know, I KNOW I get crazy sometimes, you don't have to beat me over the head with all that shit, I'm not retarded, I remember it fine. It's like some switch gets hit and I go nuts, like I'm Dr. Jekyll and Mr. Fucking Hyde and I don't know what it is but I'd do anything not to be that way, I'd take a steak knife to my brain if I knew what part to cut out. I don't want to be that way, baby, BELIEVE me, I want to be better for you, I want to be NORMAL, I want to take you back from your parents and forget this ever happened.

I know they're telling you I'm no good, that you have to finally leave me for real, but what do they know? Do they know how good it was between us like ninety-nine point nine nine percent of the time? Do they know that, thanks to them, you're no peach either (especially with a few cocktails under your belt)? The time you scratched that girl's face and threw her on the floor just because she was standing too close to me at the bar, did you mention that? Or the time you got drunk and swore that Jenny and I were fucking and screamed at her in front of everyone until she started crying and eventually admitted she only liked girls just to get you to quit and then her roommate moved out as a result of her being a lesbian and she couldn't cover the rent by herself and had to move back home? I bet you didn't mention that, or the fact that I stood by you through all of it, no matter how many of my friends told me what a complete fucking WHACK-JOB you were.

I want to remind you that this all started with one twist of the wrist (YOUR wrist) baby, and I know what you're saying, you're saying it started before that, with me and Kelly, but there's nothing between me and Kelly and besides, you can't just go and burn a guy. I don't know what's going on between you and her, but there's nothing between us, CHRIST she's practically like my sister and when I spent the night at her place, it was on the COUCH, and it was only because I had too much to drink and unlike SOME people, I don't want to lose my license. I'm not trying to say that this is your fault but I'm not trying to say this isn't your fault, or that it isn't my fault either, because I think we both got nuts and I think we're both fucked up and I think that's why we shouldn't split because if we can't understand each other, WHO is ever going to? You with some Beaver Cleaver type and me with a prom queen, come on, who are we kidding? They wouldn't last a week with the likes of us.

We were made for each other baby, so just hurry up and say goodbye to your fucking folks and come drop the charges and get me out of this shit hole of a cell before I have to kill the stinking old man in the corner who keeps looking at me and rubbing his crotch and we'll go home and we'll have a bonfire and light off some fireworks, the BIG shit you like from the catalog and we'll sit in the lawn chairs just like it's Fourth of July only it'll all be for us, star crossed and crazy exploding lovers, and if the neighbors complain, we'll be NICE for a change and apologise and invite them over and it will be the start of something new for us, something different and BETTER. We'll try, REALLY try, and it will work this time, I KNOW it. I PROMISE.

Love,

Gerald

M. G. VASSANJI

My Friend,

It's drug mischief that's brought you back . . . so painful. Or I would not trouble you. Again. It was so long ago. Another world. I betrayed you then, didn't I . . . you couldn't have forgotten that . . . wherever you are.

I see a boy walking diffidently up the curving hill of United Nations Road in Dar es Salaam, eyes fixed on the ground in front of him . . . Remember?

You would look away into the sun's glare determined to avoid me, your face scrunched up, and when you could bear it no longer you'd turn your head back, just in time to miss me passing in that glorious blue Citroën like a princess in a chariot. But one day our eyes met. I had you. Do you want a lift? – I said. And the shy dark boy dripping sweat looked startled, allowed himself just one step closer and stopped just long enough to sink his eyes in mine . . . and spoke in a dry voice, *No thank you*, and walked on. What did you feel? Your heart went thump, thump, thump, *I* could feel it. I, who was insulted. The next day you were not there, and the whole week; my driver sneaking sly looks at me in the mirror as I shamelessly scanned the sidewalk. I who was the insulted party. You were teasing me? *No. Shy, only shy; I was so embarrassed*, you replied – when you did finally appear on that road and accepted my lift. Where shall the driver drop you? *Just there, opposite the mosque is fine.* Here? – or closer . . .? *No – yes . . .* You didn't want me to see your home, did you? And I, naïve European girl, couldn't understand why. How nervous you looked, each time we let you out, and without even a glance behind you ran as if for your life!

You're so white; I mean – not pink. Is that what you first noticed about me? Not pink? *No – that hair – no, before that –* Yes? *The car – it's so majestic, the best car on the road.* You noticed the car first and not me? *But your hair – blazing, like a fire!*

Flatterer. Yes, the brown head of curls, and the green eyes, how could you have missed them in the Citroën. The eyes are dimmer, but the hair is short and black, fashions change; and yes, dyed; and yes, thin too. You truly didn't know where I came from; Sweden you mentioned once, and I pretended as if it were true; you didn't know the flag on the car hood, the blue and white with the star in the middle that had been the badge of my people for so long, and how that endeared you to me. European, sure, but a Romanian refugee, smuggled through the border aged two.

I had not a friend in town, and this boy comes along; shy, serious, thoughtful. That's the first thought that came into my mind when I saw you – what is he thinking in that head? And he's had his hair cut. It looks funny. What is there to think about so seriously with that haircut-head of his? And dark, he doesn't care about the sun roasting him, turning him darker. His skin will wrinkle sooner, Mummy might have said. I told her I had met this nice boy from the boys' school who had agreed to teach me Kiswahili, and after some discussion she and Father agreed. You can bring him after school on Saturday . . . The first time you came to our house you fell from the rattan chair. I laughed, I cried, for you. Almost everybody fell off that ill-designed chair, how could you have known. I could have told you but didn't. Forgive a girl her whimsy.

You taught me calculus, my friend, I taught you Shakespeare; you did my physics for me, I gave you tennis . . . And when I said let's sit out in the sun and came out in my yellow bathing suit, your brown face turned maroon. I am sorry. But didn't you borrow my mother's *Lady Chatterley; just to find out what the fuss is about*, you said. Sure. That too. I told her a friend had borrowed it.

Sure there was the exotic to you; the dark. And I was lonely. Not that there wasn't other game in town. Little, but there. Hofner, also from Israel; the American twins who arranged a tryst under Selander Bridge to do the dirty on us diplomats' daughters. But you were my special; your name I'd say over and over at night, happily; a king's name; *no, an imam's*; . . . but precious music all the same, always, Hoo . . . ssen, Hoo . . . ssen . . ., until that Scud-firing monster came along and put his stamp on it.

The war came; the sixty-seven one. And we were *non grata*, more or less, because of my father's job. He was a spy. African governments did not like us any more. And you never saw that Citroën again. I disappeared. No goodbye, no notice. How rude, how heartless. But not heartless, please believe me. I had no choice. Mother told me, What's the point? You are going far away where he can never belong. And you are both young. Et cetera. What I might have told my own children later. And yours.

It's the drugs, you see that have stirred you up like a genie from some dark recess of the mind . . . of the heart? . . . Yesterday I saw a boy blow himself up into shreds and here I am. I am well, just in shock, but it's the drugs. The boy's young face. And this precious thought: I wish I could send it to you, this thought of love and friendship; this sorry apology. I wish I could write it before it disappears. Again.

Tova

Tel Aviv

TESSA BROWN

Dearest Randolph,

I am writing in reference to the string of voice mails you recently left me. Although I understand that there were outside forces acting upon you, your messages nonetheless sounded rash and not fully thought out. I want to take this opportunity to go over some of your main points and offer a response, since your means of communication left me no obvious path by which to do so. I assume, of course, that you have all of our previous communications for reference, including, but not limited to, letters, electronic mail, phone messages, and transcripts of conversations crucial to the progress of our relationship.[1]

Message 1: Confusion

(a) [Exhalation] Jess [sic], it's Randy [sic]. (b) I've been thinking a lot about us and, well, I just don't know if it's the best

[1] I will be referring in particular to the communications of the past six months, in addition to various communications from over the course of the past four years, including (but, again, not limited to) Thanksgiving with your family in November of 2002 and the events related to your 2003 trip to Atlantic City.

thing for me, well, for both of us right now. (c) I know we've talked about it – well, kind of – but I really think I need to take a break. Call me back. Bye.

1A. *[Exhalation] Jess [sic], it's Randy [sic].*

Your introduction ('Jess, it's Randy'), preceded as it is by a pronounced exhale, suggests that you are unsure about how to proceed; perhaps you feel socially or otherwise obligated to distance yourself from me. Consider your motives in calling: If you are responding to pressure from friends and/or family, please remember that the only feelings on which this relationship is contingent are yours and, of course, mine. I here refer to a comment from your mother that states, 'Randy, are you sure about this one? She seems, oh, I don't know, *eccentric*.'[2] This comment and others lead me to believe that you are acting on the advice of your peers and relatives, who have led you to believe that they have your best interests at heart.[3]

[2] Overheard in the kitchen of the McKellen residence, on the evening of November 25, 2002, at approximately 9.02 p.m. Central Time.

[3] I would also like to point out, with, of course, no disrespect intended, that your mother is a frigid bitch who has had it out for me since the moment we met. Additionally, do not assume that your family life has given you a good understanding of what a healthy relationship is, especially in light of the fact that your father has been screwing, for the past eight months, your brother's fiancée.

1B. *I've been thinking a lot about us and, well, I just don't know if it's the best thing for me, well, for both of us right now.*

You make clear that you are confused about the direction of our relationship and the benefits it bestows upon each of us. The advantages of our partnership arise in all spheres of our lives. First, recall that the acquisition of your current job at Benson Atwater, Inc., was based on an interview procured for you by the husband of my dear friend. Second, consider the incontrovertible sexual benefits you have been receiving from me, arguably since our sixteenth date and undoubtedly since our twenty-third.[4] And finally, since we began seeing each other, you have lost thirteen pounds, raised your annual income by more than $10,000 a year, and present a much more appealing odor than prior to the commencement of our relationship.[5] Further, if you are cheating on me, as I presume you are, I would also add that no woman besides me would have engaged in sexual intercourse with you four years ago.

1C. *I know we've talked about it – well, kind of – but I really think I need to take a break. Call me back. Bye.*

Your dismissal of the conversation to which this sentence refers

[4] These dates are based on the first time you were given oral sex, on October 5, 2000, and the first time we had intercourse, on November 12, 2000. Additional sexual favours were granted over the course of the relationship that I believe have more than fully met your sexual needs and desires.

[5] These figures are based on analysis of weight gain/loss patterns, average annual incomes, and hygiene habits of the past seven years.

makes clear that you have not been investing the energy that a successful relationship demands of the parties involved.[6] Putting more effort into our sexual life would also help things out. You may or may not be aware of this, but you have really been dropping the ball in the bedroom lately.[7]

Message 2: Doubt

(a) Jess [sic], it's Randy [sic]. We really need to talk. Frankly, things haven't been going so well lately. (b) You can't say you don't feel it, too. (c) Oh – and sorry about all that stuff with your guinea pig. Bye.

[6] Excerpt from conversation on September 3, 2004, at approximately 7.09 p.m. Eastern Standard Time:

Randolph: I can't believe we've been together more than four years.

Jessica: I can.

Randolph: But, do you ever think about what things would be like if we'd never met?

Jessica: How sad and lonely your life would be? I try not to dwell on it. I'm just glad we did find each other.

Randolph: Do you think everyone has only one person who's made for them?

Jessica: Oh, Randolph, what a sweet thing to say!

Randolph: Do you think maybe we aren't each other's?

Jessica: Do you want to know what else is out there? Floozies. Gold diggers. Drug addicts. Think about what I've done for you. Don't you see that your life would be worse without me?

Randolph: I guess you could look at it that way, but –

Jessica: Yes, you could.

[7] Yes, I've been faking it.

2A. *Jess [sic], it's Randy [sic]. We really need to talk. Frankly, things haven't been going so well lately.*

Actually, Randolph, things have been going great, but you insist on sabotaging our healthy, thriving relationship because you subconsciously want to ruin your life. I've been worried about you for a long time now. You seem to enjoy harming yourself. This is called masochism. I believe it has a great deal to do with your mother. I would suggest distancing yourself from her while the wounds heal.[8]

2B. *You can't say you don't feel it, too.*

You are right, Randolph; I can't say I haven't felt it. I have felt the tension in our relationship from the stress your self-loathing behaviors have caused. I have felt the tension caused by your staggering home at four in the morning reeking of alcohol. I have felt the friction caused by our emotional estrangement. But I digress. This tension stems not from some deep-rooted problem but rather from the healthy growth of our relationship. Strong partners work through problems together, which is why I am here to help you work through yours. I know that you have issues with intimacy, with women, and with erectile efficiency, plus an anal-expulsive fixation,[9] but I am here to guide you as we address these profoundly disturbing 'issues', of which you seem to have an endless supply.

[8] I understand from firsthand experience that she unwantedly imposes herself on you. I therefore support any decision you make regarding moving or changing our telephone number without granting contact information to the abovementioned.

[9] Need I mention this noxious habit of yours?

2C. *Oh – and sorry about all that stuff with your guinea pig. Bye.*

Let us clarify what 'all that stuff' is: Your dog, jealous of my beautiful guinea pig from the start, mauled Tootsie II, while you, horrified by what your 'best friend' Boxer's vicious hatred could do, stood idle. I was sympathetic enough to be conscious of your feelings and have Boxer put down while you were at work the next day, in order to save you unnecessary heartache. Further, to support you through the grieving process, what could have been better than an adorable new guinea pig? I understand your surprise on finding Boxer gone, replaced by Doodles, a beautiful new guinea, but I assure you that it is for the best. When you finally come to your senses and return home, you will be moved by the tenderness that exists between Doodles and Tootsie II – now a triple amputee.

Message 3: The Worst Mistake of Your Life

(a) I think I'm going to crash with Jay for a while, and I'd appreciate it if you didn't come by or call me. (b) Um, bye.

3A. *I think I'm going to crash with Jay for a while, and I'd appreciate it if you didn't come by or call me.*

It is here that I realize what a strong influence your friends, especially Jay, must have had on the decision you claim to have made independently.[10] There have been numerous actions on their part over the course of our relationship that have made it quite clear to me (as I assume was their goal) that I do not meet their 'standards' for you.[11] I believe the fact that you are 'going to crash with Jay' strongly supports my hypothesis that the opinions of your 'buddies' have been critical in convincing you to leave me. I implore you to rise above their petty lies.

3B. *Um, bye.*

Whenever you do something you know is wrong, you speak about it with a proliferation of 'um's. For example, two years ago, when your friends whisked you away to Atlantic City for the weekend, your explanation upon return was riddled with 'um's – fifty-three, actually, in a four-minute period. These 'um's increased exponentially when I exposed, from deep within your jacket pocket, a casino gambling chip and a

[10] Jay in particular is an exceptionally destructive man. I refer specifically to a disturbing episode in which, while organizing your drawers, I came upon a photo of my Tootsie I in Atlantic City, pushed into the cleavage of some trashy hotel-bar waitress and being forced to take a shot of tequila, with Jay smiling maniacally in the background. I only pray that this alcohol was fatal, and that my beautiful guinea pig was not subjected to further abuses before she perished in that cesspool of sin. Had I reported Jay to PETA or a similar organization, he most likely would have been shot.

[11] These include, but are not limited to, the following:

- The 'Still a Bachelor' party they have thrown for you on the evenings preceding all four of our anniversaries;
- The 'RANDY IS RANDY' shirt they made you for your birthday last year;
- The whip I received in the mail three weeks ago;
- The prostitute who arrived at our apartment last Thursday.

cocktail napkin with a phone number on it.[12] From the 'um' in your phone message, I can therefore infer that you are fully conscious of the mistake you are making.

Concluding Remarks

You may or may not have already noticed that all of your bank accounts are frozen and your credit cards are inactive. I also disabled your cellular phone. I regret having to take such extreme measures, but I feel that this is entirely in your best interests. I wanted to prevent any rash purchases on your part as you attempt to fill the emotional void you surely are experiencing right now. Further, I felt it necessary to encourage you not to leave the state or communicate with Jay and his cohorts.

Speaking of Jay, by this point you are probably aware that he has been jailed on the charge of possession of marijuana with intent to distribute. The repercussions that this will have on his personal and professional lives are potentially devastating, and it is with his and your futures in mind that I reiterate the importance of keeping some distance between yourself and what is soon to be a convicted felon.

The next few years will be quite difficult for Jay, and while he struggles to put his life back together I hope you will find the energy and wisdom to rededicate yourself to our relationship. I look forward to the progress we will undoubtedly make in the coming months.

With love, and hope for your future,

Jessica

[12] And no, Randolph, I do not believe that this was Jay's cousin's cellphone number.

DOUGLAS COUPLAND

People say that when you're in love you enter a new parallel universe that runs alongside our everyday world – a small universe where nothing else can intrude – a republic of two, hypnotic, exclusive and bubbly, like you're living inside a punch line that just won't end. But I don't think this is true. I think that being in love simply makes you feel even more connected to the rest of the species – it makes you belong to the world as fully as do birds and animals and flowers. I think that the real *other* universe is the one that erupts when the love goes away – what remains when the world crumbles and you're left floating with nothing real to grab on to, and this is the world I'm living in right now. It's a place where the rules are different. It's a place where the only things that make sense are gestures that frighten or confuse people who live in the real world.

For example, this afternoon I could see a squall coming in off Vancouver Island, black and inevitable like a cartoon warlord's empire. And then an hour later the rains came. I got to thinking of the hot tarry smell of roads just after a shower that follows a drought. So I walked up to the highway, four lanes each way, just before rush hour, and began to walk backwards along its shoulder. If you were driving west and you approached me, you'd only see the back of my head, dripping wet, and my legs taking me the wrong way. Seeing this, you'd know that I was a soul in trouble, a soul obviously headed in the wrong direction, a soul who lives in this different loveless world.

But then the sun came out and I looked to my right, off the highway's edge, and there were all of these trees – birch and alder and vine maples – glistening, as though varnished. Because of the drought the colours hadn't changed the way they normally do. The wet leaves looked brittle and transparent, like glassy candies, and they lured me off the highway and into the woods.

And then I felt wonderful. I felt the way I feel after I'm halfway through my third drink, which is the way I wish all moments in life felt: heightened and charged with the sense that anything could happen at any moment – that the reason being alive is important is because just when you least expect it, you might receive just what you least expect.

Then the woods felt as though they were made of glass shards. I had this feeling that all these coloured shards ought to be tinkling like wind chimes and my head got all tickly on the inside, and then the world went silent. I had to sit down on a rock. I had this feeling that surely the early pioneers must have felt about the beauty of the New World, that the only way to explain it was that there had to have been an eighth day of creation. What else could have generated such an astonishing world?

And sitting down I also began to think about life, and about how our lives can seem so plotless and formless, and this makes us desperately need to feel as if we're a part of a grander story. And I got thinking about writers – how all writers know when they're about to finish a book – the last chapter, the last paragraph, the penultimate sentence, the final sentence and then the final words, THE END. And I got to thinking that there has to be some sort of psychic compression that happens in a writer's brain when they know they're about to hit that final wall. Surely all writers must compress something out of themselves that they hadn't expected – that a diamond has to be left behind, even a microscopic diamond.

And so I walked back to the highway, got in my car and drove to the library. I went into the fiction section, got one of those little book carts, and then I selected a hundred novels at random. I took them to the photocopier and copied the final two pages of each. I stapled them together and then took them home and I read them all.

Did I find any diamonds? I don't know. I *did* find that the one thing many story endings have in common is that when they end, the narrator is moving either towards or away from light or darkness – literally – carrying candles into dark rooms or running a red light at an intersection.

And so here in my parallel universe I think about you and I think about the light and the darkness that defined us back when we lived in the real world – the way you burned your fingers on the kerosene lamp at the lake two years ago; the way you made me go shoeless and walk through the sea foam full of phosphorescent organisms up the coast last year; the way you always had to duct-tape over the one chink of light that drilled into your eyeballs every morning from up near the curtain rod; and the night we shone flashlights through our fingers to convince ourselves that we're made of blood.

And so now I live alone in my parallel loveless world, looking for light sources and patches of black, hoping for a signal or an omen, wondering whether it will be a spark or a flame or a shadow or a tunnel, all the while feeling utterly unsure of which direction I'll be headed into once that signal arrives.

BIOGRAPHIES

Chimamanda Ngozi Adichie was born in Nigeria in 1977. She is from Abba, in Anambra State, but grew up in the university town of Nsukka where she attended primary and secondary schools. Her short fiction has been published in literary journals including *Granta*, and won the International PEN/David Wong award in 2003. *Purple Hibiscus*, her first novel, was shortlisted for the Orange Prize and the John Llewellyn Rhys Prize, longlisted for the Booker Prize and was winner of the Hurston/Wright legacy award for debut fiction. Her second novel, *Half of a Yellow Sun*, won the Orange Broadband Prize for fiction in 2007. She was a Hodder fellow at Princeton University for the 2005–6 academic year. She lives in Nigeria.

Anonymous is a well travelled man/woman of the world who has been known to swing, ménage, fall in love and – on occasion – to write.

Margaret Atwood's books have been published in over thirty-five countries. She is the author of more than forty works of fiction, poetry, critical essays, and books for children. Her novels include *Bodily Harm*, *The Handmaid's Tale*, *Cat's Eye*, *The Robber Bride*, *Alias Grace*, which won the Giller Prize in

Canada and the Premio Mondello in Italy; *The Blind Assassin*, winner of the 2000 Booker Prize; and *Oryx and Crake*. Margaret Atwood lives in Toronto with writer Graeme Gibson. They are the joint Honourary Presidents of the Rare Bird Club of BirdLife International.

Chris Bachelder was born in 1971. He is a frequent contributor to the publications *McSweeney's Quarterly Concern* and the *Believer*. He is the author of three novels: *Bear v. Shark*, *Lessons in Virtual Tour Photography*, and *U.S.!* His work also appears in *New Stories from the South 2006*, the *Oxford American*, *The Cincinnati Review*, and *Mother Jones*.

Peter Behrens is a Canadian novelist and screenwriter who lives in Maine and Los Angeles. Behrens was a Fellow at the Fine Arts Work Center in Provincetown, Massachusetts. His short stories have appeared in *Tin House* and the *Atlantic Monthly*, and in numerous anthologies. His novel *The Law of Dreams* received rave reviews in *The New Yorker*, the *New York Times* and the *Washington Post*, and won the 2006 Governor General's Literary Award for Fiction, Canada's highest literary honour.

David Bezmozgis was born in Riga, Latvia, in 1973. In 1980 he emigrated with his parents to Toronto, where he lives today. His first book, *Natasha and Other Stories*, won the Jewish Quarterly Wingate Literary Prize for Fiction, the Commonwealth First Book, Regional Prize, and was shortlisted for the *Guardian* First Book Award in the same year. His stories have appeared in many publications including *The New Yorker*, *Harper's*, *The Walrus*. David's stories have also been anthologized in *Best American Short Stories 2005, 2006*. David is a Guggenheim Fellow and a Sundance Institute Screenwriting Fellow.

Joseph Boyden is a Canadian writer with Irish, Scottish and Métis roots. His first novel *Three Day Road* won the Rogers Writers' Trust Fiction Prize and the McNally Robinson Aboriginal Book of the Year Award and was shortlisted for the Governor General's Literary Award for Fiction. He is the author of *Born with a Tooth*, a collection of stories that was shortlisted for the Upper Canada Writer's Craft Award. He divides his time between northern Ontario and Louisiana, where he teaches writing at the University of New Orleans.

Tessa Brown is a senior at Princeton University, where she is writing a joint thesis under the Religion and Creative Writing departments. Her fiction has appeared in *Harper's* magazine and *New Sudden Fiction*, and she has written book reviews for the *Forward*. She grew up in Chicago, which she still calls home.

Leonard Cohen is a writer and composer. His artistic career began in 1956 with the publication of his first book of poetry, *Let Us Compare Mythologies.* He has published two novels, *The Favourite Game* and *Beautiful Losers*, and ten books of poetry, most recently *Book of Longing.* He has recorded seventeen albums, including *Songs From a Room*, *Songs of Love and Hate*, *I'm Your Man*, *The Future* and *Ten New Songs.* He divides his time between Los Angeles and Montreal.

Douglas Coupland has written ten novels, including *Generation X*, *Life after God*, *Microserfs*, *Polaroids from the Dead*, *Girlfriend in a Coma*, *Miss Wyoming* and *jPod.* His writing has been translated into twenty-two languages, and appeared in over thirty countries. He is a regular contributor to the *New York Times*, the *New Republic* and *ArtForum.* His most recent novel is *jPod*, which was longlisted for the 2006 Giller Prize.

Geoff Dyer was born in Cheltenham, England, in 1958. He was educated at the local grammar school and Corpus Christi College, Oxford. He is the author of three novels: *Paris Trance*, *The Search*, *The Colour of Memory*; a critical study of John Berger, *Ways of Telling*; a collection of essays, *Anglo-English Attitudes*; and four genre-defying titles: *But Beautiful* (winner of a 1992 Somerset Maugham Prize, shortlisted for the *Mail on Sunday*/John Llewellyn Rhys Memorial Prize), *The Missing of the Somme*, *Out of Sheer Rage* (a finalist, in the US, for a National Book Critics Circle Award), *Yoga for People Who Can't be Bothered to Do it* (winner of the 2004 W.H. Smith Best Travel Book Award), and, most recently, *The Ongoing Moment* (winner of the ICP Infinity Award for Writing on Photography). He is also the editor of *John Berger: Selected Essays* and co-editor, with Margaret Sartor, of *What Was True: The Photographs and Notebooks of William Gedney.* In 2003 he was a recipient of a Lannan Literary Fellowship; in 2005 he was elected a Fellow of the Royal Society of Literature; in 2006 he received the E.M. Forster Award from the American Academy of Arts and Letters. He lives in London.

Michel Faber is a novelist and short-story writer. Born in Holland, he moved with his family to Australia in 1967 and has lived in Scotland since 1992. His short story 'Fish' won the Macallan/*Scotland on Sunday* Short Story Competition in 1996 and is included in his first collection of short stories, *Some Rain Must Fall and Other Stories* (1998), winner of the Saltire Society Scottish First Book of the Year Award. His most recent short-story collection is *The Fahrenheit Twins and Other Stories* (2005). His first novel, *Under the Skin* (2000), was shortlisted for the Whitbread First Novel Award and he has also won the Neil Gunn Prize and an Ian St James Award. Other fiction includes *The Hundred and Ninety-Nine Steps* (1999), a novella, *The Courage Consort* (2002), the story of an a cappella singing group, and the highly acclaimed novel *The Crimson Petal and the White* (2002).

Neil Gaiman has long been one of the top writers in modern comics, as well as writing books for readers of all ages. His *New York Times* bestselling 2001 novel for adults, *American Gods*, was awarded the Hugo, Nebula, Bram Stoker, SFX and Locus awards, was nominated for many other awards, including the World Fantasy Award and the Minnesota Book Award, and appeared on many best-of-year lists. *Anansi Boys* débuted on the *New York Times* Bestseller list in September, 2005. He has written screenplays (*Mirrormask*); the script for *Beowulf*, with Roger Avary, and is co-author, with Terry Pratchett, of *Good Omens* which spent seventeen consecutive weeks on the *Sunday Times* (London) bestseller list in 1990. He is also the creator/writer of monthly cult DC Comics horror-weird series, *Sandman*, which won nine Will Eisner Comic Industry Awards. He has written children's books, plays and television series. Born and raised in England, Neil Gaiman now lives near Minneapolis, Minnesota.

Damon Galgut was born in Pretoria in 1963 and lives in Cape Town, South Africa. Galgut is the author of several novels and one short-story collection. His débu novel, *A Sinless Season*, was published when he was just seventeen. His other novels include *The Beautiful Screaming of Pigs*, winner of the 1992 CNA Literary Award (South Africa's highest literary honour), *A Small Circle of Beings*, and *The Quarry*, which was adapted as a feature film that won the award for Best Film at the 1998 Montreal Film Festival. Galgut's last novel, *The Good Doctor* (2003), was a finalist for the International IMPAC Dublin Literary Award and for the Man Booker Prize, and won the Commonwealth Writers' Prize for best book from the region of Africa.

Panos Karnezis was born in Greece in 1967 and came to England in 1992. He studied Engineering at Oxford and worked in industry before starting to write in English. He studied for an MA in Creative Writing at the University of East Anglia. His first book, the critically acclaimed *Little Infamies* (2002), is a collection of connected short stories set in a nameless Greek village, and his second book, *The Maze* (2004), a novel set in Anatolia in 1922, was shortlisted for the 2004 Whitbread First Novel Award. His second novel *The Birthday Party* was published in July 2007. Panos Karnezis lives in London.

A. L. Kennedy has published five novels, two books of non-fiction, and four collections of short stories. She has twice been selected as one of *Granta*'s Best of Young British Novelists and has won a number of prizes including the Somerset Maugham Award, the Encore Award and the Saltire Scottish Book of the Year Award. She lives in Glasgow.

Etgar Keret was born in Tel Aviv in 1967 and is one of the leading voices in Israeli literature and cinema. He has published four books of short stories and novellas, four graphic novels and one feature screenplay. His books, bestsellers in Israel, have been published in twenty-six different languages. His first film, *Malka Red-Heart*, won the Israeli 'Oscar' for best television drama, as well as acclaim at several international film festivals, and his most recent, *Jellyfish*, won the prestigious 2007 'Camera d'Or' Award, at the 60th Cannes Festival. His first collection of stories to be published in the UK was *The Nimrod Flip-Out* and his second collection, *Missing Kissinger*, was published in 2007.

Keret teaches in Ben Gurion University's Hebrew Literature department.

Hari Kunzru is the author of the novels *The Impressionist* (2002), *Transmission* (2004), *My Revolutions* (2007), and the short story collection *Noise* (2005). His work has been translated into twenty-one languages and won him prizes including the Somerset Maugham award, the Betty Trask Prize of the Society of Authors and a British Book Award. In 2003 *Granta* named him one of its Best of Young British novelists. He sits on the Executive Council of PEN and is a member of the editorial board of *Mute* magazine.

Nick Laird was born in 1975 in Northern Ireland. He was a scholar at Cambridge University, spent a year at Harvard University as a Visiting Fellow and worked as a lawyer. He is the author of one novel, *Utterly Monkey*, which won the Betty Trask Prize, and his first poetry collection, *To a Fault* published by Faber, was shortlisted for the Forward Prize (Best First Collection). He has received several prestigious awards for both poetry and fiction, including the 2005 Rooney Prize for Irish Literature. His poetry and reviews have appeared in the *Times Literary Supplement*, *Poetry Review* and the *London Review of Books*. He published a second poetry collection with Faber, *On Purpose*, in August 2007. He lives in Rome.

Phil LaMarche's first novel, *American Youth*, was hailed by the *Guardian* as being a 'superbly edgy portrait of individual infighting and a community's uneasy, prideful attitude towards gun culture and nationhood'. LaMarche was a writing fellow in the Syracuse University graduate creative writing program, awarded the Ivan Klíma Fellowship in fiction in Prague and a

Summer Literary Seminars fellowship in St. Petersburg, Russia. His short story *In the Tradition of My Family*, was published in the 2005 *Robert Olen Butler Fiction Prize Stories* anthology and has been made into a film by Later Productions. LaMarche lives in central New York State.

Ursula K. Le Guin was born in 1929 in Berkeley, California, the daughter of writer Theodora Kroeber and anthropologist Alfred L. Kroeber. Le Guin is the author of more than three dozen books, including the multi-award-winning novels *The Dispossessed* and *The Left Hand of Darkness.* She was awarded a Newbery Honor for the second volume of the Earthsea Cycle, *The Tombs of Atuan*, and among her many other distinctions are the Margaret A. Edwards Award, a National Book Award, and five Nebula Awards. She lives in Portland, Oregon.

Jonathan Lethem is the author of six novels, including *Motherless Brooklyn* (1999), which won the National Book Critics Circle Award, the Salon Book Award and *Esquire*'s Novel of the Year, and *The Fortress of Solitude* (2003). His latest book of essays is *The Disappointment Artist* (2004). In September 2005, he was named as one of the recipients of the MacArthur Fellowship, often referred to as the 'genius grant'. He lives in Brooklyn, New York.

Sam Lipsyte's most recent novel is *Home Land,* winner of the *Believer* Book Award and a *New York Times* Notable Book for 2005. He is also the author of *The Subject Steve* and *Venus Drive.* His work has appeared in many newspapers, magazines and journals, including the *Quarterly*, *Open City*, *N+1*, *Slate*, *McSweeney's*, *Esquire*, *Bookforum*, the *New York Times* and the *Washington Post.* He teaches at Columbia University in New York City.

Gautam Malkani was born in west London in 1976. He is a journalist at the *Financial Times* and is the author of the critically-acclaimed novel, *Londonstani.*

Valerie Martin was born in Sedalia, Missouri, and grew up in New Orleans, Louisiana, where her father was a sea-captain. She is the author of seven novels, including *Mary Reilly, The Great Divorce, Italian Fever,* and *Property,* three collections of short fiction, and a biography of St Francis of Assisi, titled *Salvation.* She has been awarded a grant from the National Endowment for the Arts, as well as the Kafka Prize (for *Mary Reilly)* and Britain's Orange Prize (for *Property*). A new novel, *Trespass,* was published in 2007. Valerie Martin has taught in writing programmes at Mount Holyoke College, University of Massachusetts, and Sarah Lawrence College, among others. She resides in upstate New York.

Hisham Matar was born in New York City in 1970 to Libyan parents and spent his childhood first in Tripoli and then in Cairo. He has lived in the UK since 1986. His first novel, *In the Country of Men,* received praise from notable figures such as J.M. Coetzee and was shortlisted for both the *Guardian* First Book Award and the Booker Prize, and won the Commonwealth First Book Prize for Europe and South Asia, the RSL Ondaatje Award, the Vallonbrosa Gregor von Rezzori Prize and the Slaiano International Literature Prize.

Jan Morris is a Welsh writer and British historian born in 1926. Morris is considered one of the most influential travel writers in the world, best known for the trilogy *Pax Britannica,* a history of the British Empire, and for her detailed portraits of Venice, Oxford, Trieste and New York City. She is the recipient of honorary doctorates from the University of

Wales and the University of Glamorgan. In 1999 Morris accepted the honour of Commander of the Order of the British Empire. Morris has published over two dozen books and is a Fellow of the Royal Society of Literature.

Audrey Niffenegger is a visual artist and a professor at the Columbia College Chicago Center for Book and Paper Arts, where she teaches writing, letterpress printing and fine edition book production. She shows her artwork at Printworks Gallery in Chicago and is the author of a number of novel-length visual books and the internationally acclaimed and bestselling novel *The Time Traveler's Wife* (2004) which was longlisted for the Orange Prize in 2004 and won the Sainsbury's popular fiction award at the British Book Awards in 2006. The recipient of numerous grants, she lives in Chicago.

Jeff Parker has published one novel, *Ovenman*, and his stories have appeared in *The Best American Nonrequired Reading 2006*, *Ploughshares*, *Tin House*, *Hobart* and many other publications. He collaborated with artist William Powhida on a collection of stories and images called *The Back of the Line*. With Mikhail Iossel he edited the anthology *Amerika: Russian Writers View the United States*, and he is the Russia Programme Director of Summer Literary Seminars in St Petersburg. Parker teaches creative writing at the University of Toronto.

Francine Prose is the author of fourteen books of fiction, including, most recently, *A Changed Man* and *Blue Angel*, which was a finalist for the National Book Award. She has taught literature and writing for more than twenty years at major universities such as Harvard, Iowa, Columbia, Arizona and the New School. She is a distinguished critic and essayist, the recipient of Guggenheim and Fulbright fellowships, and was a Director's Fellow at the Center for Scholars and Writers at the New York Public Library. Prose lives in New York City.

James Robertson is the author of three novels, *The Fanatic* (2000), *Joseph Knight* (2003), which was awarded the two major Scottish literary awards in 2003–2004 – the Saltire Book of the Year and the Scottish Arts Council Book of the Year – and *The Testament of Gideon Mack* (2006), which was long-listed for the Man Booker Prize in 2006. He has also published stories, poetry, anthologies and essays. He served as the Scottish Parliament's first writer in residence in 2004 and was selected for a prestigious Creative Scotland Award in March 2006. He lives in Angus.

Graham Roumieu is the creator of *In Me Own Words: The Autobiography of Bigfoot* (2003), *Me Write Book: It Bigfoot Memoir* (2005) and the forthcoming *Teenstache*, *Bigfoot: I Not Dead* and *101 Ways To Kill Your Boss*. Roumieu's illustrations have appeared in the *New York Times*, *Harper's* and the *Wall Street Journal* and his work has received recognition from the Society of Publication Designers, the Society of Illustrators New York, American Illustration, and Communication Arts.

Mandy Sayer won The Australian/Vogel Literary Award with her first novel, *Mood Indigo*. Since then, she has been named one of Australia's Best Young Novelists by the *Sydney Morning Herald* and has published seven books, including the memoir *Dreamtime Alice*, which has been translated into several languages and won the National Biography Award. In 2006, her second memoir, *Velocity*, won the South Australian Premier's Award for Non-Fiction and *The Age* Book of the Year Award. Her latest novel, *The Night has a Thousand Eyes*, is a literary thriller of three children on the run from their murderous father. Sayer has BA and MA from Indiana University and a Doctrate from the University of Technology, Sydney. She lives in Sydney.

Lionel Shriver has written for the *Economist*, the *Wall Street Journal* and the *Guardian*, among other publications. She is the author of eight novels, including *We Need To Talk About Kevin* (2005) which won the Orange Prize in 2005, and *The Post-Birthday World*, published by HarperCollins in 2007. She lives in London and New York.

Adam Thorpe was born in Paris in 1956. He has written five collections of poetry and nine works of fiction. His first novel, *Ulverton*, was published in 1992; his second book of short stories, *Is This the Way You Said?*, appeared in 2006 to critical acclaim, and his most recent novel, *Between Each Breath*, in 2007. He lives in France with his wife and three children.

Miriam Toews was born in Steinbach, Manitoba in 1964 and currently lives in Winnipeg. She writes both fiction and non-fiction in the genres of novel, memoir, magazine, newspaper and radio and her books include *Summer of My Amazing Luck*; *A Boy of Good Breeding*; *Swing Low: A Life* and, most recently, *A Complicated Kindness* which was shortlisted for the 2004 Giller Prize and won the Governor General's Literary Award for Fiction in 2005.

Carl-Johan Vallgren was born in 1964. He is a musician and the author of eight books, including *The Horrific Sufferings of the Mind-reading Monster Hercules Barefoot*. His novels have been published in twenty-one countries. He currently lives in Stockholm.

M. G. Vassanji was born in Kenya and raised in Tanzania. He is the author of eight works of fiction, including *The Gunny Sack*, winner of a Commonwealth Prize, *The Book of Secrets* and *The In-Between World of Vikram Lall*, both winners of the Giller Prize. His most recent novel is *The Assassin's Song*. He lives in Toronto with his wife and two sons.

Jeanette Winterson OBE is the author of the novels *Oranges Are Not the Only Fruit*, *Boating for Beginners*, *The Passion*, *Sexing the Cherry*, *The PowerBook*, *Lighthousekeeping*, *Written on the Body*, *Art and Lies*, *Gut Symmetries*; a book of short stories, *The World and Other Places*; two books for children, *The King of Capri* and *Tanglewreck*; and a book of essays about art and culture, *Art Objects*. Her latest book is *The Stone Gods*.

Matthew Zapruder is the author of two collections of poetry: *American Linden* (2002) and *The Pajamaist* (2006). He is also the co-translator of *Secret Weapon*, the final collection by the late Romanian poet Eugen Jebeleanu (2007). His poems and translations have appeared in many publications, including the *Boston Review*, *Open City*, *Bomb*, the *New Republic* and *The New Yorker*. He teaches in the MFA Program in Creative Writing at the New School, and works as an editor with Wave Books. In autumn 2007 he became a Lannan Literary Fellow in Marfa, Texas. He lives in New York City.

Juli Zeh was born in 1974 in Bonn. She has worked for the UN in New York, Krakow and Zagreb, and now lives in Leipzig. Her first novel, *Adler und Engel (Eagles and Angels*, 2001*)* was awarded the Deutschen Bücherpreis for best first novel, the Bremer Literaturpreis, and the Rauriser Literaturpreis for the best novel by a German-speaking author. Her writing has been translated into over twenty languages.

ACKNOWLEDGEMENTS

Acknowledgements are due to Poppy Hampson – for skilful editing and sympathy – and Alison Samuel at Chatto & Windus, Rachel Cugnoni, Beth Coates and Liz Foley at Vintage, Jane Kirby and Monique Corless in the Random House rights department, Louise Dennys, Michael Schellenberg and Angelika Glover at Knopf, Amber Qureshi at Free Press, Martin Knelman, Bernadette Sulgit, Sara Knelman, Becky Toyne, Bernard Schiff, David Berlin, Deborah Kirshner, Antonio De Luca, Brian Morgan, Eric Pierni, Catherine Osborne, Robin Robertson and Jess Atwood Gibson. A special thank you to Leonard Cohen, whose writing on love is inspiring, and a deep bow to Margaret Atwood, whose support for this idea has been invaluable. Most of all we are enormously grateful to the contributors.